ALSO FROM COHESION PRESS

COMING SOON

SNAFU: Judgement Day
– Amanda J. Spedding & Geoff Brown (eds.)
A Hell Within – James A. Moore & Charles R. Rutledge

SNAKED
DEEP SEA RISING

SNAKED
DEEP SEA RISING

Duncan McGeary

COHESION PRESS
HERE TO STAY

www.cohesionpress.com

SNAKED: DEEP SEA RISING
© 2017 Duncan McGeary
Cover design by Dean Samed/Neostock

ISBNs:
Print: 9781925623185
ePub: 9781925623178
Kindle: 9781925623192

All rights reserved.

Orders by U.S. and Canadian trade bookstores and wholesalers.
Independent Publishers Group
814 N. Franklin Street
Chicago, IL 60610
P (800) 888-4741
F (312) 337-5985
All other regions, contact the publisher.

COHESION PRESS
HERE TO STAY
Mayday Hills Lunatic Asylum
Beechworth, Australia
www.cohesionpress.com

CONTENTS

It is said that the darkness once came out of the ocean, and it killed everything and everyone but the People. But that was not the worst. For not long after, the ocean itself rose and washed everything away, and the world was begun anew.

CHAPTER ONE

T he kraken has been found," Mary Stewart said over the phone.

"Again?" said Charlie Wice, as he pulled into a rest stop. "He used to be so elusive."

"Afraid so. It's near your house, so you can check it out before you come into the office."

Charlie envisioned Mary sitting in her comfy office at the University of Washington, her knitting neglected while she made the call. Department heads came and went, but everyone knew where the real power resided – in the little, harmless-appearing, white-haired lady at the huge, ornate desk.

Mary took great joy in sending Charlie on wild monster chases. People were always finding sea monsters on the beach. Usually they were half-eaten mammals such as whales or dolphins, and sometimes they were everyday creatures like squids or sharks. The ocean tides and scavengers sculpted some pretty strange cadavers. Though most of them didn't make it this far inland.

But every once in a long while a true sea monster appeared, a creature from the deep that somehow managed to wash up on the outer shore before being consumed. Often shifting pressures as they rose from the deep-sea distorted their bodies, but if you knew what you were looking at, if you could reconstruct the shape of the bodies, well, that made up for all the false sightings. Charlie lived for the day when he'd find something truly new, something from the deep ocean trenches no one had ever seen before. So he always responded to these calls, even when he knew he was probably wasting his time.

"St Aloysius Island," Mary said. "A Mister Ed Taylor. He said he'd meet you at the bridge."

Charlie grimaced and rolled his eyes. "Got it." *Shit, Ed Taylor.*

He pulled away from the rest stop and turned north. St Aloysius Island was close to his house so he'd make it the first stop of the day. He wasn't looking forward to the meeting. Ed Taylor stalked the county planning commission, of which Charlie was the chairman. He'd let Kristine talk him into it. "It's your civic duty, Charlie," she'd said. "Every other successful man in the area has served his time on the commission. It's expected."

For Kristine, the operative word was *successful*. Why hadn't he seen it? When they were courting, they'd made jokes about how she would be his trophy wife. It wasn't until after they were married that Charlie realized it was true.

So he served his term on the planning commission, doing his duty, but he'd be damned if he'd ever volunteer for anything like that again, partly because of gadflies like Ed who never saw a zoning change he liked, and who was certain they were being overrun by *outsiders.* Charlie wasn't sure if that was code for people of color or not. It didn't necessarily have to be. Ed didn't like anyone, no matter the color of their skin.

St Aloysius Island was close enough to the shore that it had a bridge leading out to it that was long, narrow, and rickety, and though Charlie had driven his big pickup across it more than once, he held his breath every time. He didn't like the huge truck the university had foisted on him, though he had to admit he appreciated how much gear it could carry.

Ed's rotund figure was waiting impatiently on the other side of the span. *What the hell, I'll park on this side and walk across.*

Charlie parked the truck, and as he crossed the beams were even more rotted than he'd first suspected. Another infrastructure project that had been delayed because of Ed's obstructionism. It would serve him right if the fat little man drove his old Volvo right off the edge.

Ed extended his pudgy hand. "Thanks for coming, Wice," he said, his voice gruff. Charlie had overheard his natural speaking voice and realized Ed always harrumphed and spoke a full octave lower when talking to officialdom.

"What you got for me?"

"Some kind of snake," Ed said. "It's creepy, whatever it is."

He led Charlie to the small, sandy beach near the bridge where the kids swam during the summer. There, in the middle of the white sand, was a black, serpentine shape. It was a big one, nearly six feet long.

It can't be. But when Charlie got a full look at it, he realized it was a sea snake, but unlike any he knew about.

Eons ago, this species had lived on land, but at some point in its evolution it had returned to the sea. They still breathed air, but they could close their nostrils for diving and would secrete salt with every breath out. Most stayed near warm-water coral reefs, but there were a few open-ocean species. These snakes could dive for hours, their lungs extending through most of their bodies. They were also among the most poisonous creatures on Earth.

Charlie whirled abruptly on Ed, who took a nervous step back. "You didn't touch it, did you?"

"I hate snakes," Ed said. "I wouldn't go near it."

"Good," Charlie said. "Even dead snakes can have a reflex bite." He crouched and took a closer look.

"What kind of snake is it?" Ed said from behind him.

"A sea snake, probably of the genus *Aipysurus*. I don't know what species. I've never seen one with a yellow stripe before."

"Is it unusual?"

"Not at all," Charlie said. "At least, not if you live a few thousand miles south of here."

"What's it doing in Puget Sound?"

Charlie shrugged. "Probably came from someone's aquarium."

"Wouldn't that be illegal?"

"Without a doubt," Charlie said, "but when has that stopped anyone? In fact, for some folks, the more dangerous the critter the more desirable it is. But... what can you do with a sea snake but look at it? So the owner probably dumped it at high tide and ran."

"Ran?"

"They are extremely dangerous. Their venom is ten times more potent than a viper's."

Ed looked nervously out over the rising tides.

Charlie looked back at his truck. *The one time I leave it behind.* "Wait here, I'll be right back."

He jogged back across the bridge, jumped in the pickup, and drove it over the ramshackle span, forgetting about the decaying timber, forgetting about everything but the sea snake. It had been too long since he'd dissected one.

Charlie steered the wide-tired truck down onto the beach and hopped out, popping the rear doors. His usual sample pails were too small, but he had a big, black garbage bag. He examined it for rips and, satisfied that it was intact, pulled it out then grabbed his rubber gloves and a shovel.

When he turned the sea snake was being lifted into the air by a pair of seagulls. They were struggling with the creature's weight. Ed had his back to them, watching Charlie.

Charlie shouted at the seagulls and they redoubled their efforts. Ed turned and began shouting too; when he started waving his arms, that was too much for the birds, and they dropped the snake and flew a few dozen yards away, squawking at the humans indignantly.

Charlie stood over the dropped creature, wondering how to go about getting it into the bag. He looked around until he found a fallen tree branch, then poked the snake with it. There was no reflex reaction. It was well and truly dead. He reached down to pick it up.

"What's with the birds?" Ed asked.

Charlie straightened and turned around. The two thieving seagulls were flopping about on the beach, their frenzied motions slowing even as Charlie watched. He walked over, Ed following him. The gulls were unmoving now except for their beaks, which opened and closed as they gasped for air. Then their bright black eyes dulled and they were still.

Charlie backed away instinctively.

"What's wrong?" Ed asked.

"I'm not sure," Charlie said. "But it appears the snake's skin is poisonous. I don't think I've ever heard of that."

It was odd and alarming. Creatures usually evolved one major form of defense, either a venomous bite or poisonous skin, but not both.

"Like a tree frog?" Ed asked. Charlie looked at him, and Ed shrugged. "I watch *Nature*."

"Yeah, but even quicker-acting, maybe," Charlie answered. If the snake's skin was poisonous, he was going to have to figure out how to get the snake into the garbage bag without it touching anything but the inside of the bag.

"Here," he said, holding the bag out to Ed. "Keep this open as wide as you can."

"Hey, that's your job," Ed said. He'd turned pale and gulped a little.

"Come on, man. I drove all the way out here because you called me."

Ed reluctantly took the bag and opened it as wide as it would go. Charlie placed the shovel under the fattest part of the snake and started lifting. It slid off with a sloshing sound, landing in the sand in a curl, as if alive. He tried again. The creature was heavier than he'd expected, and there didn't seem to be any way to get a fulcrum on it.

He tried several more times until he finally he managed to get the snake completely off the ground. "Get ready," he said through gritted teeth.

He gingerly turned around. Ed was standing there with his eyes closed, holding the bag too high. "A little lower," Charlie said.

Ed opened his eyes and lowered the bag just enough for the snake's head to clear it. Charlie turned the tip of the shovel, and the snake plopped down into the bag.

Ed paled further, and the bag started to slip out of his fingers.

"Careful!" Charlie grabbed the edges of the bag before it could hit the ground. *Thank God I have gloves.* "You all right?" Charlie asked.

Ed really wasn't such a bad guy, just a little undiplomatic. In fact, he'd probably been right about some of the land disputes, certainly about the Sanders family who had convinced the commission that their resort would bring in business for the area instead of becoming a rich man's playground with little interaction with the surrounding community.

Charlie closed the bag, then took the shovel to the water and slammed it into the sand. He'd let the seawater wash over it for a while. "All done," he said, turning to Ed. "I'd shake your hand, but..."

Ed didn't appear to even hear him. He was looking at the shovel, and beyond, at the ocean. "What if there are more?" he asked worriedly.

"Don't worry, it probably didn't survive more than ten minutes in water this cold."

"I... I, ah, think I might have seen one last night, alive and wriggling," Ed said.

Charlie had been turning away, getting ready to put the black bag into the back of the pickup, but at this, he turned around. "What?"

"I think there was one on my dock," Ed said. "Only it was alive. I went into the house to get a shovel, but by the time I got back, it was gone."

"Why didn't you mention this..." Charlie held up his hand. "Show me where."

"It's just a little ways," Ed said. "We can walk."

"I'll drive, if you don't mind," Charlie said. "All my gear is in the truck."

"Okay, but you'll have to take the loop," Ed waved toward the one-way street that wound around the small island. "I'm the last house."

Charlie made sure the bag was tightly sealed with duct tape, and propped it in the bed of the pickup between the side and several buckets. He got in the truck and waved at Ed. "I'll meet you there."

Ed cut across the beach and up onto the grassy sand dunes. He was mortified that he'd almost dropped the bag in fear. He really wasn't a coward. He knew that about himself, but he had a primordial reaction to slithering things.

He knew Charlie didn't like him much. Most people didn't. If it wasn't for his wife, he'd be lost. His Kathy liked him. She wanted to spend time with him, and thought he was funny and smart and good. He could be himself with her, and they had spent thirty-five blissful years together.

He'd quit exercising years ago, had let himself gain weight because he really didn't want to live after she was gone. He was five years younger, so he thought there was a pretty good chance they'd go out close together.

They had inherited the beachfront property from Ed's parents. He'd spent his summer months there – all his growing-up years – and when he'd retired, they'd made it their year-round home. And then the barbarians had come. *Outsiders.* Rich bastards who cut down anything in their way and paved everything else. The locals had let them run roughshod over everyone.

"Why don't you run for the planning commission?" his wife had asked.

He'd tried not to laugh. "I don't have the temperament, sweetie." *No, politics are for mealy-mouthed people like Charlie Wice.*

Ed waited down by the dock. He could see Kathy at the kitchen window, unaware he was watching her. Her whole body seemed like a smile to him, and he felt the same love for her wash over him that he'd felt during their courtship. It had never diminished.

He heard faint barking and saw their little Corgi, Elizabeth, scratching at the sliding doors.

Charlie came around the side of the house, his massive pickup barely clearing the opening between the house and the shed. *The bigger the truck, the smaller the penis.*

Ed led Charlie to the end of the short dock where his boat was moored during the summer.

"Right here," he said, pointing to the slight downward dip in the dock where a winter storm had managed twist the wood. "It was still alive."

"Really?" Charlie frowned as if he didn't believe it. Then his mouth opened in surprise, his eyes widening slightly. Ed turned around, expecting a sea snake to be darting toward them.

Instead, the sea below was full of dead creatures. Fish, crabs, and every other kind of tidal animal floated in the dark water. Though Ed couldn't see anything, he was certain only a snake could have made the water swirl like that.

Charlie turned on his heel and went back to the truck. Ed heard clanking and slamming, and then the biologist returned with a couple of white buckets. He got on his knees on the dock and bent over.

"Jesus," Ed said. "What are you doing?"

"Getting water samples." Charlie swooped one bucket through the water and lifted it up onto the dock. He grabbed the second container. "Might as well get a few of these animals, too, see if we can find out what killed them."

"We know what killed them."

"No, it's just a coincidence," Charlie said. "I'm telling you, that snake was dead minutes after it was put in the water."

"Snakes," Ed said. "There was more than one. Maybe there was a bunch."

"Then there are a bunch of dead snakes," Charlie said, stooping and lifting the two buckets by their handles and returning to the pickup where he loaded them in back. "Call me if you see another one, Ed."

"Of course."

"I mean it, Ed. Don't get all bullheaded about it."

"I told you, I hate snakes. The second I see anything, you're the first person I'm calling."

"Good," Charlie said. "I'll be back. I want to test this water. Something weird is happening."

Ed watched him drive away then turned to the house with a sigh. *I should have just left it alone.* He really didn't want people around his cottage. He liked his privacy. Now, who knew how many times he'd have to deal with Charlie Wice and his black garbage bags.

He went into the house, feeling a sudden urge to wash his hands. Once there, he decided to go all the way. He stripped out of his clothes and dropped them in the washer, and then started the shower.

He was toweling off when he heard his wife cry out. "Ed? Did you close the door all the way? I think Elizabeth got out."

He froze, the towel clutched to his chest, and felt his heart skip a beat.

"Kathy?" he shouted. "Stay inside. Let me do it!"

He dropped the towel, still wet, and grabbed his pants. He lost his balance and slammed against the shower door. Barefoot and shirtless, he ran out of the bathroom as he heard the sliding door shut.

His bare feet squeaked on the wood floor as he ran down the hallway. He skidded into the living room. Kathy was running down the grass toward something thrashing on the ground. It was Elizabeth. Ed saw a flash of bright yellow, and then he was running.

"Stop!" he shouted, but Kathy had already reached the dog's side. She grabbed the big, black snake in the dog's mouth, yanked it free, crouching over the now-unmoving Elizabeth.

Ed reached Kathy just as she toppled over.

She stared up at him with a scared, confused look. "Ed?" she managed to say, and then it was as if her throat closed over the words, and she was silent. She wasn't even gasping, though her body was whipping from side to side with the effort to breathe.

Ed put his own mouth over hers and tried to blow in, but the air pushed back out again, as if it had only penetrated a few inches before being repelled.

And then he felt his own body tighten, as if someone had tied strings to all his parts and pulled. His throat closed, and he took his last breath.

He'd known. Of course he'd known.

He lay down beside his motionless wife and closed his eyes. With the last of his strength, he reached out and clutched Kathy's hand.

CHAPTER TWO

They had the whole bay to themselves. As far as the eye could see, there was nothing but high, cresting waves. It was the best surf action Liam had seen all season. A few moments earlier, Devon had grabbed a roller Liam had passed on. For once, he was wrong. Devon rode the swell all the way to shore, the best surfing Liam had ever seen his best friend do. He could hear Devon whooping and hollering even out here, above the crashing of the breakers.

Liam had woken that morning, looked out his third-story window and seen clear skies. Rare enough on the Puget Sound, but especially rare in September. It was a quirk of geology that produced big waves this far inland, a narrowing of the waters striking a curve in the shoreline just right. Probably the only place close to Seattle where anyone could surf.

And he and Devon had it all to themselves.

He'd told himself he was only going to get a few more chances this season, and had immediately called Devon, who'd met him down on the beach. His friend was staying in one of the outer cottages because Liam's dad insisted that only family stay in the big house.

Devon was paying a dollar a month rent because John Sanders had to abide by the rules of the resort and only have paying customers. Just a few, just enough to meet the letter of the law and skirt the spirit of it.

It was Liam who had led his billionaire father to this place.

All because of the surfing.

His dad didn't care much about the surfing, except for how it filled a paragraph of the business plan. No, the great real-estate mogul had seen a deal: cheap land, spectacular views, and most importantly, a compliant local government. He'd ramrodded the resort through local and state regulations and built his big house, and then, almost as an afterthought, built the half-dozen cottages that earned the development the title of 'destination resort'.

They'd named it 'Coast Salish Resort'. The Native American 'Salish Casino' was just down the road. The Indians hadn't been happy about the name appropriation, but it was a savvy marketing move.

The Sanders family and their friends pretty much owned the entire island as well as the stretch of beach on the mainland across from it.

Dark clouds started to form out on the horizon, but then dark clouds almost always threatened, and only sometimes actually delivered a storm. Still, time and some great waves were a-wastin'.

Liam took the next wave, which was a mistake. It quickly began to peter out, and he bailed on it early. The water near the jetty was calmer, and he splashed closer to the giant boulders that lined the structure. In the distance, at the very tip of the jetty, was the abandoned lighthouse that looked like something out of ancient times.

Its base was constructed atop of huge granite blocks. Twenty feet up a steep staircase, the rounded lighthouse was boarded up.

I ought to ask Dad to buy it. The ultimate surfer hangout.

On the other side of the jetty was the public beach, which sat below the town, whereas the beach Liam claimed as his own was surrounded by high cliffs. It was supposed to be public, but it was de facto private.

He paddled against the tide, resting every few hundred feet. *I should hire some local kids to Jet Ski us out,* but immediately dismissed the thought. He didn't want those wankers hanging around. Besides, instead of being grateful, they'd probably hate the Sanders family even more. Ungrateful bastards. Hell, Liam spent hundreds of dollars a week in the local quick markets and fast food joints. He tipped well and treated the workers with respect despite the resentment in their eyes.

Resentment, but also envy. The girls especially could be persuaded to drop their animosity with a little cash and a fast car.

An especially cold current flowed past Liam's dangling feet, and he shivered. That was the downside to the Washington coast. It was unbelievably frigid all year long. There was a deep underwater chasm not far away. The waves broke where a shelf of land extended into the deep, and it was the chasm that made the waves big. Liam preferred to focus on the surface, on the waves, and not to dwell too much on what lay beneath. Still, every once in a while, a tendril of seaweed, a particularly cold or warm current, or the sight of a fish swimming only a few feet below gave him the supreme willies.

He left the room when his family watched any documentary on sea life, yet he still dreamed of the monsters of the deep. He knew his imagination was still haunted by the variety and strangeness of the real ocean dwellers. He closed his eyes and thought of the warm sands of the beach, the trees, his dogs, the little hideaway he had in the attic for when the blackness overwhelmed him.

Nope, all he saw was a big, gaping, ringed-toothed mouth heading directly for him. He pulled his feet onto the board, gasping as he shuddered. He was so freaked out that he didn't notice Devon paddling up.

"Man!" his friend shouted. "I think I saw a shark. A big one."

Liam managed not to let out a squeal, even as a joke. Because it wouldn't have been a joke, and Devon would have realized it. "For fuck's sake, don't sneak up on me like that," he said.

For some reason, Devon always shouted when he was out on the waves. Most of it was pure excitement, and sometimes the waves really were loud, but mostly Devon just couldn't help it.

"Dude, I've been in your line of sight for the last five minutes," he shouted.

"Yeah, well. I was thinking."

"Shit," Devon said. "You know what? That's your problem. You don't enjoy what you got. You're rich as fuck, and the ladies like you, and you surf like a pro."

Liam laughed. Of those three attributes, the one that impressed Devon the most was his surfing ability. *Probably why he's my friend.*

Devon looked worriedly out over the waves. "I saw a shark, man. I'm not kidding."

"You *always* see a shark," Liam said. "Worst thing that ever happened to you was when you saw *Jaws.*" Liam had looked up the odds of getting attacked by a shark. He'd looked up the odds for everything – sharks, jellyfish, stonefish, stingrays, and every other kind of dangerous creature. The chances of a shark attack, especially on the Washington coast, were vanishingly small, lower than in most coastal states, lower than in Oregon.

Still, it could happen, and despite his dismissive tone, Liam couldn't help but look around himself. Sometimes sharks thought surfers were seals. He glanced over at Devon in his black wetsuit. *Hell, if I was a shark, I'd think he was a seal too.* "You wanna quit?" he asked.

"Hell no! Like you always say, the walk back to the house is more dangerous, right?" Devon punctuated his words by grabbing the next wave, and again he picked a good one.

Liam watched him with envy, yet he felt almost no desire to surf himself. Truth be told, he liked just lying on his board, letting the waves gently rock him. The clouds parted. The sun was spending its five minutes of shining for the day, and he closed his eyes and soaked it up.

He didn't know how long he'd been lying on the board when he heard a popping sound and sat up, nearly tipping over into the water. Bubbles were hitting the surfboard and popping several yards out into the water. He wasn't sure, but it seemed as if the board was being pushed upward. A sense of dread filled him, and in his mind's eye, he saw the famous *Jaws* poster, the one with the girl swimmer and the shark's open jaws widening to take a chunk out of her.

He looked down into the water even as his mind told him not to.

It was exactly as he'd imagined; the huge jaws of a shark opening beneath him, its cold, soulless eyes gazing into his. He shouted, his voice steadily rising into a scream. The shark kept coming.

Holy shit, this is really happening.

Then there was gentle thud as the shark's snout hit the bottom of the board. Liam realized the shark wasn't moving. It rolled lazily onto its side and floated there, an arm's length away. Its cold, dead eyes were just that. Cold and dead.

The bubbles stopped. For a moment, the ocean was preternaturally still. Something swirled deep in the water, something black. It looked like the eye of a hurricane, and it was coming straight at him.

Devon came up to him at that moment, paddling furiously. "What's wrong?" he shouted, then cried "Fuckin' ay!" when he saw the shark.

"Get on your board! *Now,* Devon!"

"What? I'm on my board."

"Get your feet out of the water, dammit!" Liam screamed.

Devon frowned, as usual not taking Liam's orders without a show of independence. He was too slow.

The black eye beneath had separated into individual motes, each swirling with the same motion and in the same direction as the larger mass. The snakes' heads were bright yellow, and they looked like flashes of lightning in a hurricane. A few broke off and wrapped themselves around Devon's still-dangling legs.

"What the...?" Devon said, trying to pull up his legs. His bare feet disappeared into the swirling black, and he screamed. He jerked first one way and then the other, and then fell back onto his board, thrashing.

Liam started to reach out to him, but the snakes surrounded his board now, and he could barely keep his balance in the churning water.

In his agony, Devon managed to pull one leg out of the water. A black snake with a yellow head had its fangs embedded deeply into his heel, its body twirling as if it was trying to take a chunk of the foot with it. It broke away, and half of Devon's heel went with it. Blood spurted from the gash and multiple piercings on his arch and sole.

Liam could only watch in horror as his best friend suddenly jerked, putting his hands to his throat. Devon turned to him wordlessly, a look of confusion and disappointment on his face as he realized he was dying.

Then, with a final convulsion, he tipped into the water and sank into the giant, swirling vortex.

Liam floated out to sea, not daring to move. He was out of sight of land now, and while the motion of the waves was longer and in some ways gentler, the troughs between the waves were also deeper, and he felt himself sliding several times. His pressed his palms to the top of the board, willing himself not to move an inch. Not even on his longest, most spectacular rides had he ever used his sense of balance as much.

He kept his eyes closed, feeling the water's motion, and countering it instantly.

His muscles quivered, and he lost his grip. He opened his eyes in a panic and scrambled to his knees. That was better. He could see the waves now, react to them more quickly. He was getting farther and farther from land. The sun was going down. If he didn't head back soon, the currents would take him past the point of no return.

But he didn't dare put his hands in the water, didn't dare start paddling toward shore. He shivered. His wetsuit wasn't helping keep the cold from his hands, feet, and face, and slowly the chill was making its way to his core. He could just give into the hypothermia. It would be a gentle death, but he'd be just as dead as if the snakes had got him.

Something banged against his board. Liam was too tired to cry out, though his heart took off on a race, leaving his thinking behind. It was a piece of driftwood, a couple of feet long and half a foot wide, almost flat, as if nature had fashioned him a paddle, giving him another chance at survival.

He snatched it out of the water and tentatively took a stroke with it. The surfboard slowly turned, and he pushed his way against the current, which was getting stronger with every moment. It was tiring, but it wasn't as tiring as lying on the board trying to micromanage every little movement.

The physical exertion made Liam's heart beat to match his fear and cleared his head. The snakes were long gone, he told himself. It wasn't as if they filled the wide, vast ocean.

As darkness fell, he cursed himself for a fool. He'd die unnecessarily because he'd refused to think. He'd shut down, like he used to do at prep school when the hazing was at its worst.

He lowered his head and paddled in earnest, and after hours of effort, he looked up. The shore was closer, but still so far away that he almost gave up. *Quit looking. I'll get there when I get there.*

He struggled to the limit of his endurance and beyond. And in doing so, realized he'd never had to toil so hard in his entire life. Never had to go the edge of anything. His money and his father's influence had always smoothed the way. He didn't have to try hard to get decent grades, and once he'd had his growth spurt, he was bigger than the boys who had bullied him. The girls had come, and with it, the popularity, and he'd taken it all for granted.

As the moon rose, Liam kept paddling until he could see the dark outline of the islands and the mainland. He put his head down and kept churning, not even sure of his progress anymore. The driftwood slipped up out of the water half the time now, and he nearly dropped it more than once.

Finally, he saw the glowing sands of a beach, and even though he was nearly the same distance from shore as he'd been when he'd last seen the snakes, he finally gave in, lay down on his board, and put both hands in the water. At the same moment, a wave lifted him, and he could tell it was a big one. He had the urge to rise up, but his body said otherwise, and he hadn't moved an inch before his muscles rebelled and he fell back onto the board and just lay there. It felt like he was flying, and he let the ride happen.

The board hit the sand, and Liam tumbled off. He tried to get to his feet, failed, and crawled the rest of the way onto the beach. He lay on the sand, which retained some of the heat of the day, and relief washed through his body. Then the confused look on Devon's agonized face came to him.

It was only now that he was on safe ground that the darkness of his illness threatened to return. He'd fought so hard to come back from it, was almost there. But Liam knew he was fragile, that it wouldn't take much to push him over the edge.

In his mind, he wasn't safe until he made it to shelter. He slowly got to his feet, putting one foot in front of the other. He left his board behind without a thought.

There were lights not far away. He shuffled toward them. It was as if his legs wouldn't work, and he landed on his knees, but the pain bothered him less than his fatigue. Then he found himself standing in the dark, wondering where he was. His eyes caught the lights, just a little closer, and he continued on.

He stumbled into the gas station market, scaring the clerk. "Phone," he said. His voice came out as croak. The warmth of the interior flowed over him, and his skin tingled.

The young clerk handed him the landline phone, and Liam stared at it. It was so unfamiliar; he wasn't sure how to use it.

"Want me to dial for you?" the clerk asked.

"No," Liam said, finally remembering to punch in the numbers. "Dad?" His voice came out soft and faint even to his own ears.

"Liam?" his dad's voice boomed. "Is that you? Where are you?"

The clerk must have heard, because he spoke up. "Ezekiel's Landing."

"How the hell did you get there?"

"Dad," Liam said. "Devon's gone. He's dead." He hated the

sound of his own voice. Over the last summer, he'd finally begun to think of himself as grown up. Now he sounded like the ten year old who'd had his bike stolen, who had gotten lost in the Olympic Forest, who had been so embarrassed after missing his school bus stop that he'd gone all the way to the end of the line.

There was a long silence.

"I'll be right there, son."

Liam gave the phone back to the clerk and turned away to hide his tears.

CHAPTER THREE

All three clients were baited up and their lines in the water. They were out of sight of land, in the middle of Puget Sound. Now all Tom had to do was sit back and let the boat do the trolling, letting his mind wander. Pete, the deck hand, would help them with the fishing part. It was Tom's job to get them out there, find the fish, and get them back without any complications.

He preferred not to go out with fewer than five paying customers, but the young married couple had been getting antsy, so rather than lose a sure four clients in hopes of a doubtful five, they'd headed out. It was enough to get Tom through the day, and it was a little less work. He was ready for that.

Tom Bailey Charter Boats, Inc was deep in debt and barely paying its daily expenses. Tom had quit answering the phone, screening out all the debt collectors. It had occurred to him that the banks couldn't really do much to someone who was already broke. They might eventually take back the *Cirdan*, but as long as he made token payments, he doubted they wanted the old hulk. *Seven years until retirement. I just have to make it seven more years.*

The ocean was calm, the sun was shining, and Tom was a contented man. Except…

He walked over to the small window he'd ported into the pilot's cabin, put his head out, and puked. It didn't matter how calm the ocean was, he always puked at least once.

"A charter boat captain who gets seasick?"

Tom turned, wiping his mouth, and saw that Gerald Monson had climbed the steep spiral staircase into Tom's private domain.

Dammit, Pete, you're supposed to stop them.

"Yeah, well," Tom said, shrugging. "It's a small price to pay."

"You ought to look into the causes," Monson said. "You should have become accustomed by now. Have you seen a doctor?"

Tom suddenly remembered that Monson's release form had listed 'medical supplier' as his occupation. Actually, Tom *had* seen a doctor, who was amazed at what he did for a living and who told him that he had an inner ear problem and he might want to look into doing something else.

"Like what?" Tom had asked. The doctor didn't have an answer. There was no answer. Tom Bailey wasn't suited for anything else but fishing.

He gave Monson a sickly smile. "Must have been something I ate." He sat in the captain's chair and twirled it around to face his customer. "What can I do for you?"

"Well, we appreciate all you're doing for us, but we were really hoping to catch something a little bigger." Monson turned and gestured at his brother, Marty Dyer – "same mother, different father" – who was leaning over the side of the boat. They'd barely left shore before Marty started throwing up.

"Bigger?" Tom asked. He looked away, knowing what was probably coming.

"Like a big shark, or a manta ray, something like that."

"It's salmon fishing season," Tom said. "We're very lucky they opened up the season at all, much less letting us have two fish each. I'll tell you what, I still have one fish left on my own limit, and you can have that."

"I read that if you put the bait lower down, you have a chance of catching something unusual... really weird deep-sea creatures," Monson said. "They say there is a chance you might even catch something no one has ever seen."

"Sure," Tom said. "But you can't eat them. You can only kill them. I'd rather not do that."

"I'd be willing to pay a little extra."

Tom stood from his chair. He was a tall man, six and a half feet of muscle with a bit of fat, bald, and a neck tattoo of Cthulhu. His head brushed the cabin's ceiling. "If you'll get back to your seat, Mister Monson, we'll be heading in within a few hours. You can book a different boat. I'll tell Pete to pull up your gear, and I'll refund your money."

Monson stepped back, almost tripping at the doorway and toppling six feet down onto the deck. *My liability insurance will cover that.*

"That isn't necessary," Monson said. "I've already caught one fish, and it was very… satisfying. Marty's so sick he won't go near a fishing pole. Don't worry about it."

"Old Pete's the best there is," Tom snapped. "You'll catch your second fish, I guarantee it."

Monson retreated. Tom took a deep breath. *Let Pete handle it.*

If it wasn't for Pete, Tom would have given up long ago. The old man had come aboard five seasons back and ever since, the company had managed to nearly turn a small profit. If it weren't for the interest on the debt eating them alive, they'd be in good shape.

Pete hadn't been Tom's first choice, but when the college kid he'd hired quit on the second day of the season – "Fish stink, man." – Tom had been desperate. He'd noticed the old man hanging around the docks, watching the boats come and go, his long, white beard tobacco-stained around his mouth, and wearing a hat that bore the faded name of a fishing boat Tom had never heard of. On a hunch, Tom approached the old guy and asked, "You know anything about fishing?"

"Yep," Pete said, the first of the many one or two-word answers Tom got from him.

They'd headed out to sea, and when Tom reached his usual fishing grounds, Pete said, "Farther."

"This area is the best for fishing," Tom said. "I've been all around these waters."

"No," Pete shook his head. "There…" He pointed vaguely out to sea. Tom decided to keep following his hunches and went in the direction the old man pointed. About half a mile to the south-east, Pete said, "Here."

It was still one of the best days of fishing the company had ever had. After a couple more of these miraculous sessions, Tom had pretty much turned over the fishing part of the operation to Pete. He still owned the boat, but Pete was the real fisherman.

When the old man had noticed his boss was getting seasick, he'd shown up with a vile concoction that he insisted Tom drink. Sure enough, after choking it down, Tom made it through a day of rough seas without throwing up once. He'd thought the elixir was miraculous, but that night, he had felt his stomach churning, and he didn't leave the toilet until daylight. When he'd come to the docks the next morning, Pete had given him a toothless grin.

He still didn't know much about the old man. "Do you have family?" he'd asked on a past charter.

"Not here," Pete said.

"How old are you, Pete?"

"Old."

So Tom quit asking. All he knew was that Pete was always waiting on the docks for him, and that he was the best fisherman Tom had ever met.

He turned back to the windows and realized he'd drifted slightly off course. He saw Ben Barker's boat in the distance. *That's the man Monson should have hired. The guy will do anything for money.*

Seven years to retirement. He'd give the *Cirdan* back to the bank and buy a cheap rowboat and fish the calm estuaries. He wouldn't care if he spent all day on the water and didn't catch a thing. Best of all, he wouldn't get seasick anymore. *Seven years...*

Monson wasn't mad at Bailey. *My own fault for not doing more research first.* He'd come all the way from Iowa with the ambition to catch a great white shark, or failing that, a manta ray. He'd talked his little brother into sharing in the driving and the costs, though Marty really didn't like leaving Iowa if he could help it.

But after driving to the Washington coast, Monson stumbled upon an article about deep-sea creatures and decided he wanted to catch one of those. Ugly bastards. He'd have it mounted and put on the wall of his office and freak out the secretaries he went through every few months.

The young newlyweds seated nearby barely seemed aware of him. They had eyes only for each other. The guy caught a small salmon, and the woman got all squealy and squeamish. He kissed the snout of the still-living fish, and she squealed even louder.

The old man who was helping them was smiling, so Monson felt like he had to force a smile onto his own face, but inside he was bored. He didn't mind being ignored. He was used to people underestimating him. When he'd started at Clarke's Medical Supplies, he'd been the lowest-ranked salesman at first. He never sold as much per day as the other salesmen. But he'd just kept selling, day after day after day, without a break. Now he owned the damned company.

Monson felt rather than heard the line on his reel spooling out in a whir. The newlyweds were making so much noise that no one noticed Monson had something on the line. Pete was busy with the happy couple, and Monson was just as glad. It was kind of demeaning to have the old guy helping him, as if he couldn't do it himself.

He let the fish run, and the reel kept on unwinding, much farther than the first fish he'd caught. When the line began to slow, he started slowly reeling it in. It felt twice as heavy as the first fish, and excitement started to build in his gut.

He pulled and reeled, pulled and reeled. The others had finally noticed, but Pete was preoccupied with a salmon the woman had caught, so Monson was left alone for the moment. The fish was so heavy that he was certain it had to be a trophy fish.

He was surprised when the salmon broke the surface. It wasn't fighting, but somehow it still dragged. He pulled it closer and closer. It was as if half the fish was missing.

It wasn't until it reached the side of the boat that he realized something was attached to the fish's side, wrapped around its bottom half.

"What the hell is that?" Marty asked, lifting his chin from the port bow of the boat.

It was a black snake, its tail still in the water, the fangs in its yellow head sunk into the salmon's dorsal fin. As he tried to lift the fish out of the water, its body suddenly shredded, leaving only the head and part of the backbone. Monson jerked it into the boat.

Pete finally noticed something unusual happening and came over, looking down curiously at the mangled salmon. His watery eyes gave Monson a questioning look.

"There was a black snake attached to it," Monson said.

"An eel?" the old man asked.

"No, dammit," Monson said. "A snake. A snake with a yellow-striped head."

Pete snorted as if he didn't believe it. "Yellow?"

"What are you?" Monson shouted. "An idiot?"

The old man flushed, clamped his toothless mouth shut, and turned away, starting to unhook the head of the salmon.

A hand clamped around Monson's neck from behind.

Tom heard yelling from the deck. At first, he couldn't figure out who was yelling at whom. Certainly not Pete, who never raised his voice, or the newlyweds. It had to be that goddamn salesman.

He reached the deck just as Monson called Pete an idiot. He grabbed the fat little man by the neck and turned him around, almost lifting him off the deck. "Don't talk to Pete that way, you little asshole," he said with a growl.

Monson started to apologize. Bailey let him go and turned to Pete. "You all right, Pete?"

Pete was bent over the railing of the boat as if throwing up. Tom had never seen such a thing. "Pete!"

The old man reared up, fell backward onto the deck, and started thrashing. Bailey crouched over him, trying to hold him down. *It must be the old man's heart.* He started pushing down on

Pete's chest and leaned over to give him mouth to mouth when the old man spewed up white foam. Tom couldn't help jerking back.

Pete stopped moving, his eyes staring upward sightlessly.

Tom swore, then pushed to his feet, walked up the spiral stairs, and turned the boat around.

Tom slept on the boat that night. He had a small cot in the cabin, and on summer nights, he often stayed there even when he didn't have to.

The medics had arrived and confirmed that Pete was gone.

"What's his last name?" one of them had asked Tom, and for a moment he'd drawn a blank. Then he remembered why he called Pete 'The Old Man in the Sea'. His last name was Hemmings.

"Do you have contact with his family?"

Tom shook his head, embarrassed. They'd probably thought he was a heartless bastard.

"Well, we'll see what we can find out."

"I'll pay for everything," Tom had said as the medics walked away.

By the time the ambulance left, it was dark. The newlyweds had left without a word, leaving their salmon behind. The goddamn salesman had tried to apologize. "I didn't mean to insult the old man," Monson had said. "But he laughed at me when I told him there was a black sea snake wrapped around the fish."

Tom hadn't really listened. "Get out," he'd said.

Later, Tom woke in the middle of the night. He remembered reading an article about a black sea snake washing up on the California coast, far from its normal habitat.

He grabbed his flashlight and went down to the deck. The fishing pole was still leaning against the railing. He pulled the line up and stared at the fish head on the hook. He reached out then hesitated.

Instead, he pulled his knife from the sheath on his belt and cut the line, letting the hook and the fish head sink into the ripples.

CHAPTER FOUR

Charlie had to pass the administration office of the Biology Department to get to the lab. He was still wearing his rubber gloves, carrying his two white buckets – one containing the remains of the black snake, the other holding the sea life samples from Ed Taylor's dock.

He had gone three steps when Mary Stewart looked up from her knitting. She gave him her stony face, by which he knew he was in trouble. She'd told him more than once to come in the back entrance when returning from a field trip, but it was so much easier to get his mail and messages on the way in.

She put down her knitting, stood, smoothed her dress, and cleared her throat. "Out! Come back when you are cleaned up!"

Charlie turned right around. *I hope I haven't pissed her off too much.* Mary was notorious for disliking the seashore and the creatures that washed up upon it. "It's a charnel house," she'd say.

Most people considered Charlie's tenure as head of the Biology Department to have been a success because he'd managed to talk Mary out of transferring to head of administration for the English Department.

Charlie put the buckets down on the hallway floor, careful not to slosh, and poked his head around the door.

"Is Carter in?" he asked.

"He's at the alumni function," Mary said. "Probably won't be back today."

Charlie grimaced. Meeting the alumni had been one of his least favorite duties when he was department head. Ken Carter loved all the politics of the position. It was almost enough to make Charlie wish department head wasn't a rotating position.

It would be all right with him if Carter had the job full time, except for one thing – Carter was tightfisted about department funding, feeling it was his duty to end every year with a surplus, and had made it known that he thought marine biology was an unnecessary specialization.

"Thanks, Mary," Charlie said, watching her face to see how much trouble he was in.

She smiled. "No problem."

He sighed and closed the door gently. He picked up the buckets and made his way to the lab. His graduate assistant, Jerry Parker, was working in the back and looked up with his usual impassive expression. Charlie felt a moment of guilt. He'd been neglecting Jerry. He'd never had an assistant he spent less time with, but then he'd never had an assistant who already seemed to know everything.

What I should be doing is teaching him how to talk to others. The kid never asked for help, never socialized with either students or professors. One day, he had marched into Charlie's office and stood there, as he was wont to do, without saying a word.

"Yes, Jerry?" Charlie had asked.

"I just wanted you to know," he'd said, "I may have a touch of Asperger's Syndrome."

No shit, Charlie had almost said. Instead, he had nodded. "Thank you for telling me."

Jerry had stood there for a moment longer, as if uncertain whether to leave now that he'd spoken his piece. "Just thought you should know," he'd said. He had turned around and marched out the door.

Charlie dropped the buckets near the row of huge sinks along the wall and walked over to where Jerry was dissecting a lamprey. "How's your dissertation coming along?" he asked.

Jerry looked puzzled for a moment. "I finished weeks ago."

"Oh," Charlie said, momentarily at a loss for words. He'd rarely had a student finish a dissertation on time, much less months early. "You want me to look at it?"

It was obvious Jerry hadn't even thought of the next step, that he'd figured he was finished.

Charlie sighed. "Jerry, writing the paper is only the beginning. You are going to need to sell it to the committee. You know, sell it to *me*."

"But you agreed to the subject," Jerry said. His voice was flat. There was no arguing with him. He'd wanted to study both DNA and cloning, with a view toward resurrecting the sea cow that had once teemed within these waters but had been extinct for a hundred years. With most graduate students, Charlie would have suggested he pick just one of these subjects, either DNA or cloning, but not both. On second thought, he'd realized that Jerry needed an intensive challenge, and that whatever they originally agreed upon, the kid would do what he wanted anyway.

Frankly, a lot of the subject was over Charlie's head, though he'd tried not to let Jerry know that. He knew from Jerry's undergraduate papers that the kid tended to leave out the fundamental steps leading to leaps of logic. So Charlie figured it would be his job to get Jerry to explain things the kid probably thought everyone already knew.

"You want to see it?" Jerry frowned, which he usually did when he realized that he had missed some social cue that should have been obvious. "I'll email it to you tonight," he said.

"Good," Charlie said. "I'll read it over the next couple of days. Come by my office at noon on Thursday and we'll talk it over." He didn't know whether he already had something scheduled, but if he did, he'd tell Mary to reschedule whatever it was. Jerry needed to be given a firm time or he wouldn't show up at all.

The kid nodded.

Now it was Charlie's turn to try to figure out how to disengage. "All right, then," he said. "I'll see you on Thursday."

He walked back to the sinks. He poured the contents of one of the buckets into one sink, and the other bucket into another. He stood there looking down at the black snake. It was bigger than he remembered, covering the bottom half of the stainless steel. The head was narrow and long, and what he'd thought was fangs were actually a circular row of teeth, like those of the lamprey Jerry was dissecting.

He sensed someone behind him, and turned, suppressing a shout. He hated being surprised like that.

Jerry had silently come over and was staring into the sink. He leaned over.

"Don't touch it!" Charlie yelled.

Jerry looked insulted. "What is it?"

Charlie was secretly relieved. He suspected that his assistant knew more species of marine life than he did, so if Jerry didn't recognize the species, chances were that it was new.

He started getting excited by the idea. *I'll get to call it what I want. Maybe I'll name it after Kristine. She'd like that.* But he had to be sure.

"Would you do me a favor, Jerry?" he said.

"Of course, Professor Wice."

"See if Carol... Professor Wheatley is in her office. Ask her if she'll come to the lab."

"Yes, sir." Jerry hurried off.

Charlie pulled himself away from the mesmerizing sight of the yellow-headed snake and turned to the other sink. He debated taking off his gloves, then decided to keep them on. He dipped a vial into the water and set it aside to have analyzed. He wasn't sure what he expected to find, but he had a feeling something malevolent lurked within this discovery.

He heard Carol's voice in the hallway. "And how is your dissertation coming along?"

"I'm done," Jerry said.

"Really?" Carol sounded truly impressed.

She entered the lab and gave Charlie the wide smile she always greeted him with. He felt his heart do a little loop-the-loop. Being around Carol always made him feel good.

He'd thought when he married Kristine that his attraction to Carol would fade. If anything, it had grown stronger. So strong that he avoided Carol as much as he could, afraid of giving himself away.

She wore her blonde hair long and straight, and it had just a touch of silver in it. She was tall and lean, and if Charlie blurred his eyes slightly, he could swear he was looking at one of the hippie chicks he'd lusted after in high school.

But even when he didn't blur his eyes, even when he saw her wrinkles, she was still attractive to him. Until six months ago, she'd been out of reach, happily married to the late David Wheatley, president of the college and one of the nicest men Charlie had ever met. David had died unexpectedly just a year before. Carol was a few years younger than Charlie, in her mid-fifties.

As Kristine became more and more demanding, Carol's easygoing ways became even more attractive. She was also one of the foremost taxonomy experts in the world.

"Jerry says you have something unusual," she said as she approached. "Oh…" She caught sight of the snake and became very still.

"Do you know what it is?" Charlie asked after a few moments.

Carol stared down at it. "Genus *Aipysurus*," she said. "Other than that, I have no idea." She turned to him with a dazzling smile. "I think you've found something new."

"I believe its skin is poisonous," Charlie said. "And the toxin is extremely fast acting." He told her about the sea gulls and the dead creatures near Ed Taylor's dock.

"From its shape, I think this is an open-ocean snake," she said. "Probably a species that never comes near land. If it has both a venomous bite and poisonous skin, that would be extremely unusual. This… this is something we've never seen before. What are you going to call it?"

"I'm thinking *Aipysurus Kristine*."

Carol laughed. "You're going to name a poisonous sea snake after your wife?"

Charlie felt himself grow cold. *Oh, my God. She's right. Kristine would definitely have taken it the wrong way.*

Carol saw his reaction. "Well, I envy you, whatever you decide. Where did you get it?"

"I got a call from St Aloysius Island. Do you know Ed Taylor?"

She nodded; she lived on one of the islands too, and most of the residents around there knew each other.

"He says there was more than one of them. Not only that, he insists that one of them was alive."

"Unlikely," Carol said. "Easy enough to see a snake move if you're expecting it."

"That's what I thought." *Better not admit that I've been wondering if it was true.*

"What's that?" she said, motioning to the other sink.

"There was dead zone near the dock where he found the snake. I took some samples just in case the snake's toxin was causing it."

"That is impossible, Professor Wice," Jerry said. "No matter how powerful a neurotoxin, the ocean would dilute it completely."

"Unless it was somehow trapped in a small area," Carol said. "Are you planning to go back out there?"

Charlie was surprised by the question. He hadn't thought about it. He figured he'd wait for the lab results, maybe post pictures of the snake online to make sure it wasn't a known species. The chances of coming across another one seemed astronomical to him. Then again, Ed Taylor had seen more than one.

"I guess I am," he said.

"May I come with you?" Carol asked.

"Sure," Charlie said. "We can go right now, if you want." He checked his watch. Kristine was hosting a meeting of some volunteer environmental group that night and had asked him to attend, but they should have plenty of time to get to Ed Taylor's place and back.

But why am I going back? What do I expect to find?

He realized what he really expected was to spend a couple of hours with Carol Wheatley, and that was more than enough. He'd never realized how much of a gap there was in knowledge between he and Kristine until he'd married her. Half the time, it seemed like they were talking two different languages.

Carol understood his work, got his references. It was a relief not to explain everything.

She was dressed in blue jeans and a peasant blouse. "Let me get my boots and a hat and I'll meet you at your pickup," she said.

"Can I come too?" Jerry asked as she walked away.

Charlie's heart fell. He realized he really didn't want anyone sitting between him and Carol. *What the hell? I'm a married man.*

"Okay," Charlie said. "Do you have protective gear?" The kid spent most of his time in the lab and sometimes had to be dragged into the field. Charlie suspected that someday Doctor Jerry Parker would be so famous that he wouldn't have to leave his office.

"Yes, sir," Jerry said. He actually seemed excited, his eyes shining and a smile on his face, which was a rare sight. He started to walk away then suddenly came back. He reached around Charlie and grabbed a large cardboard box. He drew the big knife he wore at his waist and cut into the box.

The knife must have been as sharp as a razor, because the section of box came out square and clean. In the last year, Jerry had become fascinated by weapons, mostly guns and knives. Charlie had been forced to order his assistant to leave his guns at home and had settled for letting Jerry carry a sheathed knife.

Jerry grabbed a large marker off one of the shelves and wrote on the cardboard, 'Dangerous! Do Not Touch!'

He leaned the makeshift sign against the faucet and walked away.

I should have thought of that.

CHAPTER FIVE

They drove to the coast, Jerry sitting between the two people he respected most in the world – Professor Wice and Professor Wheatley. Charlie and Carol, as they both insisted on being called and which Jerry could sometimes force himself to remember.

He felt his body tensing at their nearness, and he closed his eyes and took deep breaths.

He was smart, he knew that. At the same time, he was an idiot. He knew that too. So he applied his smarts to his stupidity, and sometimes he could almost seem normal. He could copy ordinary so well in fact, that he'd learned to let people know that it was an act, in case they expected something from him that he couldn't deliver.

He'd gone on a date once – literally once – and it had gone well for most of the evening, and then he'd said or done something that had changed the look on the girl's face, and even he could read the expression: profound disgust. He wanted to apologize but he didn't know what he'd done wrong. Still didn't.

It was the last time he'd ever asked a girl out. Her dropping him off at the dorm without another word had stunned him like nothing else ever had, worse than all the teasing in grade school, worse even than the well-meaning patronizing in high school.

Around the university, he'd seen others like him. People who knew about Jerry's condition tended to think he couldn't read emotions, but he could. He could see when an emotion was there, he just couldn't always tell what it was. And right now, he was sensing very strong feelings between the people on either side of him. It radiated out of them; love or lust or something similar.

He wanted to look at them, but they were too close. He couldn't meet their eyes when they were so close. It was hard enough at a distance, something he had to force himself to do.

I've made another social mistake. I've gotten in the way of two people who probably wanted to be alone.

"I, uh, don't have to come," he said. "You can drop me off at the dorm."

"What are you saying?" Charlie asked. "Don't you want to come?"

"Yes, I do," he said. "But... maybe you want to be alone."

Both professors froze at his comment, and there was a long silence.

"Don't be silly," Carol said, finally. She laughed, but even Jerry could tell it was forced. "Besides, we'd have to turn around."

Charlie spoke up, and he sounded sincere. "I've been wanting to spend some quality field time with you, Jerry. I've been neglecting you. You're so smart, it seems like you don't need any supervision and I need to remember that there are things I can still teach you."

Jerry didn't answer, and he kept his eyes on the road winding ahead of them. He sensed they were looking at him and then at each other, exchanging messages he couldn't read, but he decided that it was too late to change anything now.

"So, Jerry, why did you decide on marine biology?" Carol asked.

He blurted out the answer without thinking. "Godzilla."

"Of course," Charlie said. Jerry snuck a glance at him, but the professor didn't seem to be mocking him.

Jerry had discovered Godzilla when he was five years old, and from that moment on, the Japanese monster was all he cared about. His parents did their best, but they were mystified by it all. They bought him toy dinosaurs, but he didn't care about dinosaurs. When he was old enough to be on his own, he'd haunted the local comic shop until the grizzled old owner had snarled at him, "You've seen everything I've got and everything I can get on Godzilla. Quit asking!"

In junior high, Jerry discovered there lurked real monsters in the depths of the oceans, and he had turned his attention to that. He still had his Godzilla collection filling his room at home, and sometimes when he visited, he felt a little embarrassed, but inevitably by the end of the visit, he would have taken some of the toys down and looked at them (well, played with them).

"With my daughter, it's Doctor Who," Carol said. "Can't get enough of him – or the various *hims* – as she always corrects me."

"How *is* Jennifer?" Charlie asked.

"She's doing well. I drop her off at the center every morning, and she seems to accept it. They've gone out of their way to bring in some Doctor Who stuff. Sometimes she forgets her dad is gone, and when I remind her, she'll cry. But I'd have to say she's almost happy."

"What's wrong with her?" Jerry asked.

"Nothing," Carol answered. "Just like there is nothing wrong with you."

So that's it. Professor Wheatley was one of the few people he'd ever met who treated him as she would treat anyone else. Almost everyone else went to one extreme or the other, being either too abrupt or too solicitous. Even Professor Wice, as nice and helpful as he was, tended to give Jerry too much leeway.

"She's autistic?" he asked.

"Severely," Carol said. "Not like you, Jerry. You've done very well."

They drove in silence most of the rest of the way. Jerry was deep in thought. Sometimes he wondered if he wasn't being selfish by pursuing his interest in marine biology, more specifically, in sea monsters. He knew he was book smart, and maybe he should have applied that talent toward finding a cure for autism or some other disease or condition.

He'd taken a few classes in that direction, but he'd rediscovered what he and everyone else already knew. He was interested in what he was interested in and nothing else.

The tires suddenly rattled as the pickup bounced across a wooden bridge. They had arrived at St Aloysius Island. Jerry had never been here, though he had been at the homes of both Professor Wheatley and Professor Wice, who also had homes on the coastal islands.

Someday, he was going to live out here too.

The professor turned to the right and circled the small island. It was getting late. The sun had dropped below the tree line, and it was at least ten degrees colder than it had been on campus. They came around a corner to a small cottage. Charlie drove the pickup down the narrow driveway and around the house, where there was a lawn extending down to a small dock.

The big tree at one corner of the house was full of ravens, which were making such a racket that they could be heard through the closed windows of the pickup.

Charlie stopped abruptly, and at the same moment, Jerry saw the lumps in the middle of the lawn. He couldn't make out the details, but a feeling of dread came over him. He wanted to close his eyes and retreat inside himself, count to one thousand like he used to do. But both of his professors jumped out of the pickup, and he knew he had to follow.

The lumps resolved themselves into the shapes of a dog with a woman alongside it, one arm around its neck. Lying next to the woman was a man. They were holding hands.

It took until they were only a few yards away before he saw the long, black snake just a few feet from dog's open mouth.

"Oh, my God," Carol said. "Their eyes..."

For a second, Jerry thought the people were wearing dark glasses; then he saw that what he'd mistaken for glasses were voids surrounded by blood. There were two ravens nearby, their legs in the air. The rest of the ravens had apparently learned from the demise of their fellow birds and were objecting loudly.

Jerry couldn't pull his gaze away. Their blackened sockets drew him in with their empty, deadened gaze. He felt as if he was both floating above the bodies and slowly sinking into them.

"Jerry?" A voice broke into his nightmare, a concerned voice, with the same tone his mom took when he went into one of his trances. Professor Wheatley took his arm and turned him toward her. "Jerry, look away."

Behind them, Professor Wice called 911.

"Jerry?" Charlie said after he ended the call. "Why don't you go down to the dock and get another water sample."

Jerry turned his eyes downslope, not quite understanding what he was being asked. There was a large sea lion lying on the dock, and somehow the sight of the creature finally brought him back to himself.

"Is it safe?" Carol asked.

"Well," Charlie said. "Old Professor Haggerty used to say, never get in between a sea lion and his meal or his mate. But breeding season is over, so it should be safe enough."

Carol let go of Jerry and pushed him gently in the right direction. "Be careful," she said.

Jerry turned around, walked to the back of the pickup. He'd brought protective gear, gloves, goggles, and overalls. He was always meticulous. The other students thought the precautions unnecessary. Most of the time, they probably were. *But not this time.*

He donned the gloves and goggles, grabbed a bucket, and marched down to the dock. At the edge of the water, he saw a couple of upside-down starfish and some sea anemones floating, dead. *Interesting.* Whatever had killed them had detached them from their rocky perches.

For a moment he forgot the horror of the dead people. The sea lion scooted down to the end of the dock, and then turned and blared its objection to his presence. Jerry ignored it and kept coming.

He could tell from the color of the water that the lagoon was already deep a few yards from the shore. Probably why the dock had been built there.

He got down on his knees and swooped the bucket through the water. There was something big floating right beneath the surface, and the swirl he created in the water was just enough for it to breach. It was a dead baby sea lion.

The dock beneath him shook, and there was a loud *thump* behind him. He started to rise, and turned just as the sea lion brought its jaws down on his shoulder, pushing him into the water.

Jerry managed to take a breath before hitting the surface and was dragged under.

He felt amazingly calm, as if it was all happening to someone else. Down they went into the darkness. The sea lion felt like dead weight, and he realized the huge creature wasn't moving. He unsheathed the knife on his belt, and stabbed it into the side of the creature's head. It didn't react. It had taken him down into the water with the last of its strength.

Still calm, Jerry re-sheathed his knife. His lungs were hurting, but he ignored it. Either he would pry open the sea lion's mouth or he wouldn't. If he didn't, he'd be carried to the bottom.

The creature's mouth was lax. It was only the long teeth buried into his shoulder that kept them attached. Jerry pulled the teeth out, ignoring the pain.

He kicked toward the surface, sure he wouldn't make it, but his body overrode his will and he gasped for breath the moment he broke the surface. Carol was on her knees on the dock, white faced. Behind her, Charlie was taking off his boots, looking ready to dive into the water.

"Don't!" Jerry said as loudly as he could manage. "Don't go into the water."

Charlie reached out for him, but Jerry turned aside from the dock and swam to shore. Carol came running up to him.

Jerry had thought he was calm, but now his hands were shaking. He felt out of control. Too much was happening too fast. He closed his eyes, took deep breaths.

"Don't touch me," Jerry said. "Either of you. There's something bad in the water." He walked up onto the grass and kept going. He walked past the bodies and on up to the house where he had spied a garden hose earlier. He removed all his clothes then turned on the faucet. He directed the water down on his head and rubbed his body with his other hand.

It was freezing cold, but no colder than the ocean had been. He was beyond caring, beyond pain. He knew he was probably going to die, but he had to try to save himself. He was vaguely aware that Carol and Charlie had followed him. They were silent, looking away as if embarrassed.

A siren whooped nearby and Jerry jumped. The ambulance came around the side of the house and stopped directly in front of him, as if the driver had been startled to see him.

Don't look at me!

His right arm went up over his head, wrapping around, and he groaned. The old involuntary responses to stress that he'd tried so hard to eliminate returned. His face was twitching, his tongue darting into the side of his mouth.

How crazy he must look! He'd always been afraid to take his clothes off in the light, and here he was outside in the daytime with other people, with a female even, and he was completely nude. There were red streaks in the rivulets of water running down his pale, thin body, and he realized the puncture wounds in his shoulder were bleeding.

The ambulance driver got out and stared at him. A female EMT got out of the passenger side and approached. "Are you all right?" she asked.

"The bodies are down there," Jerry said, pointing down the lawn. His arm jerked, wanting to cradle his head. With conscious effort, he resisted.

"They're dead," Charlie said. "Nothing you can do for them. You need to help Jerry first."

"Don't touch the clothes," Jerry said to his professor. He let the EMTs take him to the back of the ambulance. He'd sprayed enough water on himself that whatever poison was on him had probably been washed away. The toxin might have permeated his skin, but it wasn't going to hurt the others.

He felt the urge to dart his hand upward again and suppressed it. He bit down on his tongue, trying to control its spasmodic movements.

They wrapped a thick blanket around him, and the woman worked on his wound.

"You're lucky," she said. "The bite didn't hit the bone and

only punctured the muscle. It should heal, but you'll need some shots. Do want some pain medication?"

"No, thank you," Jerry said. The EMT was cute, with short hair with bangs, dark, sparkling eyes, and a trim, athletic body. He concentrated on looking at her because it calmed him somehow. She had a name tag that said Mindy. She was the kind of woman he could never say more than a few words to before his tongue tangled up. "Do you have something I can wear?" he managed to ask.

"I think Campbell has an extra jumpsuit," she said. She opened a chest attached to the ambulance and pulled out a pair of bright blue overalls, which were huge on him but at least covered him up. He felt himself relaxing, and the warm blanket seemed determined to put him to sleep.

"Lay back," Mindy said. "Rest. It's pretty common after a bit of excitement that you'll feel sluggish."

Jerry leaned back for a moment and felt dizzy, and then it was as if he was being dragged back down into the water, which in his mind's eye became the black holes of empty eye sockets.

He sat back up. "I'm fine," he said, moving to the back of the ambulance and standing. "I've got to help my friends."

Mindy looked uncertain. The driver, Campbell, was down by the bodies, loading them up on gurneys by himself. "Are you sure, Jerry?"

He nodded, grateful that she seemed genuinely concerned. He tried smiling at her, knew it came out wrong because she looked away frowning.

Carol was standing near Campbell, talking to him. Charlie was by the side of the house, rubber gloves on his hands, gingerly putting Jerry's clothes into a black garbage bag.

Jerry was seeing it all, taking it in, but most of his attention was focused inside, on a part of himself he'd never felt before. His body was awash with emotions: fear of dying, love for his companions, worry about his parents. Oh, he'd always felt a muted version of these emotions, but it was as if someone had opened a lid in his brain and let them all out, strong and full and completely normal.

The analytical part of his mind continued to work too, and he realized that whatever toxin was in the water – which might still kill him – had done something else to him.

Why am I still alive?

The toxin seemed to have a different effect on different people. Was it because... because of his autism? Or was the water diluted enough to have affected only a part of him?

He'd always been told he was smart, and it did seem as though he remembered everything he read or was told. But he also had vague concepts floating around in his brain that he could never quite express.

Now all the circuits were closing, all the dim theories coming together, and he saw his future as bright as a sunny day.

He burst into tears, grateful and suddenly very frightened.

CHAPTER SIX

The boat stank. Ben Barker, the owner of the *Knotty Girl* , caught Monson wrinkling his nose. "We've been catching so many fish, we haven't had time to clean up," he said.

"Riiiiigghhtt," Monson said, drawing it out. There was blood and gore in every crevice of the boat, and some of it looked to be years old, but he'd been lucky to find another boat so quickly. As he'd walked away from the disaster of his morning excursion, he'd noticed the sign at the end of the dock. 'Deep Sea Fishing.' By midafternoon, they were already underway.

What the Barker brothers may have scrimped on looks they'd apparently spent on outboard engines. The boat was amazingly fast, over fifty miles per hour. By late afternoon they were heading farther out into the open ocean.

The water was darker out here. Monson could sense the depths, could imagine the creatures below. He'd show Tom Bailey that the right amount of money could get one anything they wanted, and Monson would rub that damn trophy fish in Bailey's face.

"Okay, I need to tell you two things," Ben said. "First of all, we probably ain't going to catch anything too exotic. You know those creatures you see on *Nature* and shit? The kind with lights on the end of their snouts? Those are mostly in the deep-sea trenches, and while the ocean is pretty deep hereabouts, it ain't a trench." He paused, waiting for a reaction.

Monson was furious. He could have been told this back on shore, and he could have saved some money. But now that he was already out here, he knew he had to try. Nobody had to teach the Barker brothers about sunk costs. Con men like them knew the concept by instinct.

Monson had no choice but to nod.

"Secondly, we aren't going to catch anything with a rod and reel. Putting a hook out would be a little like dropping a rock off a cliff and expecting to hit a deer. So we're going to use a net. Not very sporting, but neither is not catching nothing. You okay with that?"

"As long as we catch something," Monson said.

"Oh, I guarantee we'll catch *something*," said Ben Barker. "Here, let me show you."

He went past Monson to the back of the boat. There was a diving ramp below a gate in the back. He opened the gate. There were three steps down to the ramp. He motioned Monson over.

Ben leaned over and unlatched something that wasn't visible on the surface. The three steps rolled up, revealing a dark well beneath. "We have loose netting down there. Anything small enough to escape is too small to keep. You can catch as much as you want, Mister Monson. Fuck the limit. We'll just put them in here."

He started to walk away then came back. "One more thing. This is going to take some time. It's kinda like flying a kite to the top of a mountain. We have a long way to go."

"Then we better get started," Monson said.

The Barker brothers produced a rig from inside the cabin that rolled out into a net with huge weights attached. The other brother, Jeremy, seemed to be in charge of the operation. They wrestled the contraption over the side of the boat.

"Now, we wait," Ben said.

The two men sat back and drank some beers, and after about an hour of the spool unwinding the nets finally stopped. Ben got up and started the boat, and they trolled for another couple of hours.

Monson had been on the *Knotty Girl* long enough that he could almost feel the boat dragging. In his mind's eye, he saw the net filling with exotic creatures, and he began to get excited. It wasn't what he'd expected, but he didn't care as long as he got something cool.

The boat stopped, and Jeremy went over to the winch and started pulling up the net. It took a little longer coming up than going down, but Monson figured that was a good sign.

When the net finally broke the surface, it looked as if there wasn't anything there. The Barkers didn't seem concerned. They pulled the net into the boat and opened it up.

Fish came spilling out. Only fish, mostly small. Normal, everyday, flopping, gasping fish.

"Shit," Ben Barker said.

"This is not what I paid for," Monson said.

"I told you I couldn't guarantee you'd get anything special."

"I paid you a great deal of money." Monson felt his face flushing, knew that he was about to fly into the kind of rage that never ended well. Normally, he'd just walk away, but he was stuck on this boat with his little brother and two very rough looking men who could drop him and Marty overboard without a second thought. Ben Barker could say it was an accident and have his brother – who looked even seedier than him – back him up.

"We can go another round," Ben said. "Stay another day and start earlier."

"I have to get back to—"

"Shut up, both of you!" Jeremy broke in. "Come and look at this."

In the net was a single fish that was bigger than the others. It wasn't a giant, but it had an odd, elongated shape. It looked prehistoric, like a true sea monster. It was still flopping about, still alive.

"Is that a coe... a colan..." Marty sputtered, finally dragging himself away from the side of the boat where he'd been throwing up. Again.

"A coelacanth," Monson said.

"A fucking coelacanth," Marty said, wiping his mouth with the back of his hand. "But they come from like the Indian Ocean, right? Or Africa?"

"Not anymore, apparently," Ben said. "I've been seeing

some awfully weird things lately." He turned to Monson with a big grin. "Congratulations, Mister Monson." Then both Barker brothers were slapping him on the back and laughing, something that never happened on Bailey's boat.

Monson wondered for a moment if the fish had been planted, then realized how crazy that was. This fish was so rare that it was probably worth ten Gerald Monsons.

"You want me to put it on ice or put it in the reservoir and try to keep it alive?" Jeremy asked.

"Keep it alive," Monson said. "We can decide later what to do with it."

He watched Jeremy hook the fish and lift it off the deck. As Jeremy carried it to the back, Monson put out his hand and stroked the prehistoric creature's side. He almost said "Sorry" out loud.

Jeremy opened the latch at the side of the stairs and reached down with the coelacanth into the darkness.

He sprang back with a cry. Something long and dark was wrapped around his arm. He tried to shake it off, and then another long, black shape slithered out of the hole and wrapped around his leg.

Monson tried to make sense of it, and then the memory of the snake attached to his salmon came to him, and he knew what it was. He stayed frozen in place as more of the snakes came pouring out of the well.

Ben Barker rushed past to help his brother, a gaffing hook in his hands. Jeremy was dancing about, frenzied, as if shocked by an electric current. He lost his footing on the slick diving deck, and let out a scream that was cut short, as if his throat had been slit. He sat down hard, and the snakes swarmed over him until Monson couldn't even see him anymore.

"Don't touch the snakes!" Monson cried out, but Ben had already reached the place where his brother had disappeared, and he was striking left and right with the gaffing hook.

"Marty," Monson shouted. "Come here!"

His brother scooted over, wiping more puke off his chin. He

looked puzzled, as if he hadn't been paying attention. "I'm never doing this again."

"Never mind that," Monson said. "Don't go near the snakes!"

"Not bloody likely," Marty shouted.

Ben Barker was trying to drive the snakes off his brother's body, but more kept coming. He hadn't cleared much of a space before he backed up to the cabin. He turned, reached inside, and grabbed a bundle. He pulled a cord and a life raft began to unfold.

The snakes were just inches away. The yellow raft was still filling with air when Ben went over the side of the boat with it, disappearing from view.

The snakes were now swarming onto the deck. Monson and Marty backed up as creatures slithered toward them. Monson's shoulders hit the mast, and he turned around, grabbed the ladder, and started climbing, not stopping until he reached the crow's nest. His brother climbed up after him. The mast swayed alarmingly, but there was just enough room.

Monson looked down, expecting the snakes to be climbing after them, but that apparently wasn't something they could do. The deck was black with them, squirming, twisting around on every open surface.

The sun was going down behind the boat, and the light hit the surface of the ocean just right so it appeared as a flatly lit sheet. There at the center, extending far into the horizon – *miles* – was something that looked like an asphalt road. But it was undulating and swaying, as if it was a giant Ouroboros wrapping itself around the world.

It was made of black snakes, stretching from the surface far down into the waters and slowing winding its way to shore.

As he stared at the sight, he caught a glimpse of something breaching the ocean waves just beyond the snakes, the same shape and color, but much larger. The black skin rippled through the water, circling the smaller snakes, and then dove out of sight.

"Did you see..." he started to ask his brother, but Marty leaned over the side of the nest and poured the remnants of his lunch down upon the writhing snakes below.

CHAPTER SEVEN

John Sanders had spent the first sixty years of his life making money. He'd spent the last five years trying to reach his son, without much success. When Liam had come to him with the idea of buying land on the coast of Washington, his immediate reaction had been to dismiss it.

Liam's face had fallen, and he'd gone to his room, not to emerge for three days.

At the end of that third day, he went to his son's room and knocked. Not his bedroom, but the semi-secret room on the top floor of the huge house, where Liam retreated when stressed. It was full of his old sci-fi books and Star Wars toys and other comforting reminders of his childhood.

"Go away." Liam's voice was muffled. He probably had his pillow over his head like he always did when he was upset.

John tried the door and was encouraged to find it unlocked. When Liam had fallen into his first depression, about the time he had entered junior high, he'd lock his door and wouldn't let anyone in.

John sat on the side of the bed. "Tell me again about your idea of a surfing resort in Washington."

"You're just humoring me," Liam said, but he removed the pillow and sat up.

Of course I'm humoring you, John wanted to say. But instead, he kept his voice calm and said, "No, it sounds like a great idea. I'm sorry. I was in the middle of something and didn't give it the time it deserved."

Then Liam's ideas came spilling out, and John felt the weight begin to lift. He was nearly in tears at the look of excitement on his son's face, eyes shining, the stress disappearing from his chin and cheeks.

Crisis averted.

When his late-wife, Peggy, had first come to him, worried about Liam's emotional and mental state, John had dismissed it as typical teenage hormones, but it had gotten worse and worse until he couldn't overlook it any longer.

Through it all, Liam's best friend Devon was the one person who seemed to be able to get through to him, to coax him out of bed and to school. Devon had gotten Liam interested in surfing.

But it hadn't kept Liam from trying to kill himself.

John couldn't understand it. His son had all the advantages that his parents had never had. He lacked for nothing.

"Is that what you think?" Peggy asked when he'd told her this. She was dressed for one of her volunteer groups, nails and hair and makeup done perfectly. It was hard to believe that beneath that perfect exterior, a cancer was growing that would take her away within a couple of years.

"You pick apart anything he comes to you with, John," Peggy said. "By the time you're done, Liam has lost interest. And even when you finally do come through, you have so many strings attached that Liam can't extricate himself. Frankly, he'd be better off without your help."

That had hurt, but when he'd thought about it, he'd realized she was right. But still, he hadn't done anything other than hire the best psychiatrists he could find, paying for a smorgasbord of medications that turned his son into a zombie.

Not long after Peggy died, just as Liam was entering high school, he swam out from the coast of New York and headed for England. If Devon hadn't noticed and gone after him on his surfboard, Liam would be lying at the bottom of the ocean right now.

That had been it. John Sanders turned his vast business interests over to various new CEOs and management teams and turned his full attention to Liam.

At the same time, Liam grew out of his awkward physical stage and became popular at school. Good looking and rich finally kicked in. Liam took up surfing with a vengeance, and despite John's doubts, he encouraged his son.

John bought up as much land as he could on the coast of Washington, ramrodded a resort through all the local regulations, and watched his son blossom.

And then came this phone call.

"Dad?" His son's voice was so weak and vulnerable that John immediately stood from his couch and waved over Perkins, his assistant, who was paying bills at the kitchen table.

"Liam? Is that you? Where are you?" John asked.

A voice in the background said, "Ezekiel's Landing."

Ezekiel's Landing? John tried to remember where that was. Miles down the coast, he was pretty sure. "How the hell did you get there?"

"Dad," Liam said. "Devon's gone. He's dead."

John didn't doubt his son for a moment. The grief in Liam's voice was enough to send shivers down his spine. "I'll be right there, son."

Liam was in the back office of the gas station, the heater on full blast, wrapped in a cheap blanket the clerk had put around his shoulders. He was shivering, white faced, his blond hair lank and his blue eyes dull.

He stood when John entered and let himself be hugged. "Take him to the car," John told Perkins. He handed the clerk a hundred-dollar bill and said, "Keep the change."

He got in the backseat with Liam, who seemed half the size he'd been that morning at breakfast. "The nearest hospital," John said. Perkins reached over to the GPS and entered the information, but Liam objected.

"I'm all right, Dad. Just take me home."

"Are you sure, Liam?" In truth, he wasn't as worried about his son's physical condition as he was about his mental state. Liam had only recently begun to show his old interests again, especially surfing. "Maybe we should have you checked at the emergency room."

"I'll be OK," Liam said. "Really."

They drove halfway home in silence before John realized they needed to report what had happened. He pulled out his cellphone and dialed 911.

Liam stared out the window the rest of the way home, scotching every attempt John made to engage in conversation. Finally, he gave up. When they pulled into the garage, Liam got out of the car and headed up to his room.

"If you need anything..." John called after him.

CHAPTER EIGHT

Charlie dropped Jerry off at his dorm, but when Jerry tried to get out of the truck, he almost fell over.

"Are you all right?" Carol asked.

"Just a little shaky still," Jerry said.

"That's it," Charlie said. "We're taking you to the hospital."

"No, really," Jerry protested. "I'm just tired is all. I feel fine."

Better than fine, but I shouldn't say anything yet about this sudden leap in mental acuity. Maybe I'm delusional. Maybe it's an illusion.

The clarity he felt didn't seem like an illusion. Anything but. But then, wasn't that exactly what an illusion would feel like?

The clearest thought he had was that this new lucidity was the result of having been exposed to whatever neurotoxin was in the sea snake. It had been greatly diluted, no doubt, but what else could it be?

He'd read a book in high school about a crazy old surfer in Jamaica who'd self-medicated with cone shell stings. They would nearly kill him but eased his chronic ailments. Perhaps it was something like that?

"All right," Charlie said reluctantly. "But I'm at least going to make sure you get to your room safely." He got out of the truck, and Carol joined him. Jerry figured he could either agree to this or be shanghaied to the emergency room.

"Why do you live in a dorm?" Carol asked.

Jerry flushed, a little embarrassed. It was the rare graduate student who didn't have his own apartment. But Jerry couldn't afford an apartment without having roommates, and he'd learned that he didn't get along with roommates.

Would that have embarrassed me before? Or would I have answered the question straight, not understanding the implications?

"It's cheaper and more convenient," Jerry said.

Carol's brow furrowed, but she remained silent.

"You want to go by the cafeteria and get something to eat?" Charlie asked.

"No, I'm fine."

He never ate in the cafeteria. He had a small fridge and microwave in his room. Jerry had managed to get a room on the bottom floor in the back corner of the dormitory nearest the road. Most of the time he could enter and leave without running into anyone. There was only one danger zone. The dorm next to his overlooked the sidewalk. As they walked up to the back door, someone shouted from an open window on the top floor of the other dorm, "Ground control to Major Tom!"

Jerry understood the reference and nearly laughed. His blue EMT jumpsuit really did look like the training uniforms astronauts wore. *I would have felt the taunt yesterday, but today I don't care.*

"Hey, fuck you!" Charlie yelled out.

There was laughter from the open window, but no one was visible. "That's no way for a professor to talk!"

"Oh, yeah?" Charlie shouted. "I recognize your voice, Simmons. Tell me about it at the next seminar."

There was a sudden silence, and the window slammed shut.

Carol had put her hand on Jerry's arm, as if concerned. He flashed her a smile. She looked surprised and let go. He inserted his key into the back door and opened it.

"Thanks for helping me, you guys," he said. The informality of that statement seemed to surprise his professors. *I'd better pretend a little longer.*

"No problem," Charlie answered. "If you start feeling bad, you call 911, you hear me?"

"Of course."

"I mean it," Charlie said. "You promise me?"

"I will call 911 if I start feeling bad," Jerry said, using the monotone he'd always used, not because he wanted to, but because he could never calibrate vocal expressions well.

Carol said, "You just take care of yourself, Jerry. Don't worry about school."

Jerry nodded and closed the door.

"Do you think he's all right?" Carol asked.

"It doesn't matter what I think," Charlie said. "Jerry will do whatever Jerry wants to do. The best you can hope for is to plant a suggestion and hope it takes hold."

"He's been in a couple of my classes," Carol said. "Seems incredibly smart. High-functioning Asperger's?"

"I wonder sometimes just how high-functioning, but yeah, he's brilliant. He's writing a dissertation that I'm *pretending* to fully understand."

They drove on for a few miles without saying anything more. It was surprisingly comfortable, as if they could each feel what the other was thinking.

"Do you want me to drop you off at your car?" Charlie asked, finally.

"I take the bus," Carol said. "Do you mind dropping me off at my house? I'm usually home when Jennifer gets dropped off. She's okay on her own as long as she stays in the house, but I still like to check up on her."

"Sure," Charlie said. He took the first off ramp heading north. He vaguely remembered that Carol's house was near the university. He'd been to a couple of parties there. As president of the university, David Wheatley had done a lot of entertaining.

"Uh, we need to head to Rampart Island," Carol said. "I moved there after David died. I may not be a marine biologist per se, but there is no better place for a biologist to be than on the coast."

"Huh," Charlie said. "We're almost neighbors."

Carol smiled slightly. "I know. I nearly dropped by a couple of times."

Why didn't you? Charlie wanted to ask, but he knew. Kristine didn't like visitors dropping by unexpectedly. The house had to be pristine before she'd entertain. But an even bigger reason was that Kristine had taken an immediate dislike to Carol. Charlie had never understood why.

Carol's residence was a cute '50s-style modern that Charlie had noticed and admired before. There was a little garage to one side, and Charlie pulled into it.

"Come on in," Carol said. "You need to meet Jennifer."

Charlie hesitated, though he wasn't sure why. But it seemed important to Carol, so he smiled and nodded.

She opened the door from the garage and yelled, "Jennifer? We've got a visitor." She whispered to Charlie, "Best not to surprise her."

Jennifer marched into the living room. She was in her early twenties and striking, with raven hair cut short, bow-shaped lips and a button nose, wide brown eyes, and creamy skin. Charlie figured Carol must have a hard time keeping the boys away from her, at least until they talked to her and realized she was a tad different.

She looked Charlie up and down. "You look like the Third Doctor," she said abruptly. "How old are you?"

"Please don't be rude, Jennifer," Carol said.

"Shut up, Mother," Jennifer said. "How old are you?"

"I'm fifty-eight," Charlie said.

She shook her head. "Too old. Jon Pertwee was fifty when he started. Although, by the time he was done, he was fifty-four." She seemed to think that made Charlie acceptable. "Who's your favorite Doctor?" she asked.

Uh, oh. Don't blow it. He wracked his brain to remember anything about Doctor Who. "Uh... Tom Baker?"

She snorted. "That's what all you old people say. Boring!"

Carol sighed and rolled her eyes. "Jennifer..."

"Well, it is," Jennifer said. "Boring."

Carol stepped over to her daughter and took her by the arm. "Go to your room for a while, Jennifer. We have business to discuss."

"What about?" Jennifer demanded.

"Marine biology," Carol said.

Charlie added, "We may have found a new species of sea—"

"Boring!" Jennifer said. She turned and left without another word.

Carol turned to Charlie, and he expected her to apologize. Instead, she said, "I think she likes you."

"What happens when she *doesn't* like someone?"

"You don't want to know."

Charlie's phone hummed in his pocket. Before answering, he checked his watch. It was 7:30, past the time he usually got home.

By the time he answered the phone it had gone to voicemail. He'd missed five calls, one from Ken Carter, the head of the Biology Department, and four from Kristine. In all the excitement, he hadn't felt his phone vibrate even once.

Oh, shit. Kristine had something planned for tonight.

He called her back first.

"Where have you been?" Kristine asked before he could say anything. "You really should answer your phone, Charlie. You don't know when it might be important."

"We've had a bit of excitement," Charlie said.

"Where are you?"

"I'm at Carol Wheatley's house."

There was a long silence on the other end. *Why on Earth did I tell her that?* He looked over at Carol. She had a comically alarmed look on her face. He nearly laughed but choked it back. He'd be in big trouble if he laughed.

"That old bag?" Kristine said at last. "Whatever for?"

"Like I said, we've had something interesting—"

"Never mind," Kristine said. "You need to call Ken Carter. He's been trying to get a hold of you."

"Oh," Charlie said. "I'll call him right now."

"You probably should," Kristine said, and ended the call.

Charlie didn't look at Carol as he tapped in Ken's number. He didn't want to know how much she'd heard. He'd become accustomed to Kristine's nagging, enough that he told himself it didn't matter. But with Carol there, it suddenly did matter.

"Hello, Ken? This is Charlie—"

"Dammit, Charlie. I've been looking for you. You need to come over to John Sanders's house right away. There's been a tragedy."

"I've been sort of dealing with my own situation, Ken."

"Whatever it is, it can wait," Ken said. "Do you know where Carol Wheatley is?"

"I'm at her house right now," Charlie said.

Again, there was a long silence. *Jesus, why is everyone so surprised by that?*

"What's happened?" Charlie asked.

"John's son's best friend was killed surfing," Ken said. "Liam says they were attacked by a swarm of sea snakes."

"Snakes?" Charlie said. He shot a glance at Carol, whose eyes widened.

"That's what they're saying. You don't sound as surprised as I thought you'd be."

"We'll be right there." Charlie pocketed his phone and shrugged. "Why does everyone think it's so weird that I'm at your house?"

Carol didn't say anything at first, then she turned and gave him an expressionless look. "I'm sure *I* don't know."

"Strange, huh?"

"Very strange," she said. "I'll go tell Jennifer I'm leaving, and we can head right out."

She left the room, and Charlie had the feeling he'd missed something important.

CHAPTER NINE

Charlie didn't have to ask Carol for directions to John Sanders's house. He didn't have to plug it into his GPS. It was hard to miss. There was an actual drawbridge out to the island, which was usually up at night but which was currently down.

There were a couple of cop cars – state police and local sheriff, and Charlie recognized Ken's BMW as well.

The huge house looked like three or four Frank Lloyd Wright houses stacked on top of each other, each level managing to jut out over the beach. It looked as if every light in the house was on, and it was almost blinding.

A deputy met them at the base of the stairs. "You the professors? This way."

She led them around to the back of the house, where there was a long room that faced the ocean, with windows running the entire length of it. They went through a sliding door. Everyone inside was already standing clustered in the center of the room.

The deputy's name, it turned out, was Sarah Ramirez. She had a no-nonsense manner that was reassuring. The state trooper introduced himself as Mark Bowie. He kept moving close to the female deputy. She kept her distance, frowning. *Some kind of history there.*

The rest were officious-looking men and women. Chairs and couches had been pushed aside. Along the back of the room, there was a table filled with a smorgasbord of food. Charlie felt his mouth water and realized he'd skipped both lunch and dinner.

Ramirez spoke in a clipped manner. "We found Devon's surfboard on the beach about half a mile down. No sign of his body."

"Excuse me," John Sanders said. He broke away and approached Carol and Charlie, hand outstretched. Behind him, a look of annoyance flashed over the deputy's face.

"Good of you to come, Professor Wice, Professor Wheatley. We need your expertise."

"I understand you had an incident with sea snakes?" Charlie asked. He wondered when to spring his own information on them. It would probably cause quite a sensation. *Listen first, then tell them.*

"Yes, but first, I noticed you looking at the food," Sanders said. "Please help yourself. That's what it's for. I knew I was pulling everyone away from their evening meals."

"Thank you," Charlie said. He walked over, Carol at his side, and they both filled plates.

"Must be nice to be rich," Carol whispered.

"Yeah, and simply crook your finger and have everyone show up on a Friday night," Charlie answered.

Deputy Ramirez cleared her throat. "We really need to get on with this, sir."

"Sure," Sanders said. "Now that everyone is here, let's start over. First, I'll tell you what Liam told me."

"Where *is* Liam?" Ramirez asked.

Sanders scowled. It was obvious he'd been asked that question more than once. "He's resting. I'd rather not involve him right now. Devon was his best friend. Besides, he told me everything that's pertinent."

Sanders proceeded to describe the swarm of snakes, how his son had kept his hands and feet out of the water and let the surfboard drift out to sea, and how he had barely made it to shore.

"He's sure they were sea snakes?" Carter asked. "Not eels or something like that?"

"They were definitely sea snakes, long and black, with yellow heads."

Carol and Charlie took a quick glance at each other. Sanders caught it.

"What is it?" he asked. "Do you know what they are?"

"We've seen them," Charlie said. "We were called to the scene of an accident this morning. Two people died. Professor Wheatley, who is an expert in such things, thinks they are a new species. But we thought they were rare."

Ramirez spoke up. "You knew about these snakes, you had people dead, and didn't raise an alarm?"

"I'm sorry, Deputy," Carol said. "But we didn't know about anything other than a black snake that had washed up on shore. Both Professor Wice and I believed it to be an anomaly. Such animals are not normally found this far north."

"Now that they've been seen alive in the water," Charlie added, "that changes everything. We do indeed need to raise an alarm. These creatures are extremely poisonous. We believe that even touching them, or touching something that has touched them, can have fatal consequences. I suggest we close the beaches."

Sanders turned to two cops. "Can you do that?"

Trooper Bowie deferred to Deputy Ramirez. "We can close the beaches temporarily for three days," she said. "More than that will require action from the governor." She turned to Bowie as if checking but it was obvious he would do as she asked.

"Where's your son," Deputy Ramirez said.

"He's unavailable," Sanders said flatly.

Ramirez's eyes flashed in annoyance. "I must insist, sir. We need to talk to him."

"What we *need* is to find out how many of these things there are," Sanders said. "We need to find out if they are just passing through or are sticking around. We need, in other words, to find out everything about them."

Ramirez wasn't willing to give up. "If anything happens because I wasn't able to speak to your son, Mister Sanders, it will be your responsibility."

"Absolutely," Sanders said. "I'll make him available soon." He turned his back on her, obviously dismissing her. She looked ready to pull out her handcuffs and arrest him right then and there, but Trooper Bowie put out a restraining hand and shook his head.

"I want to know everything that's happening," Sanders said to Carol and Charlie. "Keep me up to date."

"Yes, sir," Carter answered for them. "We'll keep you posted."

And with that, the meeting was over. Ramirez left the room without another word, obviously angry. Bowie followed, looking over his shoulder with a 'What can I do?' expression.

Carter headed for his car. Charlie and Carol hurried after him.

"I'll need the *Serenity*," Charlie said to him.

"*We'll* need the Serenity," Carol added.

Carter stopped next to his BMW and stood there, fidgeting. Finally, he said, "It's been rented out."

"You rented out the *Serenity*?" Charlie said. "To who? Is that even legal?"

"I rented it out to a documentary crew, and yes, it is legal. How else do you think I manage to meet the budget every year?"

That was a challenge to Charlie, who had never managed to balance the budget during his tenure as department head. In fact, buying the *Serenity* had come out of his budget. All Carter needed to do was keep it up.

"Look, I'll give you the money to rent a charter, whatever you need," Carter said.

Yeah, when it comes to what John Sanders wants, suddenly money is no object. But they needed to get out into the ocean, to see what was happening out there. There was no point arguing about it now.

"We'll head out at first light," Charlie said.

They drove the rest of the way home in silence. Charlie pulled up in front of Carol's house, and they sat there for a time, not looking at each other. Finally, she put a comforting hand over his. "You're a good man, Professor Wice."

He felt warmth flow over him. He wanted to take her in his arms, just to hug her, nothing else. He had a feeling it would be the most comforting hug he'd ever had.

She got out of the car. "Goodnight, Charlie."

As Charlie drove home, it was as if Carol's presence was still in the seat beside him. He liked that.

The two of them had been sliding by each other for years, passing in the hallways, giving each other small smiles, sitting at adjacent tables at meetings. It was as if they both decided they had too much in common, that their attraction was too strong to risk anything closer.

She had been happily married to David Wheatley while Charlie found himself still single in his fifties and not too excited about reentering the dating pool.

Kristine had come along, the sister of one of his colleagues, and they had hit it off. She was twenty years younger than him, but it didn't seem to matter. She was vivacious, sexy and funny. And, just like that, he had fallen in love.

They married within six months, and within two more months, Charlie knew he had made a mistake. Kristine was watching a hip-hop video, and Charlie mentioned he wished they still had dancers like Fred Astaire.

"Who's Fred Astaire?"

"You know, the guy with the top hat and tails?"

She looked at him blankly.

He said, "Fred Astaire and Ginger Rogers?"

She shook her head. He'd searched for them online, showed her a few videos, and then she'd claimed that *of course* she knew who they were, she'd just forgotten.

Charlie found himself tensing up the closer he got to home. He shook his right arm out, and then his left arm, and took a deep breath. Would she be up waiting for him? Did he want her to be?

The lights were out in the house. He crept into the bedroom, got undressed, and pulled back the sheets. In the moonlight, he could see Kristine's sleek, voluptuous form, so different from Carol's rail-thin body.

Why the hell am I comparing the two?

He crawled into bed. She had her back to him, and he could

tell she was awake, but neither of them said anything.

As Charlie fell asleep, a vision of Carol's smiling face came to him, and he felt a warm feeling flow through his body, relaxing the homecoming tensions.

I'm in love with another woman.

CHAPTER TEN

Jerry went to his desk, eager to use his newfound perspective in his work. When he'd entered his room, the surge of relief he normally felt at being shut away from the world didn't come. Instead, he looked around his cluttered space and felt a tinge of claustrophobia.

He didn't have a music player or a TV because that would have taken room away from his books, which were stacked in every corner. He liked the quiet. As useful as computers and e-readers were, he still preferred paper books whenever possible. They were comforting.

Charlie's suggestion about the cafeteria had made him hungry. As he opened the mini-fridge, he realized he was thinking of his professor by his first name, which had been something Charlie – and Carol, for that matter – had insisted on but which Jerry had never felt comfortable doing.

Strange. Calling them Charlie and Carol is so much easier.

He grimaced at the food choices. To him, food was fuel, nothing more. So he lived on peanut butter and bread, washed down by lemonade. Every couple of days he would force himself to eat some other food group; pickles or carrots, an apple, or some beef jerky.

I could put some peanut butter on an apple. Or maybe pickles on my peanut butter. Live it up! Experiment. Or… I could call for a pizza.

He had a sudden hankering for pizza. He'd only eaten it once or twice in his life, and even then he had picked off the toppings, leaving just the tomato sauce and the crust. The last time he'd done that, the other people at the table had needled him so mercilessly it was the last time he'd eaten in public.

He turned to his desk. The hard copy of his dissertation was lying there, complete, pristine, ready for Charlie to read and judge. But he suddenly realized it wasn't complete. His mind was already churning through the changes he wanted to make. He sat at the computer.

First he went to YouTube and searched for David Bowie. He'd never done that before, but now he started by playing 'Space Oddity'.

Ground control to Major Tom.

Ground control to Major Tom.

Take your protein pills and put your helmet on…

Jerry looked up, his eyes blurry, his fingers tingling. He was amazed to realize that three hours had passed. He'd rewritten almost half the paper that had taken him months to write. But now the ideas were starting to become a little hazy.

He'd forgotten to eat. When he stood, he almost fell over. Physically exhausted, he still managed to make a sandwich, then sat there chewing it and drinking his lemonade. *Something is different.*

His heart sank, and he dropped the remains of his sandwich onto the plate. *I'm losing it. Whatever* it *is. It's leaving me.*

Jerry stood, stripped off his astronaut suit, and threw on jeans and a T-shirt. He grabbed his coat and headed out.

It was after midnight when he arrived at the biology lab. There was no one there. It wasn't unusual for Jerry to be there, however. He did most of his best work in the deep of night.

He was relieved to find the sea snake still hadn't been removed. Jerry was certain Professor Wice would have come and taken it away. It would need to be put in the freezer soon or it would decay too much to be useful.

But not yet.

He donned rubber gloves, took a swab, and applied it to the snake's side then put the sample into a beaker.

I'll start with the most diluted solution I can and work my way up. He set out six different beakers and proceeded to dilute the solution six times. He had worked out the dosage when he'd been in his *clear* state, and he was pretty sure it was safe.

If it was all an illusion, I guess I'll find out the hard way.

By the time he was done, the last solution contained so little toxin that he doubted he would feel it. But maybe he'd still get some useful information. It was strictly forbidden to experiment on yourself, of course. No scientist would accept the results. But he could follow all the proper procedures later.

That was, if he still had the kind of mental clarity he needed in the first place.

Jerry looked down at the solution and knew this was the wrong thing to do. It was the new, daring version of himself who wanted to do it, and that version was rapidly fading away.

I should confer with Professor Wice. I'm a mere graduate assistant. I have no right.

He didn't know how long he stood there. It was only because he had the urge to go to the bathroom that he moved away. He walked down the long aisle to the hallway, still in turmoil. The two sides of himself were fighting a battle royal. Meanwhile, the vessel of those two personalities needed to relieve itself.

As he stood at the toilet, his old self finally gained control. *This is completely inappropriate. I will call Professor Wice immediately.*

He went back to the lab, his head down. At first, he didn't recognize the stranger standing near the sinks. As he approached, he realized it was Liam Sanders, son of the billionaire John Sanders. The biology lab they were standing in was named after the man.

The Liam he remembered had been cocky, acting bored by the whole biology thing. This Liam looked beaten down. He was slumped over, and his blond hair looked oily, his clothes dirty. He'd turned from California surfer dude to street urchin.

Jerry suddenly realized the guy was looking into the sink.

With a surge of adrenaline, Jerry's new personality returned in force. "Don't touch it!"

Liam turned in surprise. "Believe me, I wasn't about to."

CHAPTER ELEVEN

Liam was in his safe space, where he should have felt secure. The room at the top of the mansion had been designed as a storeroom, but he'd taken it over upon moving in.

Suddenly, he wanted out.

His father had questioned him gently, but persistently, looking doubtful yet accepting the story and giving him a final hug. "Do you want me to call Doctor Hoskins?" he asked.

"No, Dad, I'm really okay. It's not… like that."

Liam closed the door to the safe place and threw himself onto the mattress on the floor. He looked inside himself, looking for signs of the *other* place, where he'd spent half of his life.

When he'd gone cold turkey off the antidepressants a couple of years earlier, all the stored-up anger had come out, and he'd probably been pretty hard to take for a while. But it was real emotion, just like the occasional joy that came over him when he surfed or the gratitude for Devon's friendship.

The grief that overcame him at this moment, as he erupted in tears, felt right to him. It felt… appropriate. He *should* be feeling sad. This wasn't the same kind of darkness, the deadening kind.

I should get up and join Dad. The last thing he wanted was for his dad to call Doctor Hoskins and to have to take the dreaded pills that covered him in a thick fog. He'd finally begun to see colors again: the bright blue of the sky, the dark green of the ocean, the yellow sand. He'd finally felt hints of the old emotions.

He got up, went to the door, and then turned around again. He couldn't face his dad's worry, not this soon. It was strange how billionaire John Sanders, which was how Liam had always thought of him, a distant and powerful figure who was somehow connected to him, had become Dad. Liam could tell John was trying, that he was feeling his way, just as Liam was feeling *his* way.

Liam sat at his desk and looked up sea snakes online. There were dozens of species, but none matched what he'd seen. They were mostly solitary, and they were supposedly not aggressive, though their bite could be deadly. But much of the time, sea snakes didn't even inject venom into humans. When they did, it apparently didn't hurt at first, and it took time, a good half hour or more, before the first symptoms appeared.

Whatever had happened to Devon had been instantaneous, and the snakes had been hyper-aggressive and anything but solitary.

Could they be something new?

Whatever they were, people needed to be warned. Liam went to the closet and rifled through the coat he'd been wearing the year he'd attended classes at the university. He'd all but flunked out his freshman year, but he didn't really care. He intended to go back, to earn his degree, if for no other reason than to please his dad.

His grade-point average was destroyed, but now he didn't care if he got straight Cs as long as he got his degree. Besides, he figured he'd learned most of what he knew from reading books. One of the only advantages of deep depression was that he'd buried himself in novels.

One of the courses he'd taken in that ill-fated freshman year had been basic biology. He pulled the lab key card out of the coat's inner pocket. It probably wasn't still valid, but he could at least try to get into the lab. If he couldn't, he'd track down one of the biology professors and tell them about the black snakes.

He opened the door and descended the stairs quietly. He heard loud voices in the kitchen.

"You knew about these snakes and didn't raise an alarm," his dad shouted. "I'll be damned if I'll let you question my son. He just lost his best friend!"

"Hold on, Mister Sanders. We didn't know anything..."

Liam had to pass by the entrance to the kitchen to get to his car. He poked his head around the corner. He recognized his biology teacher, Professor Wice. Standing next to him was that good-looking, middle-aged lady professor, Carol Wheatley.

He scooted past the doorway.

Turn around and ask them. There are your answers right there.

But he kept going, though he wasn't sure why. He wanted to find out for himself; he wanted it to be something he did on his own. He didn't want anyone getting in the way. They would pick his brain and shunt him aside, and he'd have nothing more to do with it.

Devon deserved more than that from him. The others didn't care about his friend the way he did.

A voice rose behind him. "We need to talk to your son."

Liam slipped out the back door.

Amazingly, Liam's key card to the biology lab still worked. There was a bank of lights still on down one side of the lab, enough for him to see his way to the computer at the back. Along the way, he passed the big sinks where the specimens that freshmen were to dissect were prepared.

He saw something black out of the corner of his eye and stopped cold. The black skin was no longer shining but appeared a dark brown. The snake seemed to be losing shape. The black eyes were now a dead, marbled blue. But there was no mistaking the bright yellow head.

Liam wanted to grab the snake by the tail and swing it against the floor until it was nothing but a bloody paste. He started to reach down, then remembered how quickly Devon had reacted to the touch and withdrew his hand hastily.

"Don't touch it!" someone shouted.

He turned to see a young man who looked familiar running toward him. The guy slid to a stop near the sink, then reached over and lifted a piece of cardboard that was lying flat on the counter. He propped it against the faucet.

'Dangerous! Do Not Touch!' it read in neat lettering.

Liam said, "Believe me, I wasn't about to."

The guy shook his head, readjusting the sign.

"I've seen them before."

"What do you mean?'"

Liam knew this guy. A couple of times when Professor Wice was absent, his graduate assistant had taught the class. Liam remembered an utterly boring monotone, a slack face, an undemonstrative posture. Parker was his name; Jerry Parker, or something like that.

But this guy had an expressive face and bright eyes, his motions were fluid and assured like an athlete's, and his voice went up and down the scale. Apparently, Jerry Parker had been as bored by his lectures as his students had been.

"Do you know what they are?" Liam asked.

"We don't know for sure," Jerry said. "Professor Wheatley thinks it's the genus *Aipysurus*, but a species this poisonous is unknown."

"So you already knew about them?" Liam said. "You guys knew and you didn't warn people?"

Jerry looked surprised, as if he hadn't thought of it. "We thought they were rare."

"Rare!" Liam exploded "There were hundreds of them in the water! Thousands!"

"What?" Jerry looked confused, as if he couldn't quite take in the information.

"My friend Devon was killed this morning by a swarm of these," Liam said.

Jerry stared at him, turning pale. Then he grabbed Liam's arm, led him to the back office, and sat him down. "Tell me everything."

Liam was embarrassed when he started crying halfway through the tale, but he looked up to see that Jerry had tears in his eyes too.

Jerry found himself reappraising Liam as the story spilled out. Liam was obviously devastated by what had happened to his friend. While Jerry's Asperger's made it difficult to relate to other people, he'd learned to read their surface details. He'd pegged Liam as a jock type, shallow and rich. But now he saw an underlying melancholy he hadn't noticed before.

"I'm sorry," Jerry said. "We didn't know."

Maybe we aren't so different after all. They'd come from different backgrounds, had completely different experiences, and yet there was a connection there.

Jerry had an idea. "Listen, do you want to help me? Get some extra credit?"

Liam looked insulted, but then out a deep sigh. "I'm not going to school right now. But if it will help stop these things, I'll do anything you want."

"Oh, well, good," Jerry said.

He started to leave the office. The surge of adrenaline had worn off. His old combination of fierce concentration and absentmindedness was returning. He had to do something fast.

At the door, he beckoned for Liam to follow. They walked back to the snake in the sink. Jerry grabbed the final beaker containing the diluted snake venom.

"Make sure no one touches the snake," he said. "I think I have the dosage right. But if I don't wake up in ten minutes, call 911. Do not try to resuscitate me, clear?"

"Wait... What?"

Jerry upended the beaker into his mouth. Then he stood there, waiting to see if he'd feel anything.

Please let it come back. Please let me be clear.

He stiffened and let out a gasp. A jolt ran up his spine, and his throat constricted. He wanted to shout out, but he couldn't move. He lost his grip on the beaker, and it dropped to the floor and shattered. He fell backward, landing hard on the floor before Liam could catch him. Then he felt Liam cradling his head in arms.

I... may have miscalculated.

CHAPTER TWELVE

Kim Grieves waited at the end of the dark alley. Joshua and Sam were an hour late, and she was beginning to realize they weren't going to show up at all. She suspected they were more interested in each other than they were in her anyway, and that was just fine.

But they had done her the favor of introducing her to urban exploration. She hadn't even known Urbex was a thing until a month ago, and now she was addicted to it. Finding old abandoned buildings had been fun. Climbing up huge skyscrapers under construction had been even more exciting. But it was exploring the places beneath the city that really got her hooked.

Who knew that below the everyday, humdrum streets of the city, there was a whole subterranean world? Not the spruced-up, guided tour version, but the real thing. After the Great Seattle Fire, the entire downtown had been raised up, leaving old downtown still intact beneath it.

Only a small part of it was open to the public. The rest remained hidden except to those in the know. It was scary and exciting and made Kim feel like she was visiting an urban fantasy world, where men in top hats and canes and women in hoop skirts still walked.

The boys had laughed at her fantasies, but she'd ignored them.

I don't need them. I'll do it myself, explore those places they're too afraid to go.

Joshua had the key to a gate that led down to the lower levels, but Kim was thin enough to fit between the bars. She started to squeeze through. Her backpack caught for a moment, but then she was in. She turned on her headlamp.

It was illegal to be down here, of course, and dangerous during the rainy season, which in Seattle was most of the year. But Kim didn't care. She was nimble, a fairy spirit really. The boys just weighed her down with their crude jokes. They didn't seem to appreciate the dark beauty of the abandoned Victorian-era buildings.

She heard scurrying in the main corridor. There were rats down here, but they didn't alarm Kim. She figured they were more scared of her than she was of them. If Sam had been along, he would have started talking loudly to conceal how frightened he was.

She continued on, past the point the boys had refused to venture. The walls were falling down, and there was a dank smell. Her heart began beating hard.

The constant stream of water that ran down the center of the corridor was a little higher than usual. She had to hop over it a couple of times to find higher ground. It hadn't rained for a few days, and there had been clear skies, so she wasn't too concerned.

Most of the rooms were empty, but occasionally Kim came across old and broken furniture, a steampunk-looking cash register, and discarded shoes; she wasn't completely sure if those were old or newer.

People lived down here sometimes, though the rains eventually drove them away. The possibility of running into one of these mole people was the only thing that really scared her.

It was getting harder and harder to distinguish between the walls of the old buildings and the earth that had come down around them. Kim came to a place where debris had washed up against a barrier, and it was impassable. She could see that the corridor continued beyond, but she'd had enough for one night. She'd try to get Joshua and Sam to come with her next time and help her clear away the refuse.

As she began to turn, something moved in the empty space beyond the barrier, and she whirled back, restraining a cry. It was low to the ground but didn't move like a rat. Instead, it undulated, as if it was swimming. She moved closer, directing her headlamp at the spot.

She couldn't see it at first. The dirt and the water were both dark, but so was the creature. Then she saw something bright yellow moving back and forth. Only when it shot forward did she realize it was a snake, as black as the inner darkness of the earth.

Nothing had scared her until now… well, maybe mole people. But not the dark, not the rats… Snakes? That was something she hadn't even considered.

Kim turned on her heel and started walking as fast as she could. Not running. If she started running, the panic would set in. She hadn't gone more than few steps before she spotted another snake in the channel of water in front of her. She hesitated and looked over her shoulder. The floor seemed to be squirming up and down and sideways. Now she did cry out, and the sound of her own frightened voice echoing off the confines of the tunnel terrified her even more.

She moved forward, hopping over the single snake in the middle of the corridor.

Pain spiked through her shin and she batted downward without thinking. The snake was already falling away from her leg. She looked at the small puncture wound. The bite hadn't really hurt that much.

Was it poisonous? She hadn't ever heard of anything like that in the Seattle area. There were no rattlesnakes, no vipers. The worst she'd ever seen were the garter snakes her brothers had terrified her with.

It wasn't the bite that affected her first. It was her hand that went numb. It seemed to be swelling. Her breathing sounded labored, but she was scared and tired and didn't think anything of it.

Just let me get above ground. I can call for help. Kim grabbed the straps of her backpack, feeling reassured by the phone in the side pocket. Then she found herself on her knees.

How did I get here? The light on her helmet was directed at the wall, and she stared at it blankly. She felt movement around her legs and fell backward, leaning against the wet brick. Snakes were slithering over her legs, and while that should have freaked her out, she couldn't actually feel them.

The lamp dimmed... or was it her vision? Darkness closed in. She tried to raise her hand to tap the light, but she couldn't move. She felt as if she was drowning, and then there was silence as her ragged breathing stopped.

Kim tried to push air out and draw it in, but her body convulsed. The snakes were now at eye level, and she realized that she had toppled over onto her side. With her eyes frozen open, yellow stripes flashed by, silhouetted by the light still strapped to her forehead.

Then the light went out completely.

CHAPTER THIRTEEN

The angels spoke to him.

Dr Lowell Henderson looked up from his computer and watched the two porcelain angels his daughter had given him touch wings. He'd set them a hair's breadth apart after discovering them as his own personal seismograph by accident a few minor earthquakes before.

He closed his eyes. The chair was cushioned, but he could still feel the slight tremor. He went to the university web page, and there it was: a nice 2.8.

Do I call him?

When the billionaire John Sanders had contacted him for advice over a year earlier, he'd referred the man to some of his graduate assistants. After class one day, he'd come into his office to find a small, trim man in the waiting room. Henderson's assistant, Chrissy, had whispered, "He said he wouldn't talk to anyone else. His name is John Sanders."

"John Sanders?" Lowell said. "*The* John Sanders?"

Chrissy looked shocked as if she hadn't made the connection. Lowell could understand why. With the fringe of white hair around his head and his bald pate, the billionaire looked like a monk. He wore black glasses and was dressed in Dockers and sandals and a button-down shirt.

"Come on in, Mister Sanders," Lowell said. "What can I do for you?"

Sanders sat in the chair in front of Lowell's desk and smoothed out his Dockers. "I don't know if you've heard, but I'm building a resort on Caroline Island. The local officials are giving me a hard time, so I thought I'd hire a few outside experts."

"What's the problem?"

"They say that I can't build near the beach because of the danger of a tsunami."

"They're right," Lowell said. "If they ask me, I'll say the same thing."

"But I'm building the house to the highest specifications… plus."

"Doesn't matter," Lowell told him, trying to keep the impatience from his voice. "We can't build anything that will hold back the ocean."

"Then why build at all?" Sanders asked.

Why indeed? The man has a point.

"If the earthquake comes – *when* the earthquake comes – no place near the Pacific Coast will be safe. The only way anyone would survive was if they got to high ground fast enough."

"Then if I build a resort with all the security measures, won't it be safer than all those bric-a-brac houses on the beach that are grandfathered in?"

"That might be," Lowell said, calculating the best way to approach this to not only his own benefit, but that of his department. "But we have to start somewhere. However, the only truly safe measure is efficient evacuation procedures. If you have those in place, Mister Sanders, I will back you up."

Sanders stood and extended his hand. "You won't regret it, Doctor Henderson."

A few months later, after Lowell submitted an opinion paper on Sanders's project, an anonymous and generous benefactor established the Lowell Henderson scholarship fund. Within days of that, the tsunami struck Japan. Sanders called the same day.

"Is that what would happen here?" Sanders asked without preamble.

"That or worse," Lowell replied. "Like I said, no building can hold back the ocean. What causes a tsunami is a fault rupture offsetting the sea floor. In Japan it went up by a hundred feet. So it's like a big paddle at the bottom of the ocean pushing water up. Also, in deep water, at fifteen thousand feet abyssal depths, a tsunami wave travels really fast, about five hundred miles per hour, like a jet plane."

"What are the odds of it happening here?"

"One hundred per cent."

"When?"

"Ah, that's the real question," Lowell said. "It could happen tomorrow or one hundred years from now. But tomorrow is more likely. We're way overdue."

"Is there no way to know when?" Sanders asked. "Can't you predict it?"

"Well, there is nothing that has proven reliable," Lowell said. "But I have my own hypothesis."

"Tell me."

"My guess is that there will be a series of smaller earthquakes, somewhere between two and three on the Moment Magnitude—"

"Moment Magnitude? What's that?"

"We don't use the term Richter scale anymore, but for our purposes, they are both measured from one to ten. To continue, a series of two or three magnitudes in the days and weeks leading up to the Big One. But there is some controversy about that. This is called the Accelerating Moment Release, or AMR, which postulates a series of foreshocks increasing at an exponential rate. But it is not exactly reliable."

"I've done some more research on you, Doctor Henderson," Sanders said. "I understand they don't have a Nobel Prize for geology, but you've been nominated for the Vetlesen Prize how many times?"

"Hard to know, it's a secret. But I've heard on the grapevine that I've been up for it every year since 2000."

"Why haven't you won?"

"Politics," Lowell said. He meant it as a joke.

Sanders laughed dryly. "Ain't it always. But if you were betting your own life and that of your family, would you believe in this AMR?"

"I already live on the highest hill in Seattle, Mister Sanders. But yes. And if I saw it happening, I would respond to it."

"I want you to call me when you have the slightest suspicion," Sanders said. "Anything over a two point earthquake. There's a five-thousand-dollar bonus if you call me right away."

"You don't have to pay me anything," Lowell said. "I'll call you if I think the Big One is imminent. In fact, I'll probably call everyone."

"That's fine, Doctor Henderson," Sanders said, "but I've found that five thousand dollars tends to help a person's memory."

"Very well, Mister Sanders, I'll call you immediately."

That had been over a year ago. Somehow Lowell hadn't expected the Big One to happen in his lifetime. Now that it apparently was happening, he hesitated. It wasn't clear cut by any means. The foreshocks were smaller than he'd expected, more spread out, and not increasing in frequency. It wasn't even enough to discuss with his colleagues. But there was something...

He called the number Sanders had given to him.

"Perkins," a voice answered.

"This is Lowell Henderson. Mister Sanders asked me to call him."

"He's rather busy right now, Mister Henderson. Can he call you back?"

Lowell almost agreed, but then decided that if he was going to do this thing, he was going to see it through. "I think he'll want to talk to me."

"Hold on."

There were voices in the background as if Lowell had interrupted a meeting. Then Sanders came on the line.

"I thought you should know there have been five earthquakes over a two in the last ten days, and a two-point-eight earthquake a few minutes ago," Lowell said.

"I didn't feel anything."

"You wouldn't if you were doing anything at all. But this is an AMR, or something awfully close."

There was a long silence on the other end. Then Sanders said, "Thank you, Doctor Henderson. I won't forget this. I'll get that five-thousand-dollar check off to you today." He ended the call without a goodbye.

Henderson stared at the phone for a few moments, then

called his wife. "Pack your bags, honey. We're taking that vacation to New York we've been talking about. See a couple of Broadway plays."

"Can we afford that?"

"I've received an unexpected bonus," he said.

She excitedly agreed. He ended the call and sat there thoughtfully for a moment. Even without the bonus, he would have been tempted to leave town. Science or no science, he had a bad feeling about this.

After getting off the phone with Henderson, John Sanders turned to Perkins. "Pack up, we're leaving."

"What about the sea snakes?"

"Not our problem," John said. He felt sorry for Devon and his family, but there was nothing he could do for them now. He'd try to help them out later, if he could. It was his own son he needed to worry about.

This whole Caroline Island venture had been a mistake. If not for the fact that Liam seemed to take great pleasure in surfing, John would have left months ago. *Fuck this. Liam can surf anywhere.* He'd put him on a jet to Hawaii or Australia, somewhere warmer and less inclement anyway.

Dr Lowell Henderson was a dry, droll fellow who didn't seem to get excited about much. But John had heard the alarm in the man's voice. Besides, it would probably be best to get back east where Liam's psychiatrist was.

His son had come home from the first visit with Dr Shirley Patterson and said, "I told her that I felt like there was another Liam inside me wanting to get out, and she said, 'Why don't you let him out?'"

"Is that good?" John asked.

"I think so," Liam said. "It feels right. But every other doctor I said that to always got all weird about it."

"That's good, then, right?"

"I asked her if I could go off my pills, and she said yes!"

That had brought John up short. He remembered how Liam had been before taking the medication. He'd been unable to function. But the pills made him sluggish and humorless, and he had gained weight. Liam had had to take other pills because the first pills made him restless, and then other pills because the second pills made his mouth dry, and...

"Are you sure?" John asked.

"Yeah," Liam said, seeming almost excited. "I mean, she wants me to do it slowly, but she thinks we should give it a try."

Liam had been a handful for a few weeks, but eventually he had stabilized, and he'd been off the pills ever since.

Now John was afraid he would relapse.

He climbed the stairs to Liam's room, not expecting to find him there. Liam seemed to sleep in his room but do nothing else there. Sure enough, the bedroom was empty. John kept climbing the stairs, which narrowed and became twisting. There was a storeroom at the very top, really just a space beneath the eaves, but Liam had taken to using it.

He knocked on the door. Liam always acted annoyed when his dad invaded his private space, so John usually stayed away.

"Liam?" he called out when there wasn't an answer.

He tried the door. It was unlocked.

Liam was gone.

CHAPTER FOURTEEN

Tom woke to his phone trilling a little sailing ditty that he'd thought was clever at the time he'd made it his ringtone, but now annoyed him. He answered it without thinking. If he hadn't been so groggy, he probably would have let it go to voicemail.

He pushed himself up onto his elbows, knocking over the half-empty bottle of whiskey, but managing not to completely drain it. He'd gone out and bought a cheap bottle of rotgut in honor of Pete, who'd seldom been sober when on land.

"Tom Bailey Charter Boats," he answered automatically.

"Mister Bailey, this is Carol Wheatley. I don't know if you remember, but you took my daughter and me out on a fishing trip last year. Actually, you might remember Jennifer, a very pretty but very rude young woman? I think she compared you to a Doctor Who villain."

"I remember," Tom said. "She called me an ignorant asshole when I told her I didn't know who Doctor Who was."

"I believe you said, '*Who?*'" Carol laughed. "I do apologize. Jennifer doesn't always catch the joke."

"I thought the whole thing was funny. I assume she's autistic, right?" Tom said, then wondered if it was proper to point it out.

"Yes. You and your crewman, Pete, were very nice and patient with her. I've always remembered that."

"What can I do for you, Miss Wheatley?" He instantly regretted asking. *Just tell her you're sick and hang up.*

"Carol," she corrected. "I'm wondering if you are available for a charter this morning. I'm a professor of biology at the University of Washington, and my colleague, Charles Wice and I need to get out on the open ocean as soon as possible."

"I thought you folks had a boat. The *Serenity*, if I remember right?"

"It's unavailable, unfortunately. I understand that it's Saturday, and that you are probably already booked. We will pay extra if you can take us on right away. We'll pay for whomever you have to cancel, and double for our own excursion."

"Very generous," Tom said. His head was slowly clearing, and along with that clarity came a profound reluctance to head out again. It seemed disrespectful to Pete's memory, somehow. "Well, Carol, this is a bad time for me. You see... Pete died yesterday."

There was a long silence on the other end. Then Carol said, her voice low and concerned, "I'm very sorry. I understand if you can't do it, Tom. I hate to bother you further, but it's important we get out there. Do you have someone else you can recommend?"

Something about the way she said it made him ask, "What's the emergency?"

"We've seen a sea creature that shouldn't be in these parts. We need to see how many of them there are, and see if we can net a live sample."

A chill went down Tom's spine, and he was suddenly completely sober. "What kind of creature?"

"A black sea snake with a yellow head."

"Miss Wheatley... Carol, not only am I available, free of charge, but I have a story to tell you."

Carol must have called while en route, because the professors pulled up to the docks ten minutes later. The man accompanying her pulled a large bag out of a big pickup with the University of Washington logo on the side. He threw the bag over his shoulder. It must have been heavy but not particularly fragile, because when he reached the *Cirdan*, he dropped it with a *thud*.

"I wasn't sure if you had a fishing net," the man said. "I understand you're a sports fisherman." He held out his hand.

"Charles Wice... Charlie."

"I've been known to use nets," Tom said. "I can't afford to ignore any type of fishing in this business." He unzipped the bag and looked in. "Your net is better, but my net is already hooked up. It will work fine. How far down do you need to go?"

"Sea snakes breathe air, so we don't have to go down too far."

Carol followed with another large bag, which was apparently much lighter. She unzipped it slightly to show Tom what was inside. It was a clear barrel with various gauges and dials attached. "If we catch one of these snakes, we want to keep it alive. This container is designed for that," she explained.

"Hell, a bucket with seawater will keep it alive," Tom said.

"I don't think you want this particular creature to escape the bucket," she said. "I probably should have given you more of a warning. This sea snake is incredibly dangerous."

"Yeah, about that," Tom said. They waited for him to continue, but instead, he said, "Listen, let's load up and get going. I'll tell you once we're underway. Why don't you get the lines, Charlie?"

I'm going to need a new crewman. Tom was shocked he was already thinking about the future. *But I'll never have another old salt like you, Pete.*

Charlie and Carol unmoored the boat smoothly, working as a team, smiling at each other. It made Tom feel good. He'd been married a couple of times, but it had never taken. "The *Cirdan* is your real lover," his second wife, Cathy, had said during her final exit out the door.

"How long have you two been together?" he asked when they hopped aboard. He could tell they were surprised by the question and neither wanted to see what the other's reaction was. "I mean, at the university," Tom said as smoothly as he could.

"Long enough that they were still giving out tenure," Charlie said. "Let's see... thirty-two years for me. How about you, Carol?"

"I came a couple of years later," she said.

Tom nodded then said, "You two make yourselves comfortable. I've got to get past the eddy before I can come talk to you."

He didn't come back down from the wheelhouse until they had cleared the bay and headed out into open ocean. "How far out do you want to go?" he asked.

"Why don't we start at about ten miles and work our way in?" Charlie said. "That's one of the things we need to discover, how close they are to land."

Carol added, "Considering they aren't supposed to be here at all."

"Yeah, I'd never seen them before yesterday," Tom said.

"Right." Charlie motioned for him to continue. "You promised us a story."

They took seats around the deck, and Tom told them about the black snake that one of his customers had claimed to see, and how Pete had gone to unhook the remains of the salmon and had been immediately struck down.

"I thought Pete had had a heart attack," Tom said. "But then I remembered the black snake and remembered that sea snakes can be extremely poisonous. I probably would have called you guys in the next day or two if you hadn't called me."

"The guy was sure he saw a living specimen?" Charlie asked.

"*Something* ate that salmon," Tom said. "You've seen dead ones?"

"Yeah, we have a specimen back at the— Oh, shit." Charlie turned to Carol. "In all the excitement, I forgot that Jerry won't be going back to the lab. The specimen is probably decaying in the sink right now. I'll call Jerry."

"Don't you dare," Carol said. "Call Ken Carter instead."

"Good idea," Charlie said.

"Better hurry," Tom said. "We'll be out of cell range pretty soon."

Charlie nodded and went to the back of the boat, dialing as he went. Carol watched him intently.

They both have wedding rings. They aren't married to each other but they wish they were.

Charlie came back, slipping his phone into his pocket.

"You reminded him how dangerous it is, right?" Carol said.

"Nah," Charlie said. "I told him to cook it. You know, we need a new department head."

Carol snorted, and they smiled at each other again.

Jesus, get a room. Tom looked toward shore, which was barely visible on the horizon. But the conversation reminded him to put on gloves and a rubber apron. He was going to need to be careful. "We're about ten miles out," he said. "Ready to let the net out?"

With both Carol and Charlie now in protective gear, they unspooled the net, and it went smoothly. *That's because of Pete.* The thought hit Tom with a pang. *The man knew how to do things.*

They trolled for about an hour, and then wound the net in. There wasn't much in the first round, but...

"Some of these fish were already dead," Tom said.

"Is that unusual?" Carol asked.

Tom didn't answer, but hit the switch on the motor and let the net spool out again. He pointed the *Cirdan* closer to shore. After a couple of miles, he pulled the net in again. This was a more normal catch.

"Can't keep any of these," he said, picking up the flopping creatures and tossing them over the side. "If we get stopped by the Coast Guard, this was all your idea, okay?"

He headed nearer to shore until he figured from the angle of the shoreline that they were about six miles out. Just before he hit the motor to the winch, the boat shuddered, and he felt a drag. No one else, except Pete, would have noticed, but Tom realized they'd caught something big, something that would either strain the engine or tear the net if he didn't slow.

Black clouds were rolling in. Ordinarily, it would have been enough to abort the trip. But he was as curious as the professors about the black snakes. He probably had time. Sometimes dark clouds were just dark clouds.

He put the boat into a full stop, and then watched as the winch engine struggled to pull the catch into the boat. His two passengers seemed to notice something was different and came over and stood by his side.

The net came over the side of the boat. "Holy shit," Charlie said. "Is that what I think it is?"

The net and its contents thumped onto the deck. The huge creature's thrashing swayed the boat back and forth.

The creature looked fearsome and ugly, like a cross between a snake and a shark, with most of the fins toward the back and a large mouth surrounded by prominent gills. Carol approached within a few feet and stared down at it.

"How far down have you been running the net?" Carol asked.

"Close to the surface, as you requested," Tom said. "What the hell is it? I've never seen anything like it."

"It's a frilled shark, the biggest one I've ever seen," Carol answered. "It's got to be at least three meters long. A new species, perhaps. They do occasionally come near the surface, but not very often." She approached so close to the creature's snapping jaws that it gave Tom the willies. "We need to get it back into the water." She turned and gave him a pleading look. "Quickly!"

Between the three of them, they managed to pull the shark out of the net by its tail and lift it over the side of the boat. At the last second, it twisted and snapped at Charlie, barely missing his arm. Then it splashed into the ocean.

"This isn't just about sea snakes," Carol muttered. "Something is driving these creatures to the surface."

"What do you think would cause that?" Charlie asked. "Because I can't think of anything right now."

"I don't know," Carol answered. "Whatever it is, it's happening fast." She turned to Tom. "We still need to catch one of the sea snakes. Shall we try again?"

Tom let the net into the water slowly. They were now about five miles from shore, and he went one mile closer before he pulled the net in. It was full of small fish, a couple of squid, and one small black snake with a yellow head, barely big enough to be kept in by the netting.

"I wonder if the babies are extra poisonous, like rattlers," Charlie mused, looking down at it. He gave Carol a big smile.

"It may be small, but it'll do," she said.

They threw the other fish in the net overboard. Several of them were already dead from proximity to the sea snake. Carol rolled the specimen jar over. Tom pinioned the snake's head with a gaffer, and they managed to catch it and drop it into the container without being bitten. There was water in the bottom half, but enough room at the top for the snake to breathe.

Charlie peered into the container, looking elated. "I would prefer an adult," he said. "We know enough to tell the authorities to be on the lookout, but I think that's all that needs to be done. I'd say in a week, we should do this again and see if the situation has changed. You can head back to shore, Captain Bailey." Charlie seemed upbeat, relieved. "Carol and I will sluice the deck with ocean water. With any luck, your boat will be as good as new by the time we reach shore."

Tom felt the tension draining out of him. The release was a surprise. He hadn't realized how nervous he was until they had completed the task. He climbed the ladder and turned the boat toward land. He looked over his shoulder to see how far the sun was above the horizon.

There, stretching like a road in the middle of the ocean, was a serpentine silhouette. The waves were flat around the black shape, as if damped down by an oil slick. The shadow had its own movement, as if it was a river running through the ocean with its own currents.

"Oh, shit, shit, shit," Tom muttered.

He cranked the engine up to full speed and set the course. Then he climbed down to the deck and stood over the two professors, who were dipping buckets into the ocean and then spilling the contents where the net had lain.

Tom pointed into the water. "You guys see this?"

The two professors stood. Instinctively, their hands reached for each other as they stared at the wriggling mass.

"I don't think you two need to worry about finding more sea snakes."

CHAPTER FIFTEEN

To the west, beneath the clouds, the ocean grew dark. Closer to shore the sun still shone. Mist lifted off the shore as Margie watched her two young sons playing in the surf. It was ungodly cold, and the water was freezing. She'd poked her toe in upon first arriving, but that was all. It was her personal superstition that it was bad luck to visit the beach and not at least touch the ocean.

They'd left their house in Seattle early that morning. She'd grabbed the wool blanket off the bed in the guest bedroom on the way out the door and now had it draped around her shoulders.

The sun was finally breaking through, and she smiled. Dave and Dan looked like otters, gleefully diving into the waves. They were eight and ten years old, but everyone thought they were twins. Their short brown hair was bleached almost blonde from the summer sun. This was probably one of the last trips they would make before winter set in.

Margie didn't own a swimsuit. She didn't even own a pair of shorts. Her legs were short and stubby, and when she saw other women with her same rotund shape wearing skimpy clothes, she'd always thought it tacky.

She could swim, yet hadn't in years. But even when she used to swim, it had never been in the ocean. Too easily could she imagine many bitey, spiky, spiny things under the dark water. It was irrational, and she'd been careful not to infect her adventurous boys with her fears, but she always had her heart in her mouth when they played in the surf as she kept a careful watch.

The sun reflected off the water, nearly blinding her. She caught a glimpse of something long and dark floating on a wave.

At first she thought it was a piece of driftwood, or perhaps a large piece of seaweed. She stood, trying to get a better look.

Whatever it was, it was moving.

She was running toward her boys and shouting before she had time to think. "Get out of the water!"

Dave was under a wave during her first shout, but Dan turned toward her uncertainly, hearing the urgency in her voice if not her words. He reached into the water, grabbed Dave's arm, and pointed toward Margie, who sprinted toward them as fast as her chubby legs would take her.

It was an astonishing sight, and both boys watched her with their mouths open.

"Get out of the damned water!" Margie shouted in her most urgent Mom voice.

They finally responded, sloshing their way toward her slowly, looking over their shoulders as if sensing something was coming. They had barely hit dry land before the long, black shape was deposited by a wave directly behind them.

The creature slithered toward them, faster than the boys were walking, and as they saw it and started running, it seemed as if the snake or eel or whatever it was, was nearly as fast. Margie scooped a handful of pebbles as she ran, and threw the biggest of them. She was surprised and gratified that it hit the black thing's yellow head. The snake stopped and coiled itself up, waving its head back and forth as if trying to assess the danger.

Margie threw the final handful of pebbles at it as she reached the boys. "Keep going higher!" she shouted.

She stopped and faced the snake for she saw now that that was what it was. It was watching her. She raised her arms and shouted, then leaned down to grab more rocks, but there was only sand. She risked a glance over her shoulder and saw that the boys had reached the sand dunes. Hopefully they'd go all the way to the car, even though it was locked.

The moment she took her eyes off the snake, it darted forward. Margie turned and ran, but she was slower than her boys, and the snake gained ground.

She reached the border of hard sand where grasses were taking hold, and almost tripped over a large rock half covered by sand. She stopped and hefted the rock. It was as big, and there was no way she could have imagined she could hoist it over her head, but that's exactly what she did.

The snake was mere feet away when she threw the rock. It caught the creature just behind the head, pinioning it to the hard sand. Its body whipsawed back and forth, but the rock held.

Margie watched it, fascinated.

I should keep running. Unlock the car and get out of here.

Out of the corner of her eye, she spied a long, solid piece of driftwood amid the grasses. She picked it up and swung it through the air experimentally. It felt sturdy.

The snake was thrashing wildly as she approached. Its eyes were a glossy black, distinguishable from its hide only because they moved. There was no way she should have been able to read anything in those dark pools, but she saw malevolence there, anger at everything and anything that moved.

She swung the driftwood down on its head. It hissed, and she stepped back and almost tripped. Then she gathered her strength and swung the driftwood down again and again until the yellow head bubbled red and lay broken. The body thrashed a few more times and then was still.

Margie walked to the car, hands shaking, trying to catch her breath. It was the fastest she had moved in ages, and it had felt good. Maybe she should take up some kind of exercise, not because she thought she'd lose weight, because she'd given up on that, but just because it might be fun.

The boys were beside themselves with excitement when she approached.

"Did you kill it?" Dan asked. "What was it?"

"I smashed its head in," Margie said.

"I want to see it, Mom!" Dave said.

"No way," Margie said. "We're done for today. We're done for the year. We're… done."

She started the car and drove away, wondering if she should

report the incident. Halfway home, she pulled off the road, got out her phone and called 911.

"Hello? I'd like to report a snake."

Kristine waited until Charlie left the house before getting up that morning. He had left a note by the coffee maker, something about taking a boat out onto the ocean for a survey. He didn't mention he'd be with Carol, but she had a feeling.

She called Ken from the landline, since it didn't keep a record of her calls. She was meticulous when she cheated, always had been. Her first husband hadn't known anything was happening until she was already gone. She'd been seeing Charlie's boss for months now, and she figured Charlie didn't have a clue.

Probably because he's doing his own cheating. But even as she thought it, she knew it wasn't true. She'd suspected that Charlie had a thing for Carol Wheatley from the first time she'd seen the two together. It had been almost funny, the way the two avoided talking to each other. But Kristine had picked up on it. She had a radar for such things.

"Hello, babe," she said when Ken answered. "Charlie's going to be gone all day."

"I know," Ken said. "I'm the one who sent him. Carol's with him, too. Maybe they'll get together—"

"Stop," Kristine interrupted. She really didn't want to hear the scenario that Ken had in mind. In fact, she really didn't want to leave Charlie just yet. For one thing, despite being junior to Ken, her husband had accumulated a much better retirement package. And he was ten years older, and that much closer to Kristine getting her hands on all of it. Charlie was fifty-eight, and that seemed ancient to her, as if he was on his last legs. She knew in her mind it wasn't true, but there was always a chance.

She realized he might last for decades more. But she'd divorce him eventually, and the more money Charlie accumulated, the more she'd get. If she could also indulge in slightly more vigorous sex with Ken Carter at the same time, so much the better. Besides, it wasn't really the sex itself that excited her, it was the naughtiness of the cheating. She actually thought Charlie was a pretty nice guy, but she wasn't interested in nice guys. Ken Carter was more her type, though she'd never in a million years marry a guy like him, no matter what she led him to believe.

"I'll meet you at the hotel," she said. Her favorite place was off the beaten track but luxurious, private, and away from prying eyes. It was too expensive for the university types who might recognize them. The hotel had once been a canning factory and was built on an old dock that extended out into the bay. In fact, looking out of the rooms, you could almost believe you were floating in the ocean.

"I can't get away for long," Ken said. "We've had an emergency, that's why Charlie needed to go out."

"What happened?" Kristine asked. She didn't really care, but knew Ken wanted her to ask.

"Some sort of sea snake nearly killed John Sanders' son," Ken said. "The more time I spend with him the better. I'm thinking if we make him happy, he'll give us some more money."

"John Sanders, the billionaire?" Kristine asked. "Why don't I come with you? I mean, I can introduce myself as Charlie's wife, show how concerned I am and all." *And see if the rich old bastard is lonely.*

"Meet me at the university," Ken said. "You can pretend you're looking for Charlie, and I can invite you to meet Sanders."

"I'll be there soon," Kristine said.

There was a danger of being seen with Ken alone, but if they met by *accident* in public, it could be explained away. In fact, she'd make sure that busybody secretary, Mary Stewart, saw them bumping into each other.

The drive was only half an hour, but Kristine needed to spend a little extra time getting ready. She needed to look like a university professor's wife, but she also needed to look available.

After her shower, she sat naked and dripping at the computer and Googled John Sanders. He was a widower, obviously devoted to his only son. He'd given up most of the control over his companies, but still owned the majority of shares. He was getting richer every second.

He needs someone to take care of him. Someone who doesn't look like a gold digger.

She changed her mind about what she was going to wear and put on her most conservative ensemble, applied minimal makeup and no perfume at all. She tried to remember the mindset she'd used to catch Professor Charles Wice. It might all change the moment she met the billionaire, but it was always better not to come on too strong at the first meeting.

Kristine checked herself in the mirror on the way out. She was beautiful and demure, the square-cut clothing not quite hiding her curves.

What was the big emergency that everyone was so excited about? Something about a sea creature almost killing John Sanders' son?

She frowned, wondering if it was important. *A shark? No, a sea snake.* She shuddered, and then decided it didn't matter. She'd express her heartfelt concern, and if Sanders was like most men, he would soak it up.

She gave herself a last smile in the mirror then walked out the door.

CHAPTER SIXTEEN

L iam cradled Jerry's head in his lap. The guy was foaming at the mouth, his eyes clenched shut. He moaned, and looked for all the world exactly like Devon had looked in those first few moments after the snakes had appeared.

What do I do? What the fuck do I do?

Liam's hand went to his pocket. *Shit.* He'd left his phone at home, which just went to show how panicked he'd been. He never went anywhere without his phone. He searched Jerry's pockets and found his, but it was locked.

Do I leave him here and run for help? Grab the first person I see and tell them to call 911?

Problem was, it was the darkest part of the morning, the time when people were least likely to be up and around, especially at the university. *They have to have security guards, though, right? Right? Maintenance people?*

He'd had plenty of time to remember what Devon had looked like when he died. He was pretty sure his friend had begun to suffer even before the snake bit him, which meant that mere contact was enough to kill a person.

Mouth-to-mouth resuscitation would be a bad idea. Liam felt a strange relief at that thought, and then shame at that relief.

Fuck that, get a grip. If he needs it, he needs it.

He laid Jerry on the floor on his back, then, on second thought, turned him on his side. The next thing that would happen was that Jerry would start gasping for breath, as if his throat was closing.

A tracheotomy? That was a crazy thought. He'd be more likely to cut an artery or something. *But what if there's no choice?*

Liam was frozen by indecision. There were no good choices.

Jerry kept breathing, though it appeared to be a struggle. Finally, Liam decided he had no choice but to leave and get help.

"Sorry, man, I've got to go get help," he said, getting to his feet. He looked at the row of beakers and shook his head in wonderment. *Jerry drank the stuff on purpose? What was he thinking?*

He turned and started for the door, and then heard a gasp behind him.

Jerry sat up, clutching his throat, his face red and his eyes bugging out. Liam hurried back to him, grabbing a dissection knife on the way.

He pushed Jerry's hands away and pointed the knife at his neck. *Below the Adam's apple?*

"No," Jerry croaked. "I can breathe."

He was breathing all right. If desperate gasping could be called breathing.

"What the fuck did you do to yourself, man?" Liam asked. "Are you *trying* to kill yourself?"

Jerry pushed to his knees, put his hand up on the counter, and pulled himself up. He stared at the beakers.

"You still here, man?" Liam asked.

"What? Oh, yeah. I was just thinking I might need to dilute the mixture a little bit more."

"You *think?*"

Jerry suddenly turned toward him, and Liam saw he was crying. "I just remembered about your friend, Devon. I'm so sorry."

"Uh, thanks," Liam said. It was such an abrupt change of behavior that he wondered if Jerry was getting sick again. "Are you all right?"

"Me?" Jerry seemed to think the question was perplexing. He was still leaning against the counter, breathing hard, his face now white and his eyes and nose red from weeping. "I have never felt better in my life."

"You almost died, man. Maybe we should go to the hospital."

"You don't understand, Liam. I have *never* felt this good."

"Then you must be one miserable bastard, because you look like shit."

"I'm *connected*," Jerry said. "That's what I'm trying to tell you. For the first time in my life, I'm feeling the way you feel. I'm feeling *normal*."

Liam stared at him for a moment, then broke out laughing. "This isn't normal, dude. I'm pretty sure this isn't anyone's idea of normal."

Jerry shook his head. "You don't appreciate what you've got, Liam. I've been autistic my whole life. High functioning, they call it. Maybe you noticed?"

"Now that you mention it, I guess I can believe it."

Jerry laughed. "I've had a hard time reading people since I was born. I've gone through life calculating what people expected of me when I wasn't off on some obsession I couldn't control."

The light of dawn shifted through the windows and lit up his face. He looked like an otherworldly being to Liam, like an awestruck visitor from fairyland. Jerry looked up at the skylight and frowned, breaking the spell. "How long was I out?"

"I'm not sure."

"Shit," Jerry said. He practically ran to the sink. "Professor Wice is going to kill me. I should have put this specimen in the cooler hours ago."

"Specimen?" Liam asked. "You mean the snake?"

"We can't be sure if the neurotoxins will break down," Jerry said. Then he became a whirlwind of activity, moving quickly around the lab, gathering plastic bags and a box. He donned elbow-high gloves and a rubber apron and cut a piece out of the snake's side, which he then set aside. Then he packed up the box with the remains and marked on the side, 'Dangerous. Do not open'.

There was an old-fashioned refrigerator near the office. When Jerry opened it, Liam saw bottles full of sea creatures, along with containers of food on the top shelf. He shuddered at the thought of someone grabbing and eating the wrong thing.

Jerry grabbed a plastic specimen bag, dropped the piece of snakeskin into it, and sealed it. "First thing we need to do is go to the chemistry lab and have this analyzed," he said. "You want to come along?"

Jerry wasn't sure why he wanted Liam along, and it looked as if Liam wasn't sure either. Then again, both of them had been deeply affected by the appearance of the sea snakes. Jerry also suspected Liam didn't have much else to do. He was a spoiled rich kid, not a care in the world, unlike Jerry, who figured he'd be paying back his student loans for the rest of his life despite living in a dorm, despite being a graduate assistant, despite being smarter than ninety-nine per cent of the other students.

It won't hurt to see what his reactions are to my behavior because this is all new and I'm not sure I'm doing it right.

"Sure," Liam said. "I'm curious too. I'll tag along as long as you'll have me."

Since most of the science departments were clustered together, the Chemistry Department was only one building over. As they walked down the path, Jerry noticed how green the lawn was, how beautiful the chestnut trees were, the gray squirrel that chattered at them, the sound of a raven cawing on the roof of the biology building – things he would never have noticed before.

A pretty girl walked toward them. Jerry smiled at her and she smiled back, and it was amazing. He usually tried to avoid these random crossings of paths with people, because he never knew how to react. He said "Hi" when he shouldn't and didn't say "Hi" when he should. He smiled at the wrong time or, more often, in the wrong way. The usual reaction from others was to see their smile fade and for them to look away.

So ordinary, so common, and it feels so good.

Everything in his life had been internal until this last day and a half. Everything had been ordered and enclosed and contained. Nothing was left to chance. He'd thought he was happy, or at least resigned to his condition, but now that he saw how much he'd been missing, he realized bliss had come from ignorance.

What if I go back to the way I was? He almost grunted from the fear that seized his heart. He glanced at Liam, suddenly jealous of the man's ordinariness.

They entered the chemistry building via the back, where the lab was located. The lab's door was locked. Through the opaque glass, Jerry thought he saw movement inside – it could be only one person here at this hour. He banged on the door. When it didn't bring a response right away, he banged louder.

"It's Saturday!" a high voice shouted.

"It's important," Jerry shouted back. "An emergency!"

The shadow that approached was the freakishly tall Dr Patrick Krause. At nearly seven feet tall, with a bald head, and in his white lab coat, he reminded Jerry of a giant stork. He looked at Liam first, then turned his eyes to Jerry. "Oh, it's you."

"I'm glad you're in early," Jerry said, ignoring the man's disappointed tone. "This needs to be analyzed right away."

Krause was the only professor to have ever given Jerry a 'B' in a college course. For some reason, the professor had taken a deep dislike to him. Jerry had a sudden insight: it was probably because Jerry reminded the socially-awkward professor of himself.

He felt a sudden and surprising sympathy for him.

"There are proper channels, you know," Krause said. "Take it to Charlie. He's your advisor, right?"

"Charlie is busy," Jerry replied. "He wanted me to ask you to rush this. It's important. People's lives may be at stake."

"Forget it," Krause said. "I've a full day planned, and I can't fit anything else in."

Jerry wedged his foot in the door as the professor started to close it. "Doctor Krause, this is *critical,*" he said, his tone leaving no room for debate. "This is a new and deadly species, and we need to know right away just how toxic it is. We need to know what it's made of."

Krause looked down on him, both literally and figuratively. "What's gotten into you, Jerry?"

In the past Jerry would have meekly walked away, but not now. "Doctor Krause—"

"All right, all right, I'll get on it. I'll have it completed by Monday."

We need it now. But he realized that for Krause, this was really hopping to it.

"You need to be careful," Jerry said. "Even touching the skin is fatal. It may be the deadliest neurotoxin ever found."

Krause raised the plastic bag and eyeballed it. "Really?"

I've got him well and truly hooked. "Thank you, Doctor Krause," he said. "If this is as important as I think it is, you'll want to be in on the discovery." *Well, what do you know? I'm playing politics. How fun.* What had been impossible to him before was now almost easy.

They left the lab, and Jerry started heading back to the biology building.

"Dude, don't you ever eat?" Liam said, stopping in his tracks and waiting for Jerry to turn to him. "I'm starving, man. Let's go to the cafeteria. My treat."

Jerry hesitated; while the cafeteria was normally a minefield for him, he realized today he wasn't afraid, and he followed Liam without complaint.

The place was starting to fill with the breakfast crowd; it was a Saturday and there were no classes. Some freshmen were there horsing around, still getting to know one another. They took a back table, and Jerry watched it all curiously, aware that the boisterousness would have bothered him before.

"What are you grinning about?" Liam asked.

"This is just an everyday thing to you, isn't it?" Jerry asked. "You don't realize how miraculous it is."

"You keep saying that," Liam said. "I think you'll find that everyday life ain't that grand."

"Maybe, but I wouldn't mind finding out for myself."

Liam watched Jerry watching everyone else. The guy was on an ecstasy trip and thought it was *normal*. He was pretty sure he'd never felt like Jerry was feeling right now, except maybe that one time Devon had given him a pill without telling him what it was. He'd never surfed like that before or since, but when he'd gotten home, he'd slept for ten hours and decided he never wanted to feel that way again. Because if he did, he'd be taking one of those pills every day, and he was pretty sure that would be a bad thing.

Devon... Shit. He shook his head; he couldn't go there now.

He looked to Jerry again. Was it up to Liam to bring Jerry down to earth? *Nah, let the guy have his fun.*

Jerry finally turned his attention to his meal, and they ate in silence for a while. Liam was a slow eater. When he finally pushed his plate away, he looked up, expecting Jerry to be long finished.

Jerry was staring, unmoving, at his plate, half his food unconsumed.

"You all right, man?"

Jerry looked up blankly. "What?"

"You feeling all right?" Liam repeated.

Jerry looked around, his eyes darting like that of a hunted animal. "How long have I been like this?"

"I don't know, maybe five minutes?"

Jerry glanced at his watch. "I need more elixir." He stood abruptly and walked out of the cafeteria without looking to see if Liam followed. In fact, Liam got the feeling that his new friend had forgotten him entirely.

Liam followed Jerry as the he stomped up the stairs. This was the Jerry Liam remembered, not like the bouncy doppelganger of the last few hours. Jerry went straight to the refrigerator and removed the box with the snake in it.

He took a knife and started to cut off a hefty chunk of the skin.

"Shouldn't you be wearing gloves?" Liam asked, alarmed.

"I'm being careful," Jerry said, stabbing the slice of skin with the knife and dropping it into a beaker. He then filled all the beakers on the counter with some solution.

"What are you doing?"

"Making more of the elixir," Jerry said, his hands moving quickly, pouring and shaking and mixing.

"*Why?* You nearly died last time!"

"No, I was never in danger. In fact, I may not have used enough. I think I need to ramp up the dosage."

"Dude, I don't think that's a good idea."

Jerry ignored him, and went to the recycling bin in the corner of the lab and fished out six empty plastic soda bottles. He poured the contents of the beakers into the bottle. There was a small amount left at the bottom of the last beaker. Before Liam could say anything, Jerry drained it.

Liam moved closer, ready to catch him when he fell. But Jerry just stood there, eyes closed, his hands grasping the edge of the counter until they turned white. After a few minutes, he opened his eyes with a gasp.

He turned and smiled at Liam. "That's better. I think I'm getting used to it." He stared at the six bottles of elixir on the counter, then went into the back office and emerged with a backpack, and loaded the bottles in. "Come on, I've got an idea. I need to try this on someone else."

"Shouldn't you be going through proper procedures?" Liam said. "Clinical trials and all that?"

"Sure," Jerry said, "but I want to make sure that what happened to me isn't atypical. I need another test case. I know just who to try it on," Jerry said. "You have a car? Mind driving me someplace?"

Liam reluctantly agreed. He thought Jerry probably needed someone to look after him. Besides, he was curious to see what would happen.

Maybe I picked the wrong major. This science thing is pretty exciting.

CHAPTER SEVENTEEN

The *Cirdan* suddenly lurched, almost throwing Tom off his feet. He had been pointing out the river of snakes to the professors, leaving the engine to take them in a generally easterly direction toward the shore. There was little traffic out here to worry about.

He ran to the ladder, clambered up, grabbed the wheel, and put the engine in reverse.

The *Cirdan* didn't respond at first, but finally began to back up. Now the black river was not only behind them, but had circled around in front too. They were caught in a loop that seemed to be rapidly closing. Tom kept backing up the boat rather than taking time to turn it around. The noose was closing almost leisurely, but the *Cirdan* barely made it through before the two streams joined.

As far as the eye could see, the black river extended south to north, all of it being slowly drawn toward shore by the tides. The snakes were between the *Cirdan* and the harbor.

Tom gazed at the black ribbon, trying to make sense of it. At first, it seemed almost solid, like an asphalt road, but as he watched, he saw how it constantly changed – up and down, side to side. If he concentrated on a small portion of it, he could see individual snakes coming up for air, small flashes of yellow like sparks from a fire.

"They're migrating," Carol said moving up beside him.

Tom jumped, almost hitting his head against the cabin ceiling. "Shit!" he cried. "Try warning a guy!"

"Sorry, I thought you heard me," Carol said. She wasn't looking at him but examining the black river. "Migrating, or gathering to breed… or both, I suppose."

The metal steps clanged as Charlie joined them. "The clouds are looking pretty threatening," he said. "Shouldn't we head back?"

"I can't go through that," Tom said. "It will clog the motors. We're lucky it hasn't happened already."

"Can't we go around?" Charlie asked.

Tom just waved his hand at the snakes, which appeared to stretch from one horizon to the other.

"They can't go on forever," Carol said. "We'd better get started."

She was right, of course. Tom had already decided to do exactly that, but for some reason, he thought maybe it wasn't going to be that easy.

"Meanwhile, we should warn people," Charlie said. "At least contact the Coast Guard." He pulled out his cellphone and then stared at it.

"We're in the middle of a dead zone," Tom said. "You won't be able to get anything out here."

"Well, use your ship-to-shore radio, then," Charlie said. He pointed toward the CB unit on the counter next to them.

Tom felt his face flushing in embarrassment. *I may lose my license over this.* He'd always figured cellphones were good enough, because, except for this stretch of the coastline, he never went that far out. The coast was almost always in view; there were almost always boats nearby. So when his old CB unit had quit, he'd planned to buy a more modern satellite phone, just as soon as he had a banner season. It had never happened.

"It's... ah... broken."

"Broken?" Charlie said. "You let us get this far from land without any way to contact anyone?"

"I've never had an emergency," Tom muttered.

"Until you did," Carol said softly.

"What about flares?" Charlie demanded. "Surely that is legally required?" Left unspoken but obviously implied was that a functional satellite phone was probably also legally required.

"Are we sure we want to draw people to us without any way

to warn them?" Carol asked.

Tom threw up his hands. "Fine! Then we'd better get to shore fast, at least faster than these snakes, and warn them ourselves."

"We just need to get out of the dead zone," Carol said.

Tom didn't say anything as he pointed the boat south. The currents generally went north from here, and so he figured the snakes were more likely to be carried out of range sooner.

The three of them were silent as they ran parallel to the phenomenon. The yellow flashes within the black were almost hypnotic once you noticed them.

"Careful," Charlie said once as Tom distractedly guided the boat too close to the mesmerizing sight. He jerked the wheel in the other direction and decided he'd better stop staring. The ribbon seemed to go on forever. Charlie checked his phone every few minutes, but by Tom's reckoning, they were no closer to shore.

If they went too far south, he wasn't as familiar with the coastline. That could be suicidal. If they weren't able to turn shoreward soon he'd have to turn around and hear farther out. They might have to spend the night at sea, surrounded by millions of deadly poisonous sea snakes.

"How far have we come?" Carol asked.

"About seven miles," Tom said. "I can't believe there are this many snakes in all the oceans in all the world."

"There is a lot we don't know about the ocean," Carol said. "Especially the deeper zones."

"Yeah, but we should have seen this species before," Charlie said. "They're air breathers. They have to come to the surface."

"You're right," Carol said. Her voice had a finality to it that made both Charlie and Tom look at her. "This is impossible, unless..."

She turned and left the cabin. Charlie shrugged at Tom and then followed her.

Charlie found Carol standing over the sea snake they had caught earlier. It was quiet until he joined her, and then the creature seemed to see them, and the specimen jar rattled violently as it thrashed within the confines of its prison.

Carol grabbed one of the chum buckets from the side of the boat. She leaned over the starboard side and dipped the bucket into the water.

"Careful," Charlie cried, but she was already straightening up. She brushed past Charlie, unscrewed a small opening at the top of the jar, and carefully poured the water into it. It filled up half of the remaining volume. Then she went back to the side of the boat and repeated the process.

Charlie opened his mouth to object and then realized what she was doing. "You're going to kill it," he said.

"Oh, dear," she said. "Wherever will we find another one?"

They stood there for a time, and then, as one, they turned to the deck chairs and sat. It was getting chilly. The clouds were continuing to roll over them like a dark woolen blanket, blotting out the light. Though it was just after midday, it felt like twilight. Charlie remembered seeing blankets in the cabin and started to get up.

"Stay with me," Carol said. She put out her hand and grasped his. She didn't let go. For the next few minutes, Charlie wasn't certain if he was more conscious of the snake or of Carol's hand.

The snake had quieted down. When the floodlight over the cabin door went on, either automatically due to the darkness or because Tom had noticed them staring at the specimen jar, the snake became active again.

Until the light came on, Charlie hadn't realized how hard he'd been straining to see the creature. "How long has it been?" he asked, kicking himself for not checking his watch.

"Forty-five minutes," Carol said. "My understanding is that sea snakes can stay underwater for twenty minutes at a time."

This is impossible. The snake was obviously still alive, though it was getting sluggish. "Maybe the water is getting deoxygenated," Charlie suggested.

"Of course!" Carol said, and jumped off the chair and grabbed the bucket. She filled it and came over. "You drain it from the bottom, and I'll pour more in."

Charlie leaned down and reached for the valve, then had second thoughts. He went to his backpack and donned some rubber gloves. "Ready?" he asked.

They coordinated the action so that the water level never dropped. Within moments, the snake was thrashing about again.

Charlie stared at the malevolent creature from only inches away. The light glared off the glass, but he could still see its dark eyes watching him. He went over to his backpack and extracted a flashlight. He turned it on and directed the beam at the black snake.

Carol crouched beside him. "Do you see it too?" she asked, her voice filled with awe.

There, just behind the yellow head, slits had opened up. The snake had gills.

"Is it an eel after all?" Charlie said. "Could we have been wrong?"

"Of course not," Carol said. She knew that he was already aware of that, that he was simply expressing his awe out loud. "Taxonomically, it is a snake in every other way. But this isn't snake or eel. This is something new."

"How could we have missed this?" Charlie said.

"The gills are pretty well hidden in the black skin," Carol said. "Besides, you didn't have a chance to dissect one yet, right?"

"No," Charlie admitted. "What with making sure that Jerry was all right and then planning for this trip, I didn't get around to it. I thought we had plenty of time, that the snakes were rare, an anomaly. Frankly, I didn't like our chances of finding another one on this trip." He laughed ruefully. "I had it in my head that I'd like a fresher specimen to dissect. Guess I don't have to worry much about that now."

"Well, I won't tell anyone we missed it if you don't," Carol said. Of course, it was already too late. They'd told the authorities about the sea snakes without mentioning the little detail that they had gills. But if this species was something totally new, something completely unknown, perhaps everyone would forgive the omission. But her ploy made Charlie laugh.

"Yeah, we knew all along, but no one asked us," he said. They exchanged smiles. This was a big deal, and they both knew it. A Nobel Prize kind of big deal.

If they survived long enough to collect it.

Charlie glanced down at the snake. It was becoming quiescent again. It would probably need fresh water soon.

Fuck it. It can fucking die. If we want more, all we have to do is cast out a net and find another hundred.

It was irrational to blame the snake. He knew this, but he couldn't help it. It seemed to radiate malevolence. It wasn't a case of live or let live, like with so many poisonous creatures. These snakes were aggressive not for defensive reasons, not because they needed to eat – though that was probably what they used their venom for in their natural habitat – but because they seemed to want to kill anything in their path.

The snake's head pulsed, and he froze. The yellow stripes on the snake's head appeared to be glowing fluorescently. In the floodlights, it might have been mistaken for a reflection, but when he got closer, he was certain the glow came from within.

"Do you see what I'm seeing?" Charlie asked.

"It's bioluminescent," Carol said, awed. "That's why we've never seen them before. These are deep-sea creatures."

"Then what are they doing on the surface?"

The overhead lights went out. From the gloom of the cabin above, Tom's voice called out. "Guys, you might want to see this."

The moment they stood, the light from the port side of the boat washed over them. A ribbon of fire split the ocean, flowing north to south. The bioluminescence of thousands of creatures lit the sky.

Charlie put his arm around Carol's shoulders. He wasn't sure if it was meant to be in reassurance or an expression of awe. In return, she put her arm around his waist and leaned her head against his shoulder. It was the most beautiful sight he'd ever seen.

"Follow the yellow brick road," Charlie said.

"Yeah, we aren't in Kansas anymore," Carol replied.

They climbed up to the cabin to join Tom, and from there, the sight was even more spectacular. The ribbon of fire stretched in both directions as far as the eye could see.

"I think it's getting thinner," Tom muttered. "If we want to try to get to shore, we have to start now. I mean, we could stay out here all night, no problem. But we better decide soon, because I'm burning up a lot of gas, and the next depot in the other direction is China."

"We have to warn people," Carol said. "Somehow."

"There is no way the authorities aren't picking this up on satellites," Tom said. "They're probably already on their way to investigate."

"That's why we need to warn them!" Charlie said. He couldn't believe how frustrated he felt. Such a simple thing, lifting up a phone and calling someone. *You don't know what you've got until it's gone.* "They have no idea how dangerous it is."

"I could try to bull our way through," Tom said. "Get a running start, blast on through. It's up to you guys."

"I say we try," Charlie said.

Carol didn't say anything, and Tom seemed to take that as acquiescence, because he headed out to sea. He went a few hundred yards and turned around. "This better work," he said. "It's going to burn a lot of gas."

He revved the engine and put the boat into gear. They shot forward. "Better hold tight," he shouted above the sudden roar.

The boat lurched violently from side to side and slapped down on the waves as they sped toward the glowing line. It was as if a god of fire had drawn a line across the horizon.

Charlie gritted his teeth. *We are not meant to cross.* They smashed into the barrier, and the engine whined. The boat jolted, and they were nearly thrown off their feet.

Then they were through and heading for shore, the glow of the snakes behind them.

Tom let out an exultant shout. Charlie turned to Carol, took her in his arms and gave her a strong hug. She hugged him back fiercely.

The engine began to sputter, and the boat slowed.

"Shit, shit, shit," Tom said.

The boat lurched, speeding up and then slowing down, then speeding up again. Suddenly, Tom reached over and hit the switch. The engine subsided and they slowed, floating silently in the dark waters.

"I don't want to burn out the engine," Tom said. "The propellers are clogged." He didn't have to say by what.

"What do we do?" Charlie asked.

"Nothing," Tom said. "We're stuck. We can hope someone sees us, but we should save the flares until they'd do us some good."

A sudden chill raced through Charlie, alarmed that they might have to spend the night on the ocean surrounded by thousands of poisonous sea snakes. He checked his watch; still early afternoon. How was that possible? The temperature had plummeted.

They drifted in the ocean, the waves slapping against the sides of the boat. Tom doled out the blankets. "May as well be comfortable."

Carol and Charlie went down to the deck. After a few minutes of being rolled around, they found a cubbyhole between several of the nets and other supplies. Carol shivered. Charlie reached over and pulled her toward him. She didn't resist. They wrapped the two blankets around themselves and gave each other warmth.

Carol finally stopped shivering and fell asleep. Charlie listened to her deep breathing and stared up at dark clouds that reflected the flashing from the bioluminescent river of snakes.

CHAPTER EIGHTEEN

Hank realized that one advantage to growing old was that it wasn't hard to wake early. *Especially early enough for fishing.* More often than not, when Barry called him while it was still dark out, he was already awake. This time was no exception.

"Fish are jumpin'!" Barry said.

"Meet you there in five minutes."

His wife didn't stir at either the phone call or his getting up and getting dressed. They'd moved to separate beds because of her restless leg syndrome. Hank found himself sleeping much better.

Barry and Hank had found a sweet spot in a nearby estuary that almost always produced, especially early in the morning. His friend already had a line in the water when Hank drove up. "Any bites?" he called over his shoulder as he extracted his gear from the trunk.

"Threw one back, nice sized."

Hank selected his favorite lure. He'd caught his best fish with this one. He walked up the estuary's muddy bank, picked a spot near the old tree trunk, and cast.

Barry liked to toss his line out into the middle of the water and wait. He'd sit back in his portable chair and drink Irish coffee and be drunk by midmorning. Hank didn't mind. Barry was more fun when he was drunk.

Hank couldn't sit like that. He needed the activity of casting his line. Fishing gave them a little bit of excitement because they never knew what would be on the other end of the line. Mostly, though, they caught small inlet fish. They used barbless hooks and threw most of the fish back. Once in a blue moon, they caught a salmon. Not often enough to fill out their tags each season, but the hope of catching one was what brought them out most mornings. Hell, the one year they'd each caught their quota early in the season, all the fun had gone out of it.

Still, Hank was excited when something powerful snatched his lure and ran with it. Barry staggered up out of his chair and stood near the bank, watching.

"Something big," he suggested.

Hank grunted and pulled in some line. It was a long, slow process. Barbless hooks were great when you wanted to let fish go, not so great when you wanted to keep them.

He saw something break the surface and frowned. As he pulled it closer to the bank, he could see its shape in the water. It was unlike anything he'd ever caught before, long and narrow.

Barry started laughing. "A fucking eel, you lucky bastard. Ever eaten one of them? They taste great, like an old boiled shoe."

"I don't know," said Hank. "It was fun reeling it in. Why don't you go back to your chair and take another swig." Hank was annoyed, and he wasn't sure why. They needled each other mercilessly, and that was half the fun. *Why am I offended this time?*

The eel was only a few feet away. Barry turned around, laughing, making his way to his chair. On a whim, Hank whipped the eel out of the water and slung it through the air toward Barry. The long, black shape wrapped itself around Barry's neck. Hank thought he saw fangs sink into his friend's cheek.

"Holy shit!" he cried, dropping his pole. He ran toward Barry, who was now on his knees, trying to pull the eel free. As Hank approached, he got a closer look at the creature. It didn't look like an eel. In fact, it looked like a snake.

Barry fell onto his back. The snake was still coiled around his friend's neck, its fangs sunk into his face. Hank pulled the snake away and tossed it. It landed and slithered back into the estuary waters.

Barry was gasping, his eyes bugging out. Hank could smell the alcohol on his breath, and then there was no breath. Barry had stopped breathing, even though he was still conscious. He actually staggered to his feet for a moment, and Hank helped him up, not understanding.

Then his old friend froze, shook from head to toe, and toppled face first into the mud.

Hank felt his own breath becoming shallower and shorter, but he didn't think anything of it at first. Then the muscles in his neck contracted, and his throat closed. Inside his chest, his heart raced for a moment, then skipped a beat.

He was still conscious when he felt his heart stop beating. He landed on top of Barry and felt himself rolling toward the water, helpless to stop himself. The last sensation he felt was the cold water washing over his skin.

Deputy Sarah Ramirez got the call at around ten o'clock in the morning: two bodies found near the Lilliard Estuary.

She had a sinking feeling. Most mornings the good old boys, Hank and Barry, were down there. She flicked on the siren and lights and rushed to the scene even though the dispatcher had said bodies.

There was a state police car already there. "Please don't let it be Trooper Bowie," she whispered just as Trooper Bowie came around the car and waved at her. *Shit.*

"Hello, Sarah," Bowie said as she got out of her cruiser.

"Trooper Bowie, call me Deputy Ramirez, or just Ramirez."

"My pardons, Deputy," he said, not sounding the least bit contrite. He had never taken her seriously as a law enforcement officer, just as he'd never gotten over her breaking up with him.

"Is it Hank and Barry?" she asked.

"Afraid so," he said. "And I think it's connected to last night's meeting at the Sanders residence."

Ramirez rolled her eyes. It took a lot of understatement to call the huge, lodge-like mansion a simple residence. But then Bowie never acted impressed by anything or anyone.

She started walking toward the bank.

"I warn you," Bowie said behind her. "It's pretty gruesome."

I can fucking handle it.

Barry Holden was on his back, staring into the sun. His hands were near his neck, a pose she'd seen in other heart attack victims. Nothing particularly gruesome about that. Sad, but not gruesome.

She heard a splashing sound and turned to see that Hank Hamilton was half in and half out of the water. The only reason she knew it was Hank was because of his long, silver hair and beard. His face was covered by something black, and she approached cautiously.

Whatever it was, moved. Ramirez yelped and jumped back. She glanced over at Bowie, who stood watching her, but not snickering. The black thing covering Hank's face was just the tail of the creature that now emerged from a hole in his neck. It had a yellow striped head with glistening fangs. The snake slowly emerged, casting its head back and forth.

Ramirez backed up and vomited into the mud. She was pissed off at her own reaction, because she felt calm. But her body apparently felt differently.

"This isn't your first body," Bowie said.

"No," she answered, wiping her mouth. "It's the fifteenth time I've upchucked at seeing one."

"Yeah," Bowie said. "You want me to catch that thing?" He had on a pair of leather gloves and was holding a plastic bag.

"No, wait for the experts," Ramirez said.

"Are you sure?" Bowie said. "The snake will be long gone by the time they get here. Besides, I already called them and no one's answering."

Damned if she was going to let Bowie be braver than her. Still… "I don't have any protective clothing."

"Just hold the bag," he said.

"We should wait for the experts," she told him. Brave was one thing, but dealing with poisonous snakes was outright stupid.

"I'll do it," Bowie said, snatching the bag out of her hands.

"Bowie, no!"

But he was already bent over and grabbing the snake behind the neck. The tail of the snake whipped around Bowie's leg. The trooper lost his balance. He started falling toward the water and put out his hands, letting go of the snake.

It immediately sunk its fangs into his forearm.

"Well, damn," Bowie said, catching his balance and taking the snake firmly and throwing it to the ground. He stomped on its head. It thrashed once or twice and then was still.

Bowie's legs went out from under him. He sat down hard. He looked up at Ramirez with a strangely calm expression. "Make sure the eggheads get this, Sarah," he said.

"I will," she answered. "I'm sorry, Mark."

He closed his eyes and fell backward, and she wasn't sure he heard her words or her crying.

CHAPTER NINETEEN

Jennifer sat up in bed. "Mom?" Her voice was loud, penetrating every room of the house.

Her mom didn't answer. Jennifer got out of bed. Her jammies were bunched up around her middle, and her slippers were under the covers, having come off in the night. She also had on a little knitted cap, which made her feel as if her head was secure and that her brains wouldn't spill out in the middle of the night.

"Mom!" she shouted even louder.

I'll take a bath. She didn't like the shower. She liked lying in the warm water, feeling it slowly grow cold. She could lie there for hours. Mom didn't like her doing that. "You'll turn into a prune," she'd say.

But Mom wasn't home. Jennifer could do whatever she wanted. It was Saturday, and the two of them should be watching cartoons together in preparation for the new Doctor Who episode that night. New in America, at least. She'd long ago downloaded the British broadcast.

Jennifer ran the bath. *Maybe I'll go out this afternoon. Mom isn't here to stop me. Serves her right.*

She'd learned that the boys liked her. A lot. They would whistle at her, slow their cars down and try to talk to her. Of course she stuck her nose up in the air and ignored them, but in truth, she enjoyed the attention. She would keep getting that attention as long as she didn't talk to them. Jennifer had learned that as soon as she opened her mouth, a weird look would come over their faces and they would retreat. So, better to strut her stuff and make them *wish* they could have her.

Jennifer felt all tingly just thinking about it. As she lay in the lukewarm water, her hand went *down there,* and she massaged herself to that wonderful feeling.

Mom didn't know. Mom must *never* know.

Once the afterglow wore off, she couldn't enjoy the bath for some reason. She was disgruntled that her mom had left without waking her.

She put on her bathrobe and stomped into the kitchen, hoping her mom was there and had only been ignoring her. There was a note on the refrigerator, but she didn't read it. She already knew her mom wasn't home, and she didn't care what the stupid reason was.

Jennifer took a stack of bowls out of the cupboard then grabbed some cereal and milk. She was making a mess of things, spilling Cheerios all over the counter, slopping the milk onto the floor. *Serves Mom right. She should be here.*

She gobbled down several bowls of cereal then had a bowl of ice cream, which she knew her mom wouldn't approve of.

I should have my own house. It wasn't the first time she'd had the thought. Mom had given her a strange look when she'd asked, but Jennifer knew she was smart. She knew about rents and mortgages and all that. She could do it.

It was unfair that she was so smart but she couldn't figure people out. She thought it was *their* fault, not hers. They acted all unreasonable and stupid.

"Mom!" she screamed into the empty house.

Her cry echoed through the rooms, and she felt a moment of loneliness, an awareness that her future could be like this every day. It was a thought she couldn't handle.

"Dammit, Mom, where are you?"

There was a knock at the door.

That never happened. No one just dropped by. It was probably one of Mom's work friends. Mom had said, "Never open the door to strangers."

Jennifer peeked out the curtains. It was two boys – young men, really – about her own age. They were gorgeous, handsome and tall, with nice bones and muscles and all those things she daydreamed about.

She marched to the door and threw it open. "Mom's not

here," she said a little too loudly. She repeated it in a softer voice. "I'm sorry, Mom's not here.

"Are you Jennifer?" the dark-haired boy with glasses asked. "I-I'm here to see you." The boy stuttered, and she saw the look in his eyes. He was surprised by her appearance, she guessed. She was used to it. First surprise, and then disappointment.

"I don't think so," she said, and started to close the door.

"Please, Jennifer, I work with your mom. Can I just talk to you for a second?"

"Okay, one second." She counted off the second in her head and started to close the door, but the guy put his hand against it.

"My name's Jerry Parker, Jennifer. I'm like you, or I was until a day ago. But something happened, and now I'm like everyone else."

"I don't understand," Jennifer said.

"Please, can we come in?"

"I don't think I should let you," she said, but she opened the door a little wider and the boy took that as an invitation, and maybe it was. He really was cute in a nerdy sort of way. The other boy looked athletic, but maybe not as smart. The dark-haired guy walked past her and sat on the couch before Jennifer could say anything. The blonde followed a little more hesitantly. He sat in one of the chairs across from the couch, which no one ever sat in because you couldn't see the TV from there.

She frowned. The nerd was sitting in her spot. No one ever sat in her spot. "That's mine," she said, pointing.

"Oh!" the one called Jerry said, "I'm sorry!" He sprang up and moved farther down the couch.

"Well, that's okay," Jennifer said, sitting down. *I should shut up. They might like me if I shut up.* Instead, she turned to the blonde guy. "Who are you?"

"Liam. I'm along for the ride."

She turned back to Jerry Parker. "Why are you here?"

"Would you be willing to take some medicine that might make you better?" he asked earnestly. "I promise, it won't hurt you."

Liam spoke up. "Jerry, you can't promise that."

Jerry held out the palm of his hand toward his friend. "Yes, I'm sure it's safe. And it will make you like everyone else. You know, if you want to be."

"You mean normal?" Jennifer tried to understand what he was saying. "Mom says I'm better than normal. She says normal is boring."

Jerry didn't say anything for a moment. His voice was soft when he finally spoke. "Do you believe that, Jennifer?"

She didn't answer

Jerry produced a small bottle from his coat pocket. He unscrewed the lid and held it out to her.

"Are you sure about this, Jerry?" Liam said, rising to his feet.

"I have to know."

Jennifer took the magic potion from Jerry; if they weren't sure she should take it, then she would show that that she could, that she *would*. It was clear, like water. She sniffed it. There was a slight fishy smell. This was just like a Doctor Who episode, she decided. Things like this happened all the time. People were cured, and miracles happened, and a normal, everyday girl became the Doctor's Companion.

She drank the potion before she could have second thoughts.

"Are you sure you told her the right time?" Joshua asked.

There was a telltale hesitation in Sam's answer. "It's always at three o'clock, right?"

Yes, but not always on Saturday. Sometimes we do it on Fridays at eight o'clock, and I'll bet anything Kim showed up last night, waited for us, and then went home.

At least, he *hoped* she went home. But he'd been calling her all day and hadn't got an answer. She wouldn't be so crazy as to go in alone, would she?

Joshua eyeballed the lock and chain. There was just enough give in the chain that he thought she might be able to squeeze through. She was skinny enough, and her nicely-shaped boobs could be flattened, right?

It was nearing eight o'clock in the evening, and even though it was the weekend, his parents still wanted him home by midnight. So if they were going to go, they needed to start.

"Did you remember the key?" he asked. It was faintly insulting, he knew, but Sam had forgotten once, necessitating driving all the way back to his house, and neither Kim nor Joshua had ever let him forget it.

Sam pulled the key out of his pocket and, looking around to make sure no one was watching, unlocked the padlock. The caution was unnecessary. Joshua had never seen anyone in the alley. Most of the back entrances of the nearby buildings looked like they hadn't been opened in years.

If Sam's dad hadn't shown them this secret entrance, they never would have found it. "Don't ever go in there," he'd warned. He was a maintenance worker, and he'd flashed the key on his keychain, half drunk, which was why he'd veered off the sidewalk after dinner and pointed out the entrance. But of course, he must have known Joshua and Sam wouldn't be able to resist.

Sam had a cool dad. Too bad they couldn't switch parents because Sam would probably have been just fine with Joshua's overprotective parents, and Joshua would have loved to have Sam's permissive ones.

Fate was cruel that way.

Meanwhile, Kim's parents were no-shows, always off on trips, leaving Kim and her brothers alone.

They had copied the key to the padlock within a week of being shown the underground entrance, and it took another couple of weeks to assemble all the necessary gear without being noticed. It was Sam who had brought Kim aboard. She had spelunking equipment in her garage from the summer her big brother had tried out the sport.

Joshua went on in, and Sam followed, hooking the padlock without latching it home. From a distance, it looked locked. But then Sam hesitated. "Maybe we shouldn't do it," he said.

"Why not?"

"I don't know. Something's wrong."

"Like what?"

"I don't know. I just feel it."

Joshua sighed. Sam went through a variation of this almost every time, though usually not this blatantly. Usually, with Kim around, he tried to act all brave, but his behavior was always a little timid. Underground exploring wasn't for the timid. You had to push through some dodgy barriers sometimes, and you never knew what would be on the other side.

That's what made it fun. Joshua's own heart was beating fast, but he found it exhilarating. He was pretty sure Kim also found it exciting. He'd been waiting all week for this, and he wasn't going to stop because Sam had a *feeling*.

I'll go by myself if I have to.

As soon as he had the thought, he was sure Kim had done exactly that. Sam had screwed up the time, and rather than go home, she'd gone on in. Maybe that was why she wasn't answering her phone, because she was pissed.

As they walked through the familiar tunnels that led to the deeper levels, they were met by a blast of humidity. Moisture ran down Joshua's helmet and onto his face. It seemed to him the rotting walls were leaning more precipitously than usual.

Has it rained lately? Maybe at night when I was sleeping? He didn't think so. He didn't remember waking up to the roads being wet. So what was causing the moisture?

He decided to stick to places they had already explored, just in case. "What do you think of Kim?" he asked.

"What do you mean?" said Sam.

"I mean, do you like her?"

"I've known her since I was like five years old," Sam said. "We've always gotten along."

Joshua rolled his eyes in the dark. Could Sam really be that dense, or was he being devious? No, dense it was. Sam seemed to think of Kim as the tom-girl she'd been instead of the very nice-looking girl she now was. A nice-looking, fun, and exciting girl.

They continued on. There was a rivulet of water running down the center of the corridor, which Joshua was pretty sure was something new. He decided they would turn around when they reached the big chamber with the five different exits, even though on most nights, that was where they began their explorations.

I've got my fix, but Sam is right. There is something off.

He heard a tinkling sound and realized it was from something landing on his helmet and trickling down: sand and pieces of concrete. At the same time, his feet slid a little on the floor of the tunnel.

"Did you feel that?" Sam asked. His voice was hushed, as if he was afraid to move.

"What?" Joshua said.

"That was a fucking earthquake," Sam said, his voice getting louder.

"An earthquake?" Joshua laughed nervously. "I barely felt it."

"Yeah, well, the next time, the whole ceiling might come down. Come on, let's head back."

"All right," Joshua said, making it sound like a huge concession. "When we reach the big chamber, we'll turn around." There was only one more turn in the tunnel so Sam followed silently.

They reached the chamber and looked around. Joshua had never figured out what it must have been above ground. Most of the tunnels were old streets, most of the rooms old houses, but what this had been, he couldn't imagine.

He reached the center of the chamber then turned around to head back. As he did so, his headlamp exposed something that didn't seem right. Sam's lamp was already shining on the same anomaly.

It was a sixth exit. It was broken and jagged, as if it had once been sealed off, but there was no doubt there was a tunnel behind it. Joshua went toward it.

"No way, man," Sam said behind him. As if to accentuate

his words, the ground shook slightly, barely enough to make the water ripple, but enough for Joshua to feel it this time.

"I've got to see where this goes," Joshua said. "Stay, or come with me."

Joshua knew Sam wasn't going to stay there alone. His friend's footsteps followed him as he ducked through the ragged entrance.

The tunnel was the cleanest Joshua had ever seen, the walls and floor smooth and unblemished. It was also dry. The air smelled different somehow, as if it came from another century. The light of their headlamps curved down a gentle slope. As they descended, the ceiling became moist again, part of it drooping as if ready to break away at any moment. Shattered walls had tumbled into their path. Joshua went on despite his friend's objections.

If Kim can do it, so can I.

They emerged on a platform, and running down a deep culvert below them was what appeared to be a river. The water was nearly to the edge of the platform and surged toward a huge wall and flowed beneath it. Joshua had been holding back his panic, trying to feel braver than Sam, but now the sight of the torrent of water in such a confined space made him freeze.

"Wow," Sam said. "I bet no one has been here in years."

Joshua didn't answer.

Sam turned, grasping his friend's arm, pointing toward the water. The light of his headlamp followed something floating down the river.

At first, all Joshua could see was the red coat, and it took a moment for his thoughts to catch up with what his gut already knew. Then he saw the blonde hair floating through the water, and the familiar yellow scarf.

Now it was Sam's turn to be foolhardy. Joshua wanted to run back the way they'd come, but Sam ran to where the water disappeared. Joshua couldn't move. He closed his eyes, felt the earth shake again, and heard Sam's shout. Suddenly he was aware of the tons of broken stone above his head, the darkness beneath.

What the hell are we doing here?

Sam snagged the red coat. Kim's bloated face floated into view. Her blonde hair covered most of it, but her milky eyes looked up at them in seeming disappointment. And snagged around her body were what could only be snakes.

Sam struggled to stay on his feet on the slick platform.

Joshua finally moved, running over and sliding to a stop next to Sam, putting out his hand.

Then the earth shook again, and it lifted him completely off his feet. The platform tipped downward and the water surged toward them.

He was in the water, Kim floating beside him, her hand seeming to grab his sleeve, pulling him downward into the black hole.

CHAPTER TWENTY

Y ou think Mary bought it?" Kristine said. They'd had to go through the secretary to rent out the truck, pretending to meet in the hallway by accident.

"I doubt it," Ken said. "But Mary didn't get to where she is by spilling secrets. She got to where she is by hoarding secrets and letting people know it."

Ken drove a huge pickup just like Charlie's, only this one was clean and uncluttered. *Like Ken's mind.* She smiled to herself, and laid a hand on Ken's thigh. Then, as they drove through the Seattle traffic, her hand moved higher, unzipping his pants, pulling out his cock and stroking it.

Ken ran a red light. She squeezed him and said, "Try not to kill us."

They turned onto one of the winding coastal roads and drove until they were alone. He pulled over. "Well?" he said.

"I've got fresh makeup on," Kristine said. "I want to make good impression. Zip up and let's go."

Ken grumbled, but made himself presentable and turned back onto the road. He would demand some kind of payment in the future for her teasing, but that was all right with Kristine.

She didn't see the house until they turned the last corner. Despite it taking up much of the space of an entire island, the architecture blended with the surroundings. They'd managed to build the broad decks almost like the promenade of a ship, rising for three levels without cutting down many of the trees. The shrubs seemed to be native and natural. It was like a cross between a Frank Lloyd Wright building and the Elvish Last Homely House from *The Lord of the Rings*.

There was a drawbridge, an actual drawbridge leading to

the house. It was the castle of a nobleman... no, a king. Only a king – or a billionaire which, as far as Kristine was concerned, was the same thing – would have the Pacific Ocean as his castle moat.

There was a burly man with very erect bearing waiting for them. He led them up the broad steps and into the front foyer. There were three different staircases, one leading up to another floor and two spiral staircases on either side of the entrance, which led off to side rooms. The first floor was one grand ballroom. Couches and chairs surrounding a huge fireplace separated out a corner of the huge room.

John Sanders was staring into the fire.

Kristine had seen pictures of him, of course. He looked older than she'd expected, more careworn. *What cares does a billionaire have?*

Sanders turned at their entrance. Ken stopped as if waiting for permission to approach, and Sanders waved them over impatiently. He nodded to Kristine. She saw the look in his eye and recognized it. It was a man appraising her looks and liking what he saw.

"This is Professor Wice's wife, Kristine," Ken said. "I ran into her at the university and thought she might like to meet you."

"And me her," Sanders said. He took her hand in his, holding onto it for a moment longer than necessary. "I'm glad to meet you, Missus Wice. Your husband is an impressive man."

She said, "I think so, too."

Sanders turned to Ken, and it was as if someone had turned off a spotlight, as if Kristine had been dismissed and forgotten in the span of a few moments. Kristine didn't like that at all. *I'm up for the challenge.*

"What have they discovered?" Sanders asked. "Wice and Wheatley. Have they found more of the sea snakes?"

"I haven't been able to get ahold of them, sir," Ken said. "They are out on the ocean, apparently out of cellphone range."

Sanders didn't move, simply stared at Ken until he was fidgeting like a little boy. "I don't understand," the billionaire said, finally. "I gave you the money for a state-of-the-art boat. The *Serenity*, I believe you named it. Surely it has modern communications."

Ken looked down at his feet. "The *Serenity* wasn't available," he said. "We chartered a boat instead."

"Unavailable?" Sanders said. His voice was calm, yet somehow all the more threatening because of it. "What could be more important than this?"

"I rented it out before this happened."

"Rented it out."

"Yes, sir," Ken said, finally looking up. "It's the only way I can meet the budget."

Again there was a long silence.

"I understand the chairmanship of the biology department is cyclical," Sanders said coldly. "When is your term up, Mister Carter?"

"It… it's not written in the bylaws, sir. It usually comes down to who wants to do the job. If no one wants to do it, then there is an informal vote, and whoever is selected is usually gracious enough to take on the job."

"It might be time for someone else, Mister Carter. I have to say, you don't strike me as a scientist. You come across as a bureaucrat. And believe me, I've had my *fill* of bureaucrats."

"I'm sorry you feel that way," Ken said. Kristine was a little surprised by his tone. For once, he wasn't being subservient. "I've been published by the major journals. I am considered an expert in my field. And for your information, no one else wants the job. Charlie? He hates it. The *bureaucracy*, as you put it."

"Nevertheless, if you want my support from this day forward, you might want to take a break."

Ken didn't answer. Kristine thought the billionaire had made a misjudgment. As much as Ken Carter liked the money Sanders could give the department, he liked his position even more.

"Perkins!" Sanders called out.

The big man with the military bearing came in immediately, as if he'd been waiting just outside the door.

"Show Professor Carter to my office," he said, then turned to Ken. "We have our own cellphone tower here. I'd like you to try to reach Wice and Wheatley again."

Ken left with Perkins. He didn't even look at Kristine. Sanders turned back to the fire, and Kristine had the impression he'd forgotten she was there.

"Ken has his pride, you know," she said. *As do I.*

"What? You sure could have fooled me. Oh, I'm sure he values his dignity, but he values money even more. I wouldn't be surprised if he's been embezzling. I think maybe I'll set Perkins on that."

Kristine wanted to object, yet… she'd wondered how Ken could afford all the lavish meals and hotels and trips when Charlie always seemed to be scrimping for money. But then again, there was Mary Stewart, and it was impossible for Kristine to believe that glorified secretary wouldn't know if money missing.

Sanders frowned into the fire, and she had the sense something else bothered him. For one thing, she thought the welfare of the Biology Department was pretty far down his list of worries.

"I'm sorry about your son's friend," she ventured.

"Yes, that was a shame," he said. He didn't say anything more.

"Is there something else, John?" Kristine asked, finally. "Has something happened?"

Sanders turned and looked at her, and it was as if he was really seeing her for the first time. "Kind of you to ask. My son is missing."

"Missing!"

"Oh, I don't think it's anything serious," Sanders continued. "He's an adult, after all."

"How old is he?"

"Liam is nineteen, no, twenty." Sanders smiled ruefully. "They grow up fast."

"You don't look old enough to have a son who's twenty," she exclaimed. In truth, he looked like he might have had his son late in life, but Kristine found that flattery almost always worked with men.

But Sanders might have been an exception because he looked as though he hadn't even heard her. "I was hoping Liam and I could fly back east together. I've had some troubling news."

"Would you like to tell me about it?" she asked.

"It really isn't your problem, Missus Wice." He smiled at her. "I've been a horrible host. Please sit down. May I get you something to drink?"

She adopted a sultry tone. "A glass of wine would be nice."

He went to a bar near the window and came back a few moments later with two large goblets filled with red wine.

She took a sip, and it went down so smoothly that she closed her eyes in appreciation. *Yeah, I could finish this whole goblet pretty fast.* When she opened her eyes, he was watching her. "This is a tremendous house," she said.

Sanders laughed, but there was a cynical edge to it. "That's the word for it, all right. But technically, it isn't a house. It's a public lodge, owned not by me, but by Sanders Enterprises. We're sort of beta testing it."

"But aren't *you* Sanders Enterprises?"

"Not so much," he said. "Not anymore." He grimaced and took a big swig of wine.

Kristine followed his example, intending to take a sip, but it tasted so good that she kept swallowing. The glass was nearly empty. Sanders snatched it out of her hand and filled it again.

"I'm already tipsy," she said halfheartedly.

"Nothing wrong with that," he said. "How would you like to see the rest of the house?"

Kristine gave him a speculative look, knowing both of them were thinking the same thing. His smile reached his eyes, and he held out his hand to help her off the sofa.

Kristine drained the second glass of wine. *I probably shouldn't do this.* She took his hand.

She had always heard that power was an aphrodisiac, but she hadn't believed it until now. The thought that this man was worth billions, that he was friends with the most powerful politicians and celebrities in the world, made her anticipate his every move. He was interested in her, she was certain.

He didn't say anything as he led her from room to room. He didn't have to. It was the little touches she noticed: the carvings and paintings, the quality of the furniture and the fixtures. It was hard to put a finger on it, but it all radiated wealth and good taste. Sanders spoke with his hands. He touched her on the arm, then on the shoulder, and then, after showing her a view of the ocean from a huge picture window, he put his arm around her.

He kissed Kristine in the library. As she closed her eyes, she felt the floor beneath her shake. She opened her eyes and saw the bookshelves swaying. A book fell to the floor with a splat.

"Did you feel the earth move?" she joked.

Sanders didn't answer. The last room he led her to was the bedroom.

He turned her toward him and kissed her hard. Kristine didn't know if was the wine or that fact that her lover was in the same house, but she had never been so turned on in her life. She wanted to fall backward onto the bed, but he held her, then roughly turned her around and ground into her.

She put her hands down on the bed and moaned. He put his arm around her neck and pulled her back up again. He nuzzled her neck and then bit it, and it was painful for a moment, and then he was pulling up her dress and pulling down her panties, all the while keeping his arm around her neck so that she could barely breathe.

She'd tried to initiate rough sex with both Charlie and Ken. Charlie didn't have a clue, and Ken, while he tried, didn't really have it in him. Sanders clearly didn't have such inhibitions.

She heard him unfastening his belt and his pants falling to the floor. He pulled away for a moment, and she ventured a look over her shoulder. He was rolling on a condom.

"You don't have to do that," she said.

She felt him freeze. Suddenly, she there was a cold emptiness behind her. She looked over her shoulder, her naked butt still in the air.

Sanders was backing away, pulling up his pants. "What the hell is wrong with me?" he muttered. "My son is missing."

He started for the door.

"That's it?" Kristine said incredulously, adjusting her clothes. "You think I'm some kind of slut?"

"If that's what you are," Sanders said. "Listen, let's just say the wine went to our heads."

She started to object, but he held up his hand, and to her own surprise, she fell silent. "I'll never say a word about this, Missus Wice. There is no need to make a scene."

She was speechless. Never before had she offered herself to man and been turned down.

Sanders called out, "Perkins!"

The bodyguard entered the room instantly.

"See Missus Wice and Professor Carter to their car, will you, please? Then come right back. We need to find Liam. I felt the tremor this time, and I don't want to be here when the Big One happens."

Perkins came over to take Kristine by the arm, but she shook him off angrily and went into the adjoining bathroom. She washed her face, to obliterate any part of that awful man still on her.

Finally, she went to the door and, again giving Perkins an angry look when he tried to take her arm, she marched out of the house on her own and walked to the pickup.

It was locked. It was only then, as she stood there waiting, that she broke into tears. Ken found her, led her to the passenger side of the pickup, and helped her in.

"Did he…?" he started to ask.

"Ken, let's get out of here."

"You want me to drive you home?"

"No, let's go to our place."

Their place might have been a hotel room, but Kristine didn't think she could face her own house yet, especially if there was a chance of running into Charlie.

"Let's just go to bed," she said. She had no interest in sex, but she thought maybe she'd let Ken hold her, have him worry about her, and maybe, just maybe, she would forget what had just happened.

CHAPTER TWENTY-ONE

W hen is something supposed to happen?"
Liam's voice cut through Jerry's thoughts. He'd been
trying to figure out the exact percentage of neurotoxin
he'd diluted. He'd sort of winged it, which wasn't at all like him.

At the last second, he'd taken the bottle out of Jennifer's
hand, still half full.

Then they'd sat there for several minutes, both boys staring
and waiting.

She finally stood and yelled, "Quit looking at me!"

"Maybe you should get dressed," Jerry said, and she
stomped away.

"Are you sure this is a good idea?" Liam asked again.

"I gave her a very weak dose," Jerry said. "Do you want to
stop?"

Liam frowned, obviously thinking on his answer. "No," he
finally said with some uncertainty. "I'd like something good to
come out of this."

Jennifer returned, dressed in jeans and a pullover sweater.
She'd brushed her hair. She didn't seem to have the least idea
how good she looked. She plopped into her spot at the end of the
couch and turned on the TV.

"I'm not missing Doctor Who," she said.

Jerry watched her carefully, running the dosage numbers in
his head again. When he came back to the present, he knew he'd
phased out.

"How long have I been sitting here?" he asked, panic
weaseling its way through him.

"A few minutes. I've been trying to get your attention."

Jerry looked at the bottle of elixir on the table next to Jennifer,
then opened his backpack and pulled out a fresh bottle instead.

He hesitated. His usual caution was returning. As exciting as the effect of the snake poison was, there was no way of knowing what the long-term effects would be.

If I wait any longer, the old Jerry will overrule me.

He drained the bottle. His thoughts begin to clear almost immediately, and he grabbed the remote and turned the TV off.

Jennifer leapt up from the couch, eyes blazing. "Give me that! Right now!"

"Drink this," he said, handing her the half-empty bottle

She stared at both him and Liam defiantly, then snorted and downed it.

Jerry calculated that she'd taken at least as much elixir as he had the first time, but she was more severely autistic. He turned away from her to speak with Liam. "What do you think? Maybe a little more?"

"I don't think..." Liam began to say.

There was a loud gasp on the couch behind them. Jennifer was rigid, her arms and legs sticking straight out, her jaw clenched, her eyes rolling back into her head.

Liam reached her first, putting his hand under her head. Jerry reached under her legs, and they lifted her and laid her on the couch.

"Jesus, is this how I looked?" Jerry asked.

"Worse," Liam said. "You were actually thrashing and foaming at the mouth."

As if on cue, saliva started running out of the sides of Jennifer's mouth, and her arms and legs began to twitch. Her head jerked from side to side.

Then, as quickly as it had begun, the fit was over. Jennifer grew still. Jerry almost leaned down to listen to her heart. Then she moaned and opened her eyes. She stared at the ceiling then slowly turned her eyes toward Jerry.

She sat up abruptly. "Oh... my... God," she said slowly. "I-I'm feeling weird."

"Relax," Jerry said. "You're all right. You're with friends."

She looked around the room as if seeing it for the first time.

Jerry wondered if this was how an infant felt when it first gazed upon the world.

"I know what we should do!" she exclaimed. "Let's go dancing on the beach!"

"Dancing?" Jerry said. "On the beach?"

"I think we better stay here," Liam said. "Control this a little. Isn't there another Doctor Who episode coming on?"

"Control it?" Jennifer exclaimed. "I want to *feel* it! Come on! There's a bonfire down at Agate Beach on Saturday nights. I can see it from the window of my room. I've always wanted to go, but Mom wouldn't let me." Without waiting for an answer, she strode to the front door, flung it open, and headed toward the ocean.

"Should we knock her over the head?" Liam asked. "Tie her down?"

"She has to come down from her high eventually." *Maybe I'll try a smaller dose next time.*

"What about the snakes?" Liam asked.

Jerry shook his head helplessly. "That's why we need to keep an eye on her," he said, following her out the door.

Liam knew some of the partygoers: fellow surfers, hangers out, rich kids taking a break between high school and college. The bonfire was near the jetty, and the kids had cleared off a section of the broken concrete surface to use as a dance floor.

Jennifer didn't hesitate, but joined right in. Jerry pushed his way over to her and began to dance with her.

Liam watched, worried despite the air of happiness filling the night air. In the distance, he could make out the old lighthouse, the moon coming up behind it.

He glanced over at the dancers. Everyone had stopped to watch Jennifer and Jerry, who were putting on a show, twirling each other about, catching each other just in time. Both of them looked happy. Both of them vibrated with health. Everyone else looked dull and uninspired next to them.

If that stuff did that much for them, what would it do for him?

Jerry had left his backpack. Liam unzipped it. There were three full bottles of the stuff. *Maybe just a sip.*

The liquid had a slightly bitter tang. This stuff had killed Devon, and he supposed it might kill him, but he had to know. He closed his eyes. In the distance, he heard applause as there was a lull between songs. 'Surf's Up' came on, and Liam let the notes flow over him.

He wasn't sure how long he sat there. When he opened his eyes, it appeared that there were fewer dancers. There was a slow dance on, and Jennifer and Jerry were draped over each other. The fire was burning low, as if no one had added driftwood to it for a while.

I don't feel any difference, dammit.

He stood and walked toward the dance platform. Before he reached it, however, there was shouting behind him, down by the water. He turned to see that most of the partygoers were congregated down there, and they were milling about.

He turned away from Jerry and Jennifer, and walked down the sands. There was something on the beach, something that hadn't been there the last time he was here, only the day before yesterday. He couldn't make sense of it.

Someone took his arm, and he turned to see Jennifer giving him a big grin. Jerry came up on the other side of him.

"What is it?" Jennifer asked, looking at the thing on the beach.

"I think… I think it's a whale," Jerry said.

It was hard to make out details, but Liam knew the instant Jerry said it that he was right. It couldn't be anything else.

The last of the sunlight was in his eyes. Away from the bonfire, Liam's vision adjusted to the point where he could see details. There were dark spots all over the whale, and long, black streaks.

He got closer and stopped cold. "Get back! Everyone get back!" he shouted. Moments later, Jerry's voice joined his, and there must have been something in their tone, because everyone backed up.

Some of the snakes were still alive, still eating the decaying flesh of the mammoth creature. Other snakes hung limply, dead. A few dropped off the giant beast and slithered toward them.

"Don't touch them!" Liam screamed, and his voice echoed over and over in his head, and suddenly he couldn't see anything, and it was as if he was falling into darkness. *Jerry's elixir?*

He felt Jennifer and Jerry's hands tighten on his arms, and in the distance he heard a girl's voice. He thought it was Jennifer, but how could that be? She was standing next to him, wasn't she?

"What's wrong with him?" the girl's voice asked.

And then he was falling.

CHAPTER TWENTY-TWO

The gentle swaying of the waves had put Charlie to sleep. The sudden lack of motion woke him.

He checked his watch. Despite the hard wooden surface, the cold, and the danger, he'd unintentionally napped for over an hour. He'd dreamt of peaceful things, hopeful things, but now, something wasn't quite right.

The boat seemed to be completely motionless, as if they had washed up on shore. It seemed almost as if night had fallen. Dark clouds covered the sky, but the *Cirdan* was bathed in light. He could see every small feature of the deck, the gunwale, the cabin... *Not right at all.*

He rolled gently out of Carol's grasp, tucked the blanket around her, and stood.

Bioluminescent light surrounded the boat on all sides.

They were in the middle of the river of sea snakes, held up by their numbers, which stretched deep into the water. It was as if he could see all the way to the bottom of the ocean. The lights were rising and falling, individual creatures moving constantly, but the bulk of them kept the *Cirdan* steady. It was as if they were riding a wave of yellow lava down a volcano, and eventually the fire was going to burn through their vessel.

Carol rose from the deck and went to his side. Her fingers tightened painfully on his arm.

The floodlights went on, and Tom called down to them. "You seeing this?"

Charlie wanted to shush him, thinking if they didn't make any noise the creatures wouldn't know they were there. Tom came to the top of the stairs and looked down at them. The glow lit his face from below, making him look ghoulish – his chin and cheekbones prominent, his mouth and eyes deep gashes.

Suddenly, the deck felt exposed. Charlie looked down into Carol's pale face and motioned toward the cabin. He cringed as their footsteps clanged on the iron steps.

Something flew past them, something long and dark. Carol cried out, and Tom cursed. Another one of the objects soared through the few feet between him and Carol, and he retracted his bare hand hastily.

"Grab the gaffers," Tom shouted. The hooked-end bludgeons were hanging on the wall between the deck and cabin. Carol snatched one up, and handed it to Charlie before grabbing a second one. As she did, one of the snakes flew over her head.

"How are they doing that?" Tom yelled.

"Look at their tails!" Carol shouted. The snakes' tails ended in a flattened, spade-shaped fin. "They're propelling themselves through the water and into the air."

Charlie's heart sank. He'd been scared before, but now dread settled over him. What chance did they have if the snakes could jump into the boat? He couldn't see any way out of this.

A snake landed at his feet, on the top stair, and he stabbed down at it with the spike on the top of the gaffer. It thrashed its tail violently, hitting Charlie's boots and the cuff of his pants. He'd worn his heavy socks, which he'd pulled up nearly to his knees so no bare skin was exposed. But he didn't know if the toxin could penetrate the pants. He couldn't see why not.

Two more snakes landed and slithered toward him. He tried pulling the spike out of the pinioned snake, but the hook caught in slats of the stairs. Then Carol was beside him, slamming her own gaffer down on the heads of the creatures and then kicking them to the deck.

"Get in here!" Tom shouted from the cabin. "Close the door."

Carol was at the threshold but waited for Charlie. He pushed her inside and followed, losing his footing and sprawling onto the floor. He heard the door slam behind him.

The windows on either side of the door were still open, and snakes slammed against the door and the wall, barely missing the openings. Charlie grabbed one window and Tom the other, and they struggled to close them. Both of them were stuck.

"I never close the suckers," Tom grunted.

Then whatever paint or gunk was keeping Charlie's window open broke away and the window slammed shut, a crack splitting it down the middle. A snake slammed against the pane of glass at the same moment, and the crack spider webbed.

Tom was still struggling with his own window, and a snake flew past his bare hands and landed in the middle of the cabin. Carol whirled and threw her gaffer and, by luck, the spike nailed the snake's head to the floor. Charlie tossed her his own gaffer, since she seemed so much better at using them than him.

Tom slammed his porthole shut with a crash, and there was a momentary silence except for the whipping of the snake stuck to the flooring. Charlie stomped on its head. It was strangely soft, as if there were no bones in it. An ocher ooze came spilling out. He wrenched the gaffer away from the snake.

An explosion deafened him. He blinked, trying to make sense of it. He heard something flopping at his feet and looked down to see a snake with its head missing, still curling about on the floorboards. There was the smell of cordite in the air, and he turned to see Carol with her arm outstretched, holding a handgun.

"Good shot," Tom shouted. "I hope you have lots of bullets."

There was an inch gap at the base of the door, and shadows flitted back and forth there, intermittently blocking the glowing light. Then a snake head poked through the opening, impossibly flat. Carol fired again, and where the snake's head had been, there was now yellow ooze.

The windows were shaking as one snake after another threw itself at the glass. The cracks were growing wider and thicker.

"Turn out the floodlights!" Carol shouted.

Tom didn't answer at first, then he said in a low voice, "Are you crazy? We won't be able to see the damn snakes."

"Either turn out the lights or I'll shoot them out!"

Tom reached over, and suddenly they were in darkness. No, not quite darkness, for there was a bare bulb still on in the cabin, but the drop-off in luminescence was so drastic that Charlie's eyes took a few moments to adjust.

Carol's face was a blur then took on shape and form. She was white faced but determined, her lips curled back in a grimace of effort.

The window that Charlie had closed shattered behind him. A snake landed in the middle of the shards, which scattered across the floor.

"Turn off the cabin light!" Carol shouted.

"There's a snake in here," Tom said. "We won't be able to see it!"

"Either one snake or a hundred," Carol said. She stepped forward and shattered the bulb with the barrel of her gun.

It was silent again outside the cabin, which made the slithering noise inside the cabin all the more alarming. A soft glow lit up the floor. Carol was holding her phone close the floor.

The snake shot toward the light, and Charlie lunged forward, stepping on its tail. It darted around with blinding speed, its fangs headed for his leg. He threw himself on Tom's cot, but didn't think he would be able to get his leg out of the way in time. There was a loud crash, and something big and solid and square landed on the snake, beheading it.

Carol turned off her phone light. Then there was complete silence.

"Thank you," Charlie said.

"No problem," Tom answered. "At least my old CB turned out to be good for something."

Carol laughed. "I was going to say the same thing about my iPhone."

As their ears grew accustomed to the silence, they realized there were small rustles outside the door, and they quickly covered the gap with a trunk that Tom had at the foot of his cot. They took the cot and propped it against the broken window.

Then they sat in the afternoon's darkness, waiting for the clouds to part.

"You have a gun?" Charlie said.

"David insisted," Carol said. "He taught me how to use it. Said I was a natural. Before he died, he made me promise I would carry it in my bag."

"I may have to rethink my entire position on guns," Charlie said.

Slowly, the darkness began to disperse as the clouds separated, first in ribbons and then in clumps. The light of day slowly took the place of the glow from the snakes until their bioluminescence faded. "It must be instinctively activated by the dark," Carol said.

Tom got up and peered out the remaining window. "There are dozens of snakes still on the deck," he said. "How many bullets you got in that gun?"

"The magazine has fifteen bullets left," she said. "I'm a hell of a shot, but that isn't enough."

"What about shooting holes in the boat?" Charlie asked.

"What's the caliber, Professor Wheatley?" the captain asked.

"Nine millimeter."

"Should be all right," Tom said. "If worse comes to worst, that's why I have a bilge pump."

Carol opened the door, checked the stairs, then moved out onto the top step. Charlie followed and squeezed in next to her, gaffer in hand.

The snakes slithered across the slick surface of the deck but seemed unaware or uninterested in the humans.

Carol lined up her pistol, and hit the next three snakes squarely in the head, and on the next six tries, she either killed or wounded her target. Then she stopped. "I want to save the last few bullets," she said.

They edged their way back into the cabin and closed the door. Tom was peering out the window. "There are a bunch of the bastards still moving around." He went to the corner of the cabin and pulled a large yellow raincoat off a hook and donned it. It was so big and bulky that he could pull his hands all the way up into the sleeves. He grasped a gaffer and swung it experimentally.

"Wish me luck," he said, going to the door.

He stomped down to the deck and approached the first snake, which suddenly shot forward and caught the hem of the raincoat. He swung at it, and it flew over the side of the boat. Other snakes he cornered against the hull and smashed to a pulp. He hooked the bodies of all the dead creatures and tossed them over the side.

The snakes surrounding the boat didn't react to their dead companions landing among them. Tom clomped back up the stairs, shedding the raincoat. "Now what?" he asked.

"Now we see where the snakes take us," Carol said. "From here on, no one touch anything except with gloves on, and whatever you do, don't touch your face with the gloves. Until we're clear and we have access to water to wash everything off, assume everything you touch is toxic, including your own clothing."

They emerged from the cabin and sat uncomfortably apart from each other. An hour passed in slow motion. Charlie was hungry and thirsty, but most of all, it seemed as if he itched everywhere. One itch, on his nose, became so powerful that it was soon the center of his existence for a while. Finally, he couldn't stand it. He went into the cabin, reached up to the highest shelf, snagged an old manual, and used it to rub his nose. Tom noticed what he was doing and joined him, followed by Carol. Soon they were scratching themselves like three bears.

Charlie sighed in relief. He closed his eyes, and as he did, he felt the boat sway slightly. Then it lurched. He reached out frantically, catching Carol, and they both slammed into the cabin wall, barely managing to keep their feet.

What could we have hit so far out?

Tom went to the door and stopped, gazing out. The lurching had come when they'd broken through the cordon of snakes.

"What is it?" Charlie asked.

"We're free," Tom said. "The river of snakes is behind us."

Carol stared out the window, and Charlie had a sinking feeling. He was getting used to the way Carol responded to things; her being quiet and still meant something had scared her. "What is it?"

"I think you'd better come take a look for yourself."

He hurried to the window. Something large rippled through the water between them and the band of snakes, as if it was herding them. The movement was majestic and threatening. The creature was black and sinuous, and though he couldn't see it well since most of it was submerged, it was big enough to create waves that slapped against the side of the boat.

He tried to compare the movement to creatures he was familiar with: whales, a pod of dolphins, a school of fish.

This wasn't like any of those. This was something different. He began to turn, to yell out to Tom, but the creature disappeared beneath the waves. At the same moment, the river of snakes suddenly rippled, and there was a flash of yellow light.

The snakes appeared agitated, and for a moment, it looked as if they were breaking up, then they tightened back into a single entity again, headed for shore.

CHAPTER TWENTY-THREE

The sun was sinking beyond the halfway point down the western horizon. Carol pulled out her phone and checked for reception. For a moment, it looked as if the phone was going to connect, then nothing.

"If we want to make it in tonight, we need to get going soon," Tom said.

"We don't have to get all the way to shore," Charlie said. "Just close enough for the cellphones to work."

"Well, neither is going to happen if I don't get the engine running," Tom said. "The currents will take us out, along with this…" He waved in the direction of the snakes, whose migration was now several hundred yards away.

Tom went to the helm. "Keep your fingers crossed," he said. He pushed the engine's starter button. There was a whine and then a shudder. Tom stood there for a while, as if trying to decide if it was a good idea to try again. "One more time," he finally said. "If it doesn't start, I don't want to burn out the motor."

This time there was brief cough, and then nothing.

Tom brushed past his two passengers and clambered down the stairs. There was a long trunk built in under the gunwale on the starboard side. It was full of fishing tackle, but at both ends, there were colorful rolled-up plastic objects and tarps. On the bow side was a square yellow bundle. "That's the raft," he said, pointing to it.

He went to the other end, which was almost to the transom, and retrieved a heavy, red, rolled-up bundle and threw it on the deck. When he untied it and laid it out, Charlie and Carol could see that it had two arms and two legs. "This is a survival suit," he said. "It's designed for these waters. A man, a person, can't last more than five minutes out here without getting hypothermic."

No one said what they were all thinking: while the suit might hold off the freezing cold, could it withstand the fangs of a sea snake?

"Only one of them?" Carol asked.

He shrugged. "I got it for my first mate, Pete. I always figured I'd go down with the ship."

He lifted one of the legs and started to don the suit, but even Carol saw it would be too small for the man.

"No way," Carol said. "We don't know anything about this boat, and more importantly, we have no way to navigate. If anything happens to you, we'll probably end up on the rocks somewhere."

"I can't ask you to go into that," Tom said.

"You're not," Carol said. "I'm volunteering."

Charlie looked horrified. "Hell, no. I'll do it."

Tom shook his head. "Sorry, pal. Pete was a small man. No way you'll fit in it."

"Doesn't matter," Carol said. "There is absolutely no reason why it shouldn't be me. Don't get macho on me, Charlie. We don't have time for it."

They stared at each other in a battle of wills. Carol figured he was thinking the same thing she was. While the survival suit might hold against the black snakes, it wouldn't be much good against the huge creature they had glimpsed. If it had been real. And it couldn't be. It just couldn't.

What choice do we have? This boat isn't moving without the propellers being cleared.

Charlie and Carol nodded at the same moment.

She grabbed the suit out of Tom's hands and started putting it on. It was too big for her, but Carol didn't say that aloud. The only way Tom and Charlie were going to let her do this was if she didn't show the slightest doubt or hesitation. It was probably already wounding Charlie's pride, but she didn't see any reason for her not to be the one to go.

Charlie was like her late husband, a gentleman with an old-fashioned sense of honor. Tom, at least, seemed to accept her offer. "The suit has buoyancy so it will take some effort to go under the surface," he warned. "I can give you some weights that will pull you down. We'll tie ropes around your chest and under your arms, and all you need to do is tug on one of the ropes and we'll pull you up."

"How does she breathe?" Charlie said.

"There's a small canister of oxygen, which will only last a few minutes. But you probably won't need it," Tom told Carol. "Just do a couple minutes' work at a time. In an emergency, the oxygen nozzle is designed so that if the suit is dragged under temporarily in heavy seas, you won't drown before coming back up. It isn't designed for long-term use. So save your breath as much as possible."

"If I can't get the props unclogged in a few minutes, I probably never will," Carol said.

They rigged her up and agreed that any kind of tug meant they should lift her out of the water. Otherwise, the weights would take her down.

Tom handed her a flashlight with a cord attached to it. "Tie this to your wrist," he said.

Finally, and most importantly, Carol donned two pairs of gloves. Tom handed her a large knife, which she tied to her other wrist. "Don't cut yourself," he said. "Or the suit." He handed her a pair of goggles. "These will probably leak, because they're mechanic's goggles, not meant for the water. But I figure they might be better than nothing."

Charlie looked as if he wanted to nix the whole deal. "Wait," he said, and ran up to the cabin. He emerged with a roll of duct tape.

"Good idea," Tom said, and grabbed the roll. He wound the tape around Carol's arms and legs until it ran out.

She tried to take a step and nearly fell over. "You may have overdone it a bit," she said. She laughed and tried to flex her arms. The tape resisted and then gave way a little. She thought she probably had enough mobility to get the job done.

"Put up the hood," Tom said. "The whole thing seals around your neck so water can't get in. Pull that tight. Now, there's a small nozzle to your starboard – sorry, your right. That's the oxygen. When you feel it giving out, it's time to come up, whether you've fixed the problem or not.

"Don't do anything stupid or dangerous," he said. "If you can't clean the propellers safely, leave it. We have enough water and food to last several days out here. Someone will come along and save us."

Tom was obviously trying to sound confident, but Carol could see he was blustering. They could float out farther into the ocean and not be found for weeks, months, or ever.

"One last thing," Tom continued. "This red tab down by your waist. This will inflate the suit all the way. If anything happens, pull it, and nothing will keep you down for long."

Carol nodded. She was really doing this. It was all well and good to bravely volunteer, but she was really doing this. Maybe she'd hoped the men would talk her out of it. If so, she'd been too convincing.

Charlie gave her a brave smile. "Very stylish. You look like a cartoon character."

"Actually, they're called Gumby suits," Tom said.

"Great," Carol said. "If I see SpongeBob I'll be sure to say hello."

They lowered her into the water, and she began to quietly panic. It was as if all her consciousness was bent on maintaining the illusion of control while her insides were going wild. She gave a thumbs-up, but it was as if someone else had done it.

I'm a marionette. First the rope under her right armpit lowered, then her left as she settled into the dark water. She floated there for a time, breathing so hard she was sure Tom and Charlie could hear it.

All I have to do is jerk on the rope.

But not until she'd gone through the *pretense* of at least trying to do what she'd volunteered to do. So far, it was as if the whole thing was happening to someone else, and the ropes held by others dictated her actions. But to go farther, Carol would have to take her fate into her own hands.

She could feel the weights tied to her feet dragging her down. If the ropes around her failed or if the men lost their grip, she would sink all the way to the bottom. She could visualize the creatures below her, swimming around her legs, just out of sight. She expected something to coil around her legs and squeeze, imagined the sharp pain of fangs sinking into her flesh.

She tried to duck underwater, and then realized she had to give the signal to the men to loosen the ropes. She took one more deep breath and looked up into Charlie's concerned face. She instantly relaxed, suddenly certain that she was going to be all right. She was wearing a survival suit and eight layers of duct tape.

A wave slapped against her, spilling over her head, and she looked nervously over her shoulder. She was safe in a normal world of normal creatures, she tried telling herself... but there were monsters out there.

Stop thinking about it!

Carol gave the signal and immediately began to sink. They let her go down about two feet. The cold hit like a hard slap to her face. All thoughts left her, along with her breath. Salt water leaked through the goggles, stinging her eyes. *What am I doing here?*

The cold sting began to recede slightly, and she began to think more clearly. *Quickly.* She pulled the flashlight up and turned it on. The propeller blades were a yard away, farther under the boat that she realized. She yanked on the ropes.

They pulled her up so fast that she gasped. She'd only been down for about thirty seconds, but it had seemed like forever. "You're going to have to give me another couple feet of slack," she said.

Tom nodded, and Carol gave the signal to lower her again. They waited until she had taken a couple of deep breaths and then dropped her down. She had the presence of mind to hold the flashlight this time, and she pulled her way to the blades. Black material was in every nook and cranny. Her heart jackhammered in her chest. She could barely see the metal of the propeller edges.

It was moving. Her heart seemed to stop for a moment, and then race to catch up. The movement was from the current, not because they were alive.

Where's the damn knife? Oh, tied to my other arm. She took hold of the handle and tried to pry some of the material away. It moved. All the breath left her, and then she almost gasped as the snake faced her and appeared to hiss at her. It shot out about six inches before its jammed body stopped it.

Carol didn't remember pulling on the ropes, but she was breaking the surface before she could gasp. "What's wrong?" Charlie asked.

She took breath after breath. Charlie reached down for her, his face filled with concern.

"I'm all right," she said, sounding calmer than she felt. "I'm getting the hang of it. Let me try again."

Reluctantly, they slowly lowered her until only her head was above the water.

"Are you sure?" Charlie asked.

Carol didn't want to answer, afraid her voice would crack and reveal how frightened she was. "I think I can do it," she answered.

This time she had hold of both the knife and the flashlight. Most of the snakes were dead, but one still lunged at her, its tail caught. She stabbed it through the head. Breathing deep, she started attacking the snake flesh that was coiled around the screws. She went slowly, making sure to guide the material away from her face.

Am I getting exposed to the toxin by being this close? She decided that if the Pacific Ocean wasn't enough to dilute the toxin, nothing was. She realized her chest was getting tight and wondered how long it had been since she had taken a breath. Only then did she remember that there was an oxygen tube just centimeters away. She took one breath.

Save it. This is going to take longer than I thought. She wasn't sure how long she hacked at the dead snakes, but her arms were exhausted just as her air gave out. Rather than take more oxygen, she pulled on the ropes.

"Almost done," she gasped when she broke the surface. She didn't say anything more, just floated there taking deep breaths. *One more time.* There were dead snakes jammed in places she couldn't reach, at least not without better tools, but she thought she'd gotten most of them.

Carol gave the signal again, and they lowered her into the water.

Like bait on the end of a line. She looked down into the water and it seemed to her that something was moving below her, something large.

There is no such creature.

She forced herself to look away and set to work cutting free the last of the organic obstruction. She decided to go to the limits of her breath and finish the job rather than dive again.

Something brushed up against her back and wiggled across her gloved hands. Bubbles poured from her mouth as she shouted, withdrawing her hand.

It was a live snake, swimming free. Within moments, several others surrounded her. Strangely, they didn't attack, but simply circled her as if trying to understand what she was doing.

Strange, they move in concert, like a school of fish. The water pushed her up and down with the same motion, as if the ocean and the creatures within it were moving as one.

She took a sip of oxygen, her lips clamping down, determined to finish the job, knowing that if she didn't finish it now, she never would. The snakes obviously didn't know what to make of her.

As long as they aren't attacking.

She pared away the last of the gunk, then let go of the flashlight and the knife. She yanked on the rope, but instead of rising, she sank. She tugged again, harder. At the same moment, the light from the flashlight, which had been shining wildly upward, blinked out. She was jerked to one side even as she sank. There was a light there, but it wasn't from the flashlight. She couldn't make sense of it.

Then, behind the light, she saw a nightmarish face: long, curved teeth, and above them, two huge eyes. *An angler fish,* her taxonomically-trained brain supplied. Instead of frightening her, the knowledge reassured her. Angler fish were not known to try to eat people. Then again, they were usually far too deep into the ocean for that.

She stopped sinking and felt the pressure of the ropes pulling her upward. But the angler fish that had swallowed her flashlight weighed her down.

The pressure in Carol's chest grew, but somehow the intellectual exercise of identifying the fish calmed her. She remembered the oxygen nozzle. She took the tube in her mouth, reached up, and pulled the wire. After two deep breaths, she took the knife tied to her wrist and cut the flashlight cord on the other wrist.

The angler fish floated away, glowing slightly from inside from the still-lit flashlight. Then suddenly, the light blinked out. Something black replaced it. She blinked. It was gone.

She then reached down and cut the cords that held the weights. She immediately started rising. Her heart pounded. She felt as if she was ready to pass out then remembered to take a quick breath. Again she felt like she was dangling on the end of a hook. Sharks infested these waters, giant squid, and something... something bigger.

She continued to float upward.

Not quick enough, dammit. She pulled the red tab at her waist, and the explosive inflation tightened her suit around her. The air pushed against the duct tape and then found other parts of the suit to inflate. It must have used the same oxygen that she breathed, because the nozzle stopped supplying air.

She grew lightheaded. Suddenly, none of it seemed to matter. She looked down into the murk and saw a long row of black snakes, undulating beneath her feet. They merged, becoming one long sidewinding creature. She saw a single striped yellow head and reptilian eyes looking up at her as if curious.

She heard her own scream muted by the water and exhaled, emptying her lungs.

Then she raced upward.

She broke the surface and saw Charlie's concerned and very red face. He was halfway over the gunwale, in danger of falling in.

"Pull me up!" she shouted.

"Get over here, Tom!" Charlie cried out.

Carol realized that, despite seeming to take a lifetime, the entire confrontation had probably lasted twenty seconds. As oxygen reached her brain, she began to doubt what she'd seen. She knew her taxonomy. There was no such creature. Fear and deprivation had created the monster out of her worst nightmares.

Tom rushed to the other set of ropes and looked down on her.

"Oh, my God," he said.

Both men pulled on the ropes at the same time. Carol was lifted out of the water and dragged over the gunwale. She lay on the deck, staring into the sky. Charlie loomed over her, and he had a strange look in his face. He raised the gaffer over his head and swung it down at her. She didn't have time to move.

The gaffer slammed into the deck next to her head, and only then did she see the yellow head of the sea snake, its glistening fangs mere inches from her face. Another one was slithering behind it. She raised her duct-taped arm instinctively and felt the pressure of the fangs biting down. Charlie grabbed the snake by the back of its head with his gloved hands and threw it out into the water.

Tom unzipped the survival suit and yanked Carol out, lifting her completely off the deck and into his arms. He staggered up the steps to the cabin and set her down.

She looked over his shoulder to see Charlie striking downward, again and again, and then she noticed a dozen sea snakes with their fangs hooked into the survival suit.

CHAPTER TWENTY-FOUR

W hat's wrong with her?" Tom asked.

Carol lay on the cot. Her blue eyes were open, and when Charlie stared into them, he saw consciousness. A blissed-out consciousness. But Carol wasn't talking. She didn't respond in any way. He checked every visible part of her and her clothing, looking for puncture wounds. She appeared untouched.

"She must have gotten some of the toxin," Charlie said. "I'd hoped the ocean water and the currents would dilute it enough to keep her safe. Dammit, it should have been me."

He felt a heavy hand on his shoulder. "She got the job done, Charlie. You wouldn't have done any better," Tom said.

Probably worse. But it would be me who was laying here, not her.
"I shouldn't have let you leave the ropes," Charlie said

"I don't see how we had any choice," said Tom. "If I didn't get some binoculars on that boat, it would have passed out of view."

The unclogging of the propellers had been going well. Carol looked determined, and she kept giving the thumbs-up. Charlie could see bits and pieces of sea snakes floating away. The situation had seemed stable enough that when they spied a boat on the horizon, both men felt Charlie alone could keep Carol steady.

"That's the *Knotty Girl*," Tom said. "The Barkers don't usually get out this far. Wonder what's going on. It looks like it's adrift."

He'd handed over the ropes holding Carol in place and had gone to fetch the binoculars out of the cabin.

"It's the *Knotty Girl* all right," Tom called out. "It looks abandoned. No... wait... there are a couple of people in that ridiculous crow's nest."

Charlie could hear a distant voice. He started to turn around to say something – what, he couldn't remember – when the ropes jerked downward out of his hands.

He managed to hang onto his own, but Tom's ropes slipped away. He lurched over the transom, barely keeping himself from tumbling into the water. He saw Carol's alarmed face looking up at him, and then she was sinking out of sight.

"She's sinking!" he cried out. "Get over here, Tom!"

He was there in seconds, but it seemed to take forever to coordinate their movements so that the ropes started going upward instead of downward. Then, within a few meters, they were unable to pull upward any farther.

"If this were a fishing line, I'd say we have a big one," Tom said. Then he looked stricken, as if he instantly regretted what he'd just said.

"Yeah, and Carol is the bait."

They pulled as hard as they could, and they felt small movements, enough for them to redouble their efforts. Then the ropes went slack and they stumbled backward, Charlie landing on his ass and Tom barely staying upright. By the time Charlie got to his feet, Carol bobbed in the water. Instead of looking frightened, she had a strangely content look on her face.

"Oh, my God," Tom said.

Charlie stopped himself from panicking at the sight of the black snakes hanging from the survival suit. The men pulled Carol out of the water in one heave. Tom grabbed her out of the suit, and Charlie set to killing the snakes as fast as he could. Fortunately, most of the creatures were hooked onto the suit by their fangs and couldn't get loose.

When Tom picked her up, she made a contented sound, and after he laid her on the cot, Charlie perched beside her, brushed back her short blonde hair, and looked into her eyes.

"We'll get you home," he said softly. He got up, grabbed a towel and some of the drinking water, and started wiping every part of her skin. He looked around. Tom was outside the cabin.

Feeling faintly guilty and embarrassed, Charlie opened Carol's blouse and wiped as much bare skin as he could. He put his hands on her bra then decided against it.

He left her jeans on as well. Whatever toxin had gotten into her had probably already done its damage, he reasoned. She wasn't dead. And Jerry had come back from it, and he'd probably gotten a higher dose.

He heard Tom yelling outside and went to the door. The captain wasn't yelling at him, but to someone on the western horizon.

"Ahoy!" Tom shouted, and the sound seemed to carry a long way. The mast of the boat that had passed by them, pulled by the outward currents, had nearly disappeared. All that could be seen was the crow's nest, and two men frantically waving their arms.

"We can't do anything if the engine doesn't start," Charlie said. "You ready to try?"

"Yeah, I've been holding onto that hope," Tom said. He had a wry grin on his face. "The longer I hope, the more likely it will work. Sailors are a superstitious lot."

He went to the wheel and held his hand over the starter button. He hesitated, looking at Charlie with raised eyebrows.

"Do it," Charlie said.

The engine let out one shuddering cough the first time Tom pushed the button. "That's encouraging... I think," he said.

He pushed again, and the engine turned over, whining and rapidly losing strength.

"Now it's the battery that's the problem," Tom muttered. He took a deep breath. "Here goes."

The engine caught immediately on the third try. A grayish-blue cloud rose over the transom and drifted over to them. The smell of gas was pungent, but the ocean wind quickly wafted it away.

"The *Knotty Girl* is heading for the river of snakes," Tom said. "God help them if they get there before we get to them." He turned the *Cirdan* out to sea.

It didn't seem as if they were making much progress at

first, but then the crow's nest came back into view along with the yelling figure. Another man was lying down, hanging onto the mast with both arms. Little by little, more of the mast was revealed, and then the top of cabin and the gunwales.

Once in sight, the boat grew rapidly until the *Cirdan* bore down on it so fast that Charlie gripped the railing and glanced nervously at the captain. Tom eased back on the engine when they were a hundred feet away.

By now it was clear why the *Cirdan* had caught up so quickly. The other boat had stopped moving because it was flush with the river of snakes.

"Look at their transom," Tom said.

The lower platform at the stern of the *Knotty Girl* was swarming with black snakes, some of which were flowing up and over the transom and onto the deck.

With the *Cirdan's* engines idling, they could clearly hear the men yelling from the crow's nest. "Get us out of here!"

"Where's Ben Barker?" Tom shouted.

"He's gone! They're both dead!" one of the men shouted.

Charlie and Tom stared at the swarming snakes, both reluctant to do anything.

"I can't just leave them," Tom said. "It's the code of the sea, man. Next time, it might be me."

"The next time you're surrounded by poisonous sea snakes?" Charlie said.

"You know what I mean."

"Yeah, I do," Charlie said with a sigh. "How do we do it?"

Tom stood at the wheel, frowning. He looked around the cabin as if taking inventory, as if there was a magical solution there. Finally, he pointed to the *Knotty Girl*. "You think you can lasso its cleats?" he asked. "We need to tow that boat away from the snakes, if we can."

"I'll try," Charlie answered. "Are the ropes long enough?"

"If I get close enough," Tom answered. "But I'd rather keep some distance, so why don't you tie a few of the ropes together."

When Charlie combined the ropes, they were longer than

he'd expected, about thirty feet or so. "Please hurry!" One of the men shouted. "Please." Charlie finished tying the last knot as the other man yelled, "Oh, God, hurry up you idiots!"

Shut up already. Or we'll leave you here.

He tied a loop at the end of the rope and twirled it a few times. It was heavy, but he thought he could probably manage it. He went back to the cabin to tell Tom.

Tom spoke before Charlie had closed the door. "I think I know these two. That bastard who's yelling wanted to catch some deep-sea creatures for trophies, and I told him to get lost. I'm not surprised the Barkers took him up on his offer. Well, Monson and his brother got more than they bargained for, that's for sure."

Charlie went to the cot where Carol was lay. Her eyes were closed, and she had shifted to her side and seemed to be sleeping. That was encouraging.

"You ready?" Tom asked. "I'll get as close as I can."

"About twenty-five feet should do it," Charlie said. He went out onto the deck, picked up the rope about ten feet from the loop, and started twirling it. He thought about taking a few practice swings, but then realized that even though the rope was plastic, once in the water, it would get heavier. His best chance would be his first.

The engine was loud, as if objecting to the slow approach. When Charlie judged they were close enough, he swung the rope. The engine slowed and he nearly lost his footing, and then he got into the rhythm of the swing and let go.

His first attempt was pathetically wide and short. And sure enough, as he pulled the rope back onto the *Cirdan*, Charlie could tell it was heavier. Somehow, though, the heaviness seemed to add to the momentum and curve of the release on his second try, and it flew over the side of the *Knotty Girl's* gunwale.

Charlie pulled the rope toward him a few inches at a time. The loop was near one of the cleats, but when he tried to direct the rope toward the hooks, it was like trying to push a noodle. It moved just centimeters in the right direction. He saw that he wasn't going to come within a foot of his goal and gave up, pulling on the rope with such force that it flew backward halfway to the *Cirdan* before falling into the waves.

He tried two more times, neither as close as the near miss. The muscles in his arms were twitching in pain, and his arms felt ready to fall off. "We're going to need to get closer!" he shouted.

The engine grew louder, and they were soon with ten feet of the other boat. Looking over the starboard side of the *Cirdan*, Charlie could see the black snakes swirling, but unlike the lower transom and diving deck of the *Knotty Girl*, the snakes had no way to get onto the *Cirdan*.

From this close, it took only one easy swing, and the loop fell neatly over a cleat. Charlie pulled on the rope to make sure the tension kept the line securely taut. He looped his end of the rope around one of the *Cirdan*'s cleats and looked toward the cabin. He couldn't see through the unbroken window. Sunset was nearly upon them, and the glare was blinding. But he figured Tom could see him, so he waved his arm.

The *Cirdan* backed up, and the rope grew tauter still. There was a groaning noise, and the *Cirdan*'s gunwale dipped, but then the *Knotty Girl* was free of the snakes, and they were heading into open water.

Charlie kept his eyes on the ocean until there wasn't a black snake in sight. Tom must have sensed they were far enough away because the engine slowed. The captain came out of the cabin and stared across the ten-foot gap to the other boat.

"You probably can't see it, but from the cabin, I can see their deck. It's swarming with snakes," he said.

"How do we get them down?" Charlie asked.

"Well, the survival suit seemed to do a pretty good job," Tom mused.

"Are you volunteering?" Charlie asked. Tom looked away and didn't answer. "If we get close enough to use the survival suit, we risk the snakes getting onto the *Cirdan*."

"I think I have a better idea," Tom said. "What if we string the rope from the crow's nest to our deck? They can slide down it."

Charlie liked the idea, not least because it put the burden on the men they were saving.

When they told the men of their plan, both immediately objected. "What if we lose our grip?" Monson said.

"Well, if you'd rather climb down to the deck and jump from there, we'll try to accommodate you," Tom answered.

Both men scowled, and then in a softer, more pleading tone, Monson said, "We're exhausted. We haven't slept or eaten or drunk anything in a day. I'm not really sure we can do it."

"I'm sorry, Monson," Tom said. "I don't think you have any choice."

Monson looked down at the other man. "I'm not sure about Marty. He's going to need help."

Charlie unhooked the rope from the *Cirdan*, and it immediately started running through his hands, burning his palms. He barely held on. When there was enough slack, he whipped the other end of the rope off the *Knotty Girl*'s cleat and pulled the loop back.

"Catch this," Charlie said, swinging the loop over his head. He let go. The rope was going to miss Monson by a couple of feet, but he reached out and grabbed it, almost toppling off his perch – only his brother's quick thinking in pulling him back, saved him. "Tie it tight!" Charlie shouted, and then turned to Tom. "We're going to need to keep the line tight, so start for shore."

Tom nodded. "I doubt this is going to work," he muttered, but he went to the cabin, and as Charlie finished tying his end of the rope to the *Cirdan*, the engines started humming again. The *Knotty Girl*'s mast tipped toward them, and both men shouted, but Tom eased up and the mast straightened while the rope stayed taut.

"Swing your belt over the rope and wrap it around your hands," Charlie said.

"I'm sending Marty over first," Monson yelled. There was a loud argument between the two, but the brother finally got to his feet and took off his belt, looping it over the rope. Monson slapped him on the back, then pushed him.

Marty shouted in surprise. He bumped over the knot, but held on as he zipped down the rope faster than any of them expected. Charlie had just enough time to lean over and grab him.

Meanwhile, Monson had looped his own belt over the rope. Then he stood there for several moments, as if in doubt.

"Hurry," Charlie said.

The man leapt off the crow's nest and whirred down the rope at speed until he hit the first knot. His left hand went downward, and he started falling. His momentum carried him most of the rest of the way to the *Cirdan*. He stretched out his arms, reaching for the top of the gunwale.

Charlie rushed forward to try to help. He saw one hand on the gunwale, three fingers clutching desperately, and lunged for it, catching the wrist as the fingers slipped off. He reached down with his other hand and grabbed Monson's shirt at the shoulder. He leaned backward into the boat, and the man came over the gunwale, landing on the deck with a crash.

Charlie leaned over, but the man was still panicked, staring at something to his left.

The specimen jar had slid down the deck and was only inches from Monson's bulging eyes. The black snake within was unmoving. The water hadn't been replaced in over a day, and the creature had probably suffocated.

"Don't worry," Charlie said. "You're safe."

The boat shuddered, and Charlie's eardrums popped. He stood up and watched a shock wave shimmer in the sunset, as if God had decided to dive into the ocean. The ocean seemed to rise and fall before his eyes, the waves changed direction, running diagonally toward the shoreline in the distance before switching back again as if jolted.

A low rumble filled the air, coming from all sides, above and below. The boat vibrated, and Charlie's feet slid along the deck, and then there was a loud roar as if a giant ocean liner was passing close.

The ocean changed color as he watched, clouds of silt rising from below and bubbling to the surface.

"What is that?" Monson said, his voice shaking.

The shock waves approached the *Cirdan* so fast that the eye could barely catch it, and then the boat tipped to port. Both men lost their footing and slid down the deck, slamming against the gunwales.

That's impossible. Charlie had attended Lowell Henderson's lectures and could almost hear the geophysicist words: "An earthquake will generate a series of shock waves, but only compressional waves, or P-waves, will propagate through the water. Someone on the surface of the ocean won't even know an earthquake has occurred."

Too bad Henderson isn't here to see this. Charlie realized the earthquake had occurred just below them. He felt a tingling in his scalp, and the blood-draining sensation flooded down his body, as if a death shroud had been thrown over him.

This is the Big One. The one they've been warning about.

Despite the warnings, they *weren't* prepared. Not for something this big. The earthquake would liquefy the sandy soil beneath Seattle. The tsunami following would sweep away the wreckage.

Carol was still out cold, probably a blessing because her daughter was in the path of the huge wave. *How will I tell her?*

And then guilt hit as he thought of Kristine going about her daily business, unaware of the danger, and no way to warn her.

He'd read estimates of the death toll from a tsunami, ranging from the alarmist to the optimistic, but tens of thousands of people were likely to be casualties if the worst came to pass.

Casualties. It sounded so bloodless. These were his family, his friends, his neighbors. Seattle was his home. And there wasn't a thing he could do about it. Ironically, a boat floating on top of the earthquake was safer than anyone on shore.

Helplessly, his heart in his mouth, he watched the shock wave heading for shore.

CHAPTER TWENTY-FIVE

Annie woke in a bed that was so big and plush and smelled and felt so good that when she came back from the bathroom she flung herself, naked, onto the covers. She turned over, spread-eagled, and laughed. It was the best room in the North Coast Indian Casino.

I'm ready to fuck the world!

Speaking of which, she was pretty sore. Billy had proven to be a vigorous lover.

"Billy?" she called, and then sat up. *Where the hell is he? Did he fuck me and leave?*

Billy, Billy, Billy. The square-jawed Indian card dealer.

She'd loved the name tag. Billy... did she know any *Billys*? So old-fashioned, just like Annie. Annie and Billy.

She'd teased him about it, flirting with him outrageously, and as the free drinks had kept coming, she'd gotten pretty blatant, so much so that she'd heard the muttered remarks of the others at the table. She'd ignored them. Annie flirted with everyone.

When she'd gotten up from the poker table to leave, Billy had been coming off his shift. He sidled up to her. She frowned at him, ready to tell him that flirting was *not* an invitation. Then he'd done something even more outrageous.

"What room do you have?" he'd asked.

For some reason she'd blurted it out. "101," she'd said. "Listen, I'm sorry if you got the wrong idea, but I was just having fun."

"That's a nice room, but I have a better one. Right on the beach. Quiet, private. You can have it. No strings attached."

"All... right..." she'd said slowly. *Well, I did say I was going to say yes to everything.* She ran her eyes up and down his tall, lanky frame, noting his long, black hair, as glossy and dark as her own, and his perfect complexion and high cheekbones.

"Come on, I'll show you," he'd said. "No strings attached."

"Okay," she'd muttered, suddenly feeling tipsy. *Did he spike my drink?* She did some internal diagnoses. *Nope, I'm as drunk as I should be.* "Lead on, Billy. Billy... I really like that name."

He'd smiled, revealing straight, brilliant white teeth. "So you've been saying."

He'd led her to a part of the beach she hadn't known existed, completely private. Behind high walls, a crescent beach with white sands waited. *Did they import that?* Because everywhere else she'd been, the sands were dark.

The room was enormous, bigger than Annie's entire apartment. He'd unlocked the door and ushered her in, and then turned to leave.

"Billy?" she'd said.

He turned, and Annie went right up to him and kissed him, and then she reached back and unzipped her dress, which dropped like a shed skin to the floor. She'd dressed in her sexiest black lingerie so she'd been expecting this, and he'd been expecting this, and it was every bit as good as she'd hoped.

And now he was gone. What was the saying? Find 'em, fuck 'em, and forget 'em? That had always been her motto. It had never happened in reverse before.

But she still had the bed, and the room, and the beach. She jumped off the bed, still naked, and opened the door. Looking both ways, she realized that no one could see her. The walls made the entire enclosure completely private.

Sadly, there was a bunch of seaweed cluttering the pristine white sand. *How unfortunate.* That stuff stank when it started to rot.

Well, I doubt I'm getting another night here. Unless Billy comes back.

Billy. Billy. Billy. Billy and Annie.

She stepped out onto the sand and walked down to the water. As she approached, the seaweed started to squirm.

She stopped dead in her tracks. A cold chill ran down her spine despite the morning sunshine.

That isn't seaweed. Those are... snakes?

She backed up and looked over her shoulder. The sand between her and the open door, which had been white moments before, was now black. The snakes writhed, revealing flashes of yellow as their heads rolled in and out of the mass.

Annie sprinted for the door, jumping from sandy spot to sandy spot, and she almost made it. Just as she stretched for her last jump, a snake seemed to levitate out of the sand, and sank its fangs into her heel.

She cried out but kept running, smashing the snake against the doorjamb as she passed. She tried to close the door, but the wounded snake was in the way. When she leaned down to move it, she suddenly felt dizzy.

Another snake writhed through the doorway. Then another. Annie realized she didn't have the strength to do anything about it. She backed away and fell against the bed. She managed to maneuver her way to its middle before she stopped being able to move at all.

She closed her eyes and felt something slimy and wet moving up her leg.

She opened her eyes and saw the red of an open mouth and glistening fangs, and felt a sharp pain in her cheek.

Oh, Billy, we never had a chance.

Derrick made his way back to the beach unit, looking over his shoulder. Before starting his dealer shift, he'd happened to notice that the ultra-luxurious room wasn't booked last night for the first time that he could remember, and then Annie had come on to him, and he didn't know what he was thinking, but he'd gone and done it.

For one thing, he was wearing Billy's nametag. He wasn't sure why, as a joke, maybe? He'd had to hold his hand over the tag every time a supervisor came by, and that was a hassle, but then Annie...

It was meant to be. She'd kept saying that. Billy and Annie.

And after the night they'd just had, he believed it.

Oh, sure, she'd dropped two thousand bucks without blinking. Oh, sure, she was a college-educated white girl. But she had a wild streak, and he had a wild streak, and while it might not last, it would be glorious while it did.

He was still wearing his dealer clothes: long black pants, shiny black shoes, and a white shirt with a tie, which was draped loosely around his neck.

He had gone to get breakfast, using up his tips from the night before on a meal for both of them. But as he approached the walls that enclosed the private beach, he started getting nervous. She'd been awfully drunk. Maybe she'd be embarrassed. Maybe she'd turn her nose up at him.

Taking a deep breath, he pushed open the gate and stopped. The white beach had disappeared, replaced by... blackness. Blackness that writhed.

He approached carefully. He'd been raised on the farthest reaches of the reservation, and he had a healthy respect for wildlife. The boardwalk on the side of the building was clear, and he jumped up onto it and trotted to the open door.

Annie lay in all her magnificent nakedness on top of the bed, but she was striped with black and red. The black was smearing the red.

The red was blood.

A black serpentine shape came out of her open mouth, carrying something red in its fangs, and Derrick gagged as he realized it was her tongue.

She stared sightlessly up at the ceiling.

Derrick dropped the breakfast tray and ran. He made it to the gate and slammed it just as a snake tried to dart through. Its yellow-striped head was severed. Its jaws opened, and then it stopped moving. He kicked the head, then ran.

The next thing he knew, he was standing outside the administration offices in a daze.

What do I say? That I stole the room? That I seduced a client?
Both were firing offenses.
She's dead. I can't help her.

But what about the snakes? Would they still be there? Would anyone even believe him?

He turned around and made his way to his locker where he changed into his street clothes. He dropped Billy's nametag on the floor in front of his friend's locker and walked away.

He got on his beat-up Honda motorcycle, but instead of heading to his studio apartment, he turned and headed toward the reservation.

Conrad Smith listened to his grandson's story intently.

It was true, he could tell from the boy's manner. Derrick didn't lie. He was a wild kid in many ways, but he didn't lie.

"There is a story," Conrad said.

Derrick fell respectfully silent. When Grandfather spoke, everyone listened.

"It is said that the darkness once came out of the ocean, and it killed everything and everyone but the People. But that was not the worst. For not long after, the ocean itself rose and washed everything away, and the world was begun anew.

"The blackness was a warning. *'Run,'* Snake said. *'Run into the mountains, for the sea god is done with you. He has come to cleanse the world.'*

"But the People ignored the warning. All but Crow, who heard the distant approach, the rumbling beneath the waters, and listened to Snake and took his family to our tribal home. There, Crow drew a line around his People and commanded the blackness not to pass.

"The ocean rose, almost reaching the top of the mountain, but Crow and his family were saved. They came back down to the seashore, and the People began anew. This tale has been passed down ever since as a warning."

Conrad's grandson appeared to believe every word of it. "What happened to the snakes?" Derrick asked.

"A white cloud descended from the skies and covered them, and the blackness vanished," Conrad said. "Only the ancient ones know what that means. I don't have a clue."

"What do we do?"

"We listen to the warning. Call your mother and your brothers. I'll try to get ahold of everyone I can. It's time for a little vacation. Hurry, Derrick. Like Crow says, we don't have much time."

Derrick ran out the door, and moments later, the rough motor of the Honda roared off into the distance. Conrad sighed and got up more slowly.

All those years of telling stories at the visitor center, and never once had any of them come true.

Until now.

Conrad believed these stories were indeed warnings to a People who didn't possess writing.

You ignore the stories at your peril.

He would use what influence he had, but he doubted most of his brethren would listen. Such stories were quaint to them, tourist fodder, nothing more.

But he would try.

CHAPTER TWENTY-SIX

Sheriff Snyder got up from behind his desk and closed the office door before raising his voice. Deputy Ramirez had never met anyone more conscious of appearances than her boss.

"I'm not closing the beaches because of one unfortunate accident," he said.

"It's more than Bowie," she said. "There was also that kid who was surfing, the two fishermen – Hank and Barry, and there might be others."

"We don't close beaches on a busy weekend because of a might-be."

Mike Snyder was tall, blonde and, admittedly, handsome. He had a habit of standing over Sarah in a way that once might have been intimidating. Now she shrugged it off. Whether he did it consciously or unconsciously, she hadn't decided yet, just like she hadn't decided how intelligent he was. Sheriffs weren't elevated by merit and promotion after all, they were elected. Right now, she was inclined to believe he was stupider than a sea anemone.

"These creatures are extraordinarily lethal," Ramirez insisted. "Professor Wice says there is enough poison in one creature to wipe out a city. I saw it happen to Bowie. It took only seconds."

"So, a grand total of two poisonous snakes," Snyder said.

"There is no reason to believe there aren't more."

"Actually, there is no reason to believe there *are* more," Snyder said. "I'm going to need more proof than that."

Proof? "Sir, one of our fellow cops is dead."

Snyder looked surprised, then suddenly contrite. "You're

right, Deputy. But all the more important we get it right. Have you talked to Professor Wice about this latest incident?"

"The professor wasn't available," she said.

The first thing she'd done after the ambulance had taken Bowie away was drive to the Biology Department at the university. She'd seen Professor Carter and a striking-looking woman leaving the building, probably his wife or girlfriend the way they acted toward each other. Sarah almost stopped him, then decided she'd rather talk to one of the other two professors who had been at John Sanders's meeting. Carter had seemed a factotum, eager to please, whereas Wice and Wheatley had seemed like real scientists.

There was a little old lady perched behind an enormous desk in the biology office. Despite the other woman's diminutive size, she hadn't been intimidated by Ramirez's badge.

Ramirez was short, but she was also stocky and strong. Most people, including felons, underestimated her strength and agility. Most of her fellow deputies, middle-aged men who had let themselves get out of shape, were probably less capable physically than she was. She'd grown up on a ranch in eastern Oregon, bucking bales of hay every summer.

She'd also graduated with top honors from her class at the academy, but no law enforcement agency had been willing to hire her until Sheriff Snyder, who was smarting from the bad press of having hired his twentieth white male in a row, was forced into diversity. Sarah had checked off two or three points, depending on how you counted it. She was a woman, and half-Hispanic and half-Native American.

Frustrated, Sarah drove back to the sheriff's office and demanded to see her boss, though it was her practice to talk to him as little as possible. She'd been given the beachfront area to patrol, which meant the most serious offense she usually confronted was underage drinking.

Her arrest record, as she was reminded in her evaluations, was light. But she didn't see any point in throwing these kids in jail or even citing them. She usually made sure they got home safely, driven by someone sober, and left them with a warning. Sometimes she took the step of contacting their parents.

Now, standing in Sheriff Snyder's office, Ramirez could tell he wasn't willing to use department resources despite the death of a fellow officer. It just went to show he wasn't a real cop. No cop would react this way. It was maddening, and she wasn't leaving his office until she got something.

"I heard about a sea snake that washed up on a California beach," he said. "They said it came from hundreds of miles south, and that it was incredibly unusual for it to be there. So if they're rare in California, they've got to be even rarer in Washington."

"Something has changed," Ramirez said. She was going to make sure he heard her, that he understood the danger.

"Changed?"

"The currents, the temperature of the water."

"Oh, bullshit. You're talking about that global warming crap?"

Too late, Ramirez remembered that the sheriff had mentioned he didn't believe in climate change.

"It could be something else," she said. Inspiration came to her. She'd heard once that wildlife acted crazy before a seismic or volcanic event. "Maybe it's an earthquake warning."

Snyder stared at her. "You're stretching, Deputy Ramirez."

"The professors told me this was a new species," she said, suddenly certain she was right. "Two people have died in less than two days—"

"Just bad luck. If it's a new species, it's got to be even rarer, right?" Snyder said. "Listen, Deputy Ramirez, I've heard your request, and I don't consider it out of line. In fact, I'll contact all our patrols and have them keep a lookout, how's that sound?"

There was a tone in his voice that told her she wasn't going to get more than that. In fact, after the conversation they'd just had, she was surprised she'd gotten that much.

"I think you are underestimating the problem, sir," she said. "I will say as much in my reports." She turned and left the office, feeling Snyder's eyes boring into her back. Despite his reassurance that he didn't consider her request out of line, she knew she was going to pay for it.

Unless something horrible happened.

As she pulled away from the sheriff's building, Ramirez automatically turned onto her normal patrol route, even though it was late in the day and she could just as easily have gone home. *I'm going to keep an eye out.*

She figured maybe she'd approach groups of people and warn them personally, but as she reached Myrtle Edwards Park, the first of her daily visits, she realized it was so busy that anything other than a bullhorn would be ineffectual. She parked in the overlook and watched the young families and bands of school kids playing for a time. It was the closet park to the population center and therefore the most likely place for something to happen.

She pulled away and drove to the next stop on her route, Discovery Park. Again, she didn't get out of her car. There was no point. The beach was packed. All she would accomplish was panic.

Well, maybe that's what's needed. She started to get out, and then clicked the door shut again. *It would cost me my job. And for what? The small possibility that I'll stumble across the one place on the entire West Coast where the sea snakes will show up again?*

Ramirez drove toward the end of her route where private residences had been grandfathered in, perched close to the beaches, and where individuals owned small islands. John Sanders and his private fiefdom were out there. Maybe she could convince the billionaire to use his influence on the sheriff to get him to close the beaches.

It was a forlorn hope because she'd sensed the billionaire had mostly been concerned because his son wanted him to be. But with Liam Sanders safe, his father probably really didn't care that much.

She turned off before she reached the Sanders resort. One of her favorite places was up here, the long Robinson Jetty and Mallory Lighthouse. It was a place that real Seattleites knew about, but few newcomers or tourists. The parking lot was a good half mile above the beach, but for some reason, she felt compelled to get out of her car and make the long walk even though the sun was setting.

She had reached the sand dunes above the beach when the path she was walking on, which was hard soil and broken rock, seemed to suddenly turn to soft sand, and she was nearly tossed off her feet.

She tried to catch her balance, but it was as if she was on a ship at sea, being rocked by huge waves. The stunted trees, which leaned to the east almost horizontally to the ground, shook and danced, and one nearby popped out of the ground with a *crack*. The shaking went on for a full minute.

An earthquake. A big one.

Tsunami!

She started running. Not everyone would understand the danger. She'd seen pictures where people ventured far out onto the exposed sea floor, thinking it a marvelous adventure.

She reached the last bend in the trail where a large cliff obscured the view of the ocean. At least, it had once been a large cliff. Now half of it was sheared away and had tumbled toward the water. People struggled upward against the broken soil of the now-buried trail.

"Get to high ground as fast as you can!" Ramirez shouted to the groups of people as she passed them. So far, they all seemed to be young and able-bodied. She reached the last stragglers.

"Anyone else down there?" she asked.

"I don't think so," a girl said. She seemed dazed, almost puzzled. "Maybe..."

Ramirez hesitated. If she went much farther, she might not make it back herself. She could see the beach now, and it looked mostly empty. The light was rapidly failing. Behind her, she heard distant sirens.

She almost turned around, but at the last moment, she thought she saw movement on the beach.

Damn. How could anyone be so stupid?

She ran the rest of the way to the beach, thankful for her stamina. She saw the huge carcass of the whale first and nearly stopped in amazement, but out of the corner of her eye, she noticed two people who leaned over something. As she sprinted toward them, shouting, she saw that there was another person lying between them.

"You've got to get to safety," she said, coming up to them. It was a young man in heavy-framed glasses accompanied by a slender and beautiful young woman who looked as if she could be a model. A huskier blonde man was unconscious on the sand.

Drugs or alcohol, Ramirez guessed. She didn't smell any booze. "What's wrong with him?" she demanded.

"I don't know," the kid with glasses said. "He just passed out. I can't leave him here."

"I'll take care of it," Ramirez said. "Get the hell out of here."

The young man looked her over doubtfully. "I'm a marine biologist. There is a tsunami coming. Soon. We don't have time to get away. At least, not all of us."

"All right, then grab his legs," she said. She leaned down to take the unconscious youth's arms.

"We tried that," the girl said. "He's too heavy."

"I'm stronger than I look," Ramirez said. "Come on, quit arguing. You, young lady, there is nothing you can do. Run to your car and get going. I'll take…"

"Jerry," the young man offered.

"I'll take Jerry and your unconscious friend…"

"Liam," the girl supplied.

"…and Liam in my patrol car."

The girl looked confused. For it a moment, it seemed as if she didn't know where she was or who she was. Her companion reached down and grabbed a backpack. He extracted a bottle of clear liquid and handed it to the girl. "Drink this, Jennifer."

"What's that?" Ramirez asked.

The guy didn't answer, just made sure the girl took a long guzzle and then finished off the bottle himself. Whatever it was, they seemed to need it and to immediately perk up.

Drugs it is, then. Not my problem. My problem is to get these kids off the beach and as far away as possible. "Come on, we're wasting time," she said. "If you aren't going to help me, I'll do it myself. In fact, it might be best if I just hoist him onto my shoulders. You two kids run... *now!*"

As if to accentuate her words, there was a strange sound, something Ramirez had never heard before. The ocean was drawing back with a long, soft sucking sound.

"You'll never make it," Jerry said. "We need to go to the lighthouse."

For a moment, Ramirez couldn't make sense of his words. She turned to where he was pointing. The huge, blocky base of the lighthouse obscured the setting sun, sending deep shadows down the jetty. It was more than two hundred yards away, but the path was flat except for a few patches of rubble. Ramirez had always wanted to go out there and look at the old lighthouse, but had never done it.

Now, she calculated the half mile of broken ground to the parking lot versus the enticing, imposing lighthouse so much closer.

"How do we get in?" she asked.

"We'll figure it out," Jerry said.

He sounded so confident Ramirez almost laughed. "Well, the lighthouse is over a hundred years old, so it must be pretty sturdy."

"Then again," Jerry said, "it *is* a hundred years old."

"Let's go," Ramirez said, lifting Liam from under his armpits. This time, Jerry grabbed the boy's feet. The unconscious youth's body seemed almost light.

At first.

Within a hundred yards, Ramirez was already stumbling. She had taken it upon herself to walk backward, to give Jerry the straightaway. Without discussing the matter, they now switched, and again made quick time until Jerry tripped and fell hard, almost dragging her down with him. Jennifer stepped up and took one of Liam's legs, and they started out again.

The water had almost disappeared from sight, and the view of the sea floor, exposed to the air for the first time, was like seeing the landscape of an alien world in twilight. A large shark, which hadn't managed to catch the receding water, was stranded near the jetty, tossing its head and tail so hard that it appeared to be shattering rocks.

Reinforcing the alien image was another creature, almost as big as the shark and with the same general shape. It was pink and looked flabby, with small fins. Its head, however, was a thing out of nightmares. It had a long, spiky snout, almost like a swordfish's, that protruded out over its jaws. Its eyes were at the base of the protuberance, and beneath it was a huge, toothy maw, open and gaping.

"A goblin shark," Jerry grunted. "Shouldn't be here."

"They were trying to escape the earthquake," Ramirez said, now completely certain it was all connected.

"Probably," Jerry said. "We should have realized it was a warning."

And then they were at the base of the lighthouse. There was a metal door set into the blocks of granite, and it had a huge, new, shiny padlock on it.

In the distance, they heard the roar of the ocean returning to take back the land it had abandoned, and more.

CHAPTER TWENTY-SEVEN

Mary Stewart had an almost photographic memory. She'd studied the Cascade subduction zone, so when the first tremor jolted through her feet and shook her massive antique desk, she knew she was in trouble.

The papers in her hand trembled, and as the room tipped, the doors to the big desk slid open. The room tilted back again, and the drawers slammed shut. She tried to rise from her chair, but was thrown forward onto the desk. She climbed up on it as it slid across the floor, slamming into the wall. Dust and plaster rained down.

The pictures on the walls turned perpendicular then crashed to the floor. She rode the desk, feeling as if she was on a small boat in stormy seas. The quake seemed to last forever.

The big window behind where her desk had been started its vibrating exodus, shattered. The buildings across from her swayed in unison. There was a heavy jolt and what sounded like a sonic boom, and she was nearly bucked off the desk.

As the desk stuttered toward the open window, she saw the street below, heard the sound of crashing cars. People on the sidewalks staggered as if drunk, looking every which way as if trying to find the source of the danger. Power lines snapped, showering sparks.

There was a small lull, and the panic came. Mary jumped off the desk, rolling along the floor. She saw the sky, then the floor, the sky, and then she was on her feet, running for the door. She could hear the strain in the walls as they move back and forth.

The floor left her feet, and she slammed into the hallway wall. The small table near the elevator moved up and down and sideways all at the same time, looking as if it was dancing.

The elevator buttons were dark, and the stairs leading down were blocked by a massive chunk of concrete with rebar poking out, threatening to skewer her. Mary climbed upward, taking the stairs, but none of the steps were where they had been a moment before.

Somehow she made it to the roof just as the tremors finally stopped. The earth was still for a moment, and then the screaming started. She reached into her pocket and tried to find the spot on the roof where she always smoked, but nothing seemed familiar. She lit a cigarette anyway, her hands shaking.

The danger was far from over. The earthquake was only the beginning.

The tsunami was coming.

She'd always been certain she'd survive the earthquake, making sure the science building was up to code. But nothing could stand in the way of a hundred foot tall wall of water.

Ever since Mary had read Ken Carter's paper on the Cascadia subduction zone and how a massive quake there would affect Seattle, Mary had been deathly afraid. She'd gone home that very night to tell Ernest, who'd laughed and said, "Hell, I'm betting an asteroid will wipe out Earth before that happens, or the Yellowstone super-volcano, or any number of other disasters."

Her husband had gone off to research the subject, and he came back and told her, in his most authoritative engineer tone, to quit worrying. "It's extremely unlikely the tsunami will reach Seattle," he said. "The Strait of Juan de Fuca will absorb most of it."

Mary had then done what she usually did and researched it herself. While it was true that the tsunami from the big subduction earthquake might not reach Seattle, there was also the Juan de Fuca fault. "What if they both happened at the same time?" she'd asked.

"Don't borrow trouble from an imaginary future, honey," Ernest told her.

But Mary couldn't stop thinking about it. She'd had nightmares about it almost every night for months until Ernest finally relented and they sold their house near Lake Washington and they moved the highest point in the area in western Seattle; highest point being relative. It was all of five hundred feet above sea level.

It wouldn't be long. At most a half hour. As Mary stood on the roof staring to the west, an aftershock nearly threw her off her feet. She could see Lake Union from the top of the Biology Building, could visualize the water's path as it flowed west until it met the Pacific Ocean. It was like a dagger pointed right at her heart.

The building swayed, felt as if it dropped several inches. She closed her eyes, every thought fleeing. *No, that can't be. Not now.* She opened her eyes as the concrete bannister nearby shuddered and cracked, the sound penetrating even her dulled eardrums.

Weird. It was as if she could hear and see everything. The waters of Lake Union rippled, and in the far distance, sirens blared. The tsunami alert – the thing she'd always feared. She'd practiced her escape a thousand times. Down the stairs, into her car, and drive east past Lake Washington and not stop until she reached the Cascade Mountains.

But now that the moment had come, Mary found she couldn't move.

What does it matter? Ernest is gone. My job is almost gone. I'm the Sphinx of the Biology Department, and no one likes me or even really knows me.

She pulled out a second cigarette and lit it.

She remembered the paper by Dr Carter almost word for word.

The effects of a megathrust earthquake, of 0.9 or larger magnitude, could be devastating to tidal life, depending on how much debris is lifted from the shore. Most species would quickly recover, however. Any sea life at more than 600 feet in depth (100 fathoms) would be unaffected.

It had been so cold-blooded and objective, but reading between the lines, it had been horrifying. The *debris* that would affect tidal pools would be coming from the human habitations on land, of course.

Professor Wice had written a critique of the paper, mostly praising it, but calling into question the assertion that deeper ocean creatures would not be affected.

Mary watched the waters of Lake Union, which connected Lake Washington on the eastern border of Seattle with the Pacific Ocean on the other side. They dropped steadily. It wasn't sudden. It was more like watching a sunset. She couldn't pinpoint when it became noticeable, just that the water level slowly dropped until the banks of the lake were high and dry and there was more mud than water.

The tsunami was on its way. She lit a third cigarette, and midway through taking a toke, she felt lightheaded.

The car horns increased. But unlike the car alarms she'd first heard, these blares were almost musical in their variety. These were people trying to escape. She walked over to the edge of the roof and looked down. The roads were clogged with stationary cars. She might have beaten the traffic if she had responded immediately, but now it was too late.

There was an old, beat-up lawn chair near the edge of the roof, and Mary sat in it and put up her feet.

She heard the roar first. It was loud, like a hurricane, like a thousand freight trains bearing down on the city, out of control, unstoppable. Then the wall of water rose over the horizon. The sun was behind it, and it was so beautiful that her heart leapt. It seemed to be moving in slow motion, an almost leisurely approach, as if Poseidon said, 'No hurry, we'll get to you soon enough.'

But she knew it was an illusion.

The buildings in the wave's path didn't crumble at first. The tsunami engulfed them, then they slowly sank out of sight. Or so it appeared from a distance, but as the wave approached, she heard the impact, heard the walls of the skyscrapers breaking under the onslaught. There were huge, rolling black slabs and smaller debris in the crest of the wave, so it wasn't just water striking the obstacles, but the broken remnants of the tsunami's first victims.

Mary's hearing was amazingly clear, as if all her consciousness was concentrated on the effort. Beneath the tsunami's roar, she heard the rumbling of broken concrete and steel and other debris grinding together in the giant whirlpool.

If I have to die, then let it be in the Gotterdammerung. Let Ragnarok come, the Twilight of the Gods, the Apocalypse.

She sat like the Sphinx, waiting for the end of days.

The last few seconds took a lifetime. Her thoughts went back to all the happy years with Ernest. She felt calm, accepting of her fate.

The building shuddered, lurched. The water surged over the roof, taking the lawn chair out from under her.

The wave struck her like the hands of a giant, and she tumbled through the air. Her breath was punched from her body, her eyes filled with grit, and her mouth sucked in water. She felt one last moment of despair, then nothing.

CHAPTER TWENTY-EIGHT

Joshua tumbled through the water, his arms and legs slamming against the sides of the tunnel. It was completely dark. He felt as if he was descending into the bowels of the Earth, deep down to where creatures waited for him. When his soul was gone, his body would continue to sink, to feed the bottom dwellers.

He wasn't sure how fast or for how long he floated. His lungs were burning, and it felt as if he couldn't hold his breath another instant, but that instant passed, and then another, and suddenly the urge to breathe went away.

That's not right. His thoughts were slow and hazy. *I'm dying.*

Someone or something grabbed his foot, and he instinctively kicked out, then immediately regretted it. Maybe Sam was still alive. Maybe his friend had reached out.

A whirlpool sent him under, and he twirled down into the darkness. His arm brushed up against something rough, and he reached out, jamming his fingers into a crevice. For a moment he held himself against the onslaught.

Then, with a frustrated cry, muffled by cascading water, he came loose and he was dragged away, helpless. He was like a leaf in rapids, unable to control the spinning. His face rose above the water for a moment, and he gulped in air and spray. Then the light and air was gone.

Joshua almost gave up then. His shoulder slammed against a wall, and it must have pushed him upward, for his head suddenly broke the surface. He gasped in air for only a second before the current caught him and pulled him down again.

He sensed a softening in the current, as if the channel widened. His head broke the surface again, and he caught a glimpse of steep concrete walls. He was in a culvert, open to the moonlit sky. He managed to stay afloat this time, to watch the concrete walls whizzing past. The water level dropped steadily.

Joshua's feet brushed the ground, and he tried to get his footing, but the current was still too strong. He was able to stay upright for moments at a time, but the water was the master here, and continued to knock him off his feet. His head barely broke the surface, and he could only stay upright for a few seconds at a time.

A gap in one of the walls appeared ahead of him. Desperately, he lunged in that direction, but the moment his feet left the bottom, the current caught him and pushed him downstream. His hands scraped the concrete walls, finding nothing to hang onto. He tried to dig his feet in, and they slid along the bottom and he slowed. With everything he had, he pushed against the flow. He was exhausted. Every moment felt like his last, as if he couldn't possibly hold on a moment longer. *I'm not going to die here.*

The walls were tall and flat, and there was no way he could climb them. The opening was his only chance.

He pushed against the current, grunting and growling with each step, leaning forward, his arms growing weak. His hands slipped on the flat surface and he was unable to stop his momentum. The aperture rushed past, and he felt his strength go. For a moment, he floated, ready to give up. He thought of insects he'd seen floating dead in open containers, unable to climb the unnatural, artificial surfaces.

"No!" he cried, unwilling to just give up. He felt renewed strength, but knew it was his last reserves. If he didn't climb out soon, he never would. It seemed so unfair. He'd survived the worst of the rapids, bashed against rough walls, and here he was in calm waters with no way of getting out.

A dark fissure opened to his left. With the last of his strength, he pushed forward until he could barely lift his legs and arms. He could barely gain traction, but an eddy caught him and pushed him in the right direction. His hand caught the edge, and somehow, *somehow*, he held on.

The opening had a broken piece of concrete protruding from its flat surface. He grabbed it and felt it partially give way, and then it held, and he was floating next to the platform. He held on for a few moments, too exhausted to do anything more. His fingers slipped, and with a surge of panic, he dragged himself up over the lip of the cleft until his chest rested on the flat surface. It was slick. The current dragged at his deadened legs, threatening to pull him away.

He thrust his arms outward, trying to hold on.

He breathed against the rock, bubbles forming in the moisture, his eyes stinging, his body completely numb. With a final push, he dragged himself the rest of the way up.

Joshua flopped over on his back, gasping for what felt an eternity. It seemed to him that the roar of the water diminished, and he rolled onto his side and stared down into the culvert. The water was a trickle along the bottom.

He pushed to his knees with a groan, every muscle aching, and turned toward the dark opening behind him. There was a rusted metal door sunk a few feet into the bank. It had a padlock on it, but the lock was equally rusted. He pried the broken piece of concrete from the platform and slammed it against the lock. His middle finger took the brunt of the blow, and he cursed and dropped the concrete. After sitting and holding his bleeding finger for several moments, he heard the water returning.

Joshua looked over the edge. The water now ran in the opposite direction, inland. He was beyond feeling alarmed, and yet there was something shockingly unnatural about the sight that pricked at his most primal fears. He turned back to the door and slammed the concrete against the lock again and again and again, ignoring the pain in his finger.

It was the hinge that finally gave way, not the lock. He pulled it the rest of the way out of the wall with his numbed fingers. His fingernails were broken and bleeding, and his middle finger throbbed. There was a ladder behind the door, and he started climbing.

The grate that served as a manhole cover was only a dozen

feet above, and it was locked. Joshua hooked his arm around the top rung of the ladder and wept. *Fuck you! Fuck you!*

He slammed his shoulder against the barrier in frustration, not because he expected it to do any good. To have survived this much, only to be denied so close to safety. He stuck his hand through the grate and felt the open air, the freedom just inches away.

"Hang on down there," came a voice from above. Joshua heard keys jangling, and then the cover opened and a man in a hard hat stared down at him. A hand was extended, and Joshua took it and felt himself being lifted.

"Dammit," said the gruff voice. "Every time there's a tsunami warning I have to come down here and check for idiots like you."

Joshua was dumped onto a city sidewalk. He looked around. He'd driven down this street a hundred times and never known there was a culvert on the other side of the wall. But that wasn't what caught his attention. In the distance, the Space Needle listed. Black smoke was rising on the horizon, and there seemed to be fewer skyscrapers than he remembered. Behind him, the retaining wall had a foot-wide crack in it.

Apparently, the tossing inside the culvert hadn't all been the currents.

"You damn kids," the man said. "You're lucky this was my last stop."

"Sorry," Joshua muttered.

The man wore a fluorescent vest that said City of Seattle on it. Under it was the name Gary. "How many times do we have to tell you kids how dangerous these culverts are? Not to mention dirty."

Joshua didn't bother defending himself. After all, he'd been doing the equally frowned-upon activity of exploring under the city. "My friend," he said, then remembered Kim's body floating by. "My friends... they're still in there."

"Then they're dead," Gary said grimly. "Do you have any idea what's happening?"

In the silence after the question, Joshua heard the sirens in the background.

"There's a tsunami coming," Gary said. "Come on, you can ride with me." The worker turned and walked over to a large city pickup truck parked on the side of the road. The street was strangely empty, though Joshua could hear traffic farther to the east. He stumbled after Gary, went to the passenger side, and managed to climb up into the seat though his arms and legs felt like putty. Looking back one last time to where Sam and Kim...

"Traffic is gridlocked," Gary said, starting up the truck. "Luckily, I know some back ways."

Gary drove westward for several blocks before turning toward the south. He drove another few blocks, and then they were in the semi-industrial zone of Seattle, near the railroad tracks. There was a service road that ran parallel to the tracks and headed east and west.

Gary pulled onto the road and accelerated. They hit a bump, and Joshua was lifted out of the seat, slamming his head against the ceiling of the cab. "Put on your seat belt, kid," Gary said. "I'm not slowing down. We're probably too late anyway."

Joshua looked over at the man. He was overweight, and his face was bright red. He was breathing so hard, it looked as if he was going to hyperventilate.

"Thank you for stopping," Joshua said.

"It's not every day you see a hand coming out of a sidewalk," Gary grunted.

They came around a corner and there was an oil drum in the middle of the road, as if it had fallen out of the bed of a truck. Gary swerved, and the pickup lost traction. It slid sideways across the railroad tracks, stuttering over the iron rails, tipping so much that Joshua's head slammed against the window. The truck came to a stop.

Gary slammed on the accelerator and shot back over the tracks and onto the road.

"Where are your parents?" the man asked, quickly getting up to the speed they'd been traveling before the oil drum.

Joshua tried to answer, but he was shivering so hard that he stuttered. His mouth was clenched tight, his teeth hurting. Without slowing, Gary shrugged off his orange vest and then the coat beneath it. "Put this on."

The coat was warm from the man's body and so big that it might as well have been a blanket. Joshua warmed up in seconds.

"So," Gary said. "Your parents?"

Joshua realized he hadn't even thought of his family, and a wave of guilt washed over him. "The west hills," he said.

"They should be all right," Gary said. "These tsunamis aren't supposed to go inland much more than a mile."

"Aren't we already a mile inland?" Joshua said.

"Yeah, but I think this tsunami is a big one. Too many waterways running through this town, it's a natural tidal path. So, you know, just to be safe, I'd like to find some hill somewhere to wait this out."

He turned off the road running parallel to the railroad tracks. A street ran alongside a fence on the other side of the railyard. There was a gate in the fence, but it was locked.

Gary accelerated. "Put your head down," he said.

The truck slammed into the gate. It wasn't like in the movies, where the metal barrier flew neatly over the pickup so that they could go their merry way. The gate attached itself to the bumper, and they ground to a halt.

Gary jumped out of the pickup in the middle of the road and started wrenching the tangled metal away. "Help me out, kid!" he shouted.

Joshua joined him on the other side, and between the two of them, they managed to pull the gate off the bumper. It clattered to the asphalt. The road was empty, lined by a row of boarded-up buildings.

"What's your name?" Gary asked as they jumped back in the truck. "So I don't have to keep calling you kid."

"Joshua. Joshua Cantrell."

"Nice to meet you, Joshua. My own kid is about your age. Goes to school in Colorado, thank God."

Up ahead, Joshua saw traffic crossing their road about two blocks ahead. Gary barely slowed. They were heading north now. They reached the intersection, and Gary slammed on the brakes. The *road* was a narrow one-way alley traveling west to east, and it was full of vehicles, and every one of the drivers sounded as though they were leaning on their horns.

Directly in front of them, there was a four-foot gap between the stalled cars. Gary pulled his pickup up to the gap, and then slowly drove into it. Both ends of the front bumper made contact. He stepped on the gas, and the other vehicles were slowly pushed aside. Metal screamed, but even louder were the outraged cries of the drivers.

"There's a bunch of business cards in my glove box, Joshua," Gary said. "Mind handing them to me?"

Joshua gave the man a handful, and Gary rolled down the window and threw the cards into the air. They fluttered through the air, landing on the back of one car and the front of the other.

"Sue me!" Gary shouted. With that, he pushed the pickup on through, sending both cars sideways. The screeching of metal was the loudest thing Joshua had ever heard.

"Jesus," he said.

"Jesus, Mary, and Joseph," Gary agreed. Then they were through and heading north again on an empty road.

"Good thing I have tsunami insurance," Gary said gleefully.

"Really?"

Gary snorted and looked at Joshua to see if he was kidding. "I think fender benders are the last things the insurance companies will be worrying about."

Joshua realized they were very close to his house, which was near the top of one of the highest points in Seattle.

"Turn here," he said impulsively. To his surprise, Gary turned into the alley, which ran next to the ritzy shopping district at the bottom of the hill. There was a theater nearby that Joshua went to almost every weekend. The alley headed upward, and instead of the backs of businesses, they were running alongside the backs of big, fancy houses. The higher they went, the fancier the houses got.

The alley ended abruptly at another cross street jammed with cars, this time on both sides.

Gary slowed and then stopped. He looked over at Joshua and laughed. "Don't worry, kid. I'm not going to try to bull our way through that. Frankly, I'm surprised we got this far."

"Come on," Joshua said. "My house isn't far from here. There's a pretty good-sized hill just a couple hundred yards away."

A couple hundred yards didn't sound like much. But both Gary and Joshua were winded within half that distance; Gary because he was overweight and out of shape, and Joshua because he'd already expended more of his body's resources than he had ever spent before. They slowed to a staggering walk.

There was a sudden silence in the distance. At first, Joshua couldn't figure out the difference. Then he realized all the sirens and car alarms to the west of them had fallen silent.

"That can't be good," Gary huffed.

Then they heard the roar. They couldn't see the wave because of the houses, but the crashing and grinding was unmistakable.

"Run!" Gary shouted.

Joshua discovered he did still have a few reserves of energy. He sprinted up the hill, passing people who were looking behind him in horror. He didn't stop or look until he reached the first bend in the road..

There he stumbled and almost fell to his knees. *Not yet.*

In the distance, the buildings that had obscured the tsunami were vanishing one by one, as if an invisible giant stomped on them. Then he saw the first of the white and blue waters, roiling with stone, metal, concrete, timber, and other debris.

Gary struggled up the hill a hundred feet below him. Joshua looked up. There was still a couple of hundred feet to go to get to the top, and every instinct told him he needed the height. There was a crowd of people up there, and they shouted and motioned encouragement.

Joshua ran down the hill and reached Gary's side. The man was just standing there, bent over, breathing raggedly and clutching his chest over his heart.

"Have a heart attack later," Joshua said. He tried to take the man's arm and throw it over his shoulder.

"Give me a break," Gary managed to say. "I'm an elephant... you're a monkey."

He kept talking, but the tsunami's roar had grown so loud, Joshua couldn't make out the words. But something that Joshua had done must have inspired the big man, because he stumbled upward again.

He went another fifty feet and stopped. The waters whooshed up the hill, and Joshua's feet went out from under him. Someone grabbed him by the arm, and he got back to his feet.

The water kept rising until Joshua was certain all of Seattle would disappear forever and become the new Atlantis.

I can't fight the ocean.

The water pushed him up the hill, but just as he neared the top, the wave crested and receded, pulling him backward hard. It was as if he was a bug beneath a vacuum. If he lost his footing, he was lost.

Gary waded through the surge as well, the big man holding up better than Joshua. As the water retreated in a rush, Gary grabbed him, and between the two, they managed to keep their feet against the undertow.

And then they were beyond it, on dry land.

Joshua turned to the person who'd helped him. It was a teenager, probably the only person on the hill younger than Joshua among the crowd, who likely came from the immediate neighborhood of mostly retirees. "Thanks," he said, then looked around for Gary.

Gary was lying on his back, but he was still breathing. Joshua hurried over to him, and Gary gave him a wink. "Still kicking," he said. Below them, the waters were receding.

The teen that had helped Joshua came over. "We need to wait for at least eight hours or until an all-clear signal, according the radio," he said. "Also, the first wave may not be the biggest."

Gary rolled onto his stomach and groaned, and then pushed himself up.

Joshua saw something bright orange where the tide had receded. He went down to it and stopped, stumped by what he was seeing. The creature looked like it came from a cartoon. It was round and had big eyes on the side of its head and a fringe like a doily along the bottom. There were two large ears on top of its head.

The aliens have landed. A giant spaceship crashed in the ocean and its occupants are washing up on land.

"That's a Dumbo octopus!" The kid who had helped Joshua stood beside him. "They live in the deep ocean. Like, really deep."

Joshua looked out over Seattle, and it reminded him of the pictures of Hiroshima and Nagasaki he'd seen in school. It was as if the ocean had decided to switch sides, to take everything on land and deposit it deep into the ocean and take everything in the ocean and deposit it on land.

There was a far-off rushing sound, and another wave appeared above the devastation. It was bigger than the previous wave. Joshua said goodbye to the Dumbo octopus and turned to run up the hill.

There was shouting from the crowd above, and they pointed at something below them. Joshua turned back and looked down the hill. A huge desk had washed up on the road, looking as big as a boat. A little old lady got off, completely drenched.

How the hell did she get there? How did she survive?

Then, without thinking, he ran toward her.

CHAPTER TWENTY-NINE

Perkins was in John Sanders office when the earthquake struck. The house seemed to jerk slightly, and then again. There was a loud groan as the frame of the house bent but held firm as it was designed. It was unsettling but not alarming. The structure was so well constructed for just this possibility that it held up well.

It was the view outside the office window that told him what was really happening. The water in the moat sloshed over the banks, which then crumbled. The ornamental plants were tossed from their placements, roots and all. It was as if the earth moved in a wave.

When it was over, his boss said, "Jasper, I need you to do me a personal favor."

It had been so long since Perkins had been called by his first name that for a moment he didn't realize his boss was speaking to him. "Sir?"

"I want you to find my son," John Sanders said. "I don't care how you do it. Find him. Get him out of the city. Don't take no for an answer."

"Of course," Perkins said. With a sinking heart he realized that Sanders was asking him to use any means, legal or otherwise. It wasn't just making sure Liam was safe.

Ever since Sanders first hired him, they'd had a good professional relationship. Perkins watched and listened, always close by, doing whatever Sanders asked, and even more often, what Sanders wanted but didn't ask.

But it had never been anything underhanded.

Unlike his former employers. When Perkins left Special Ops, he'd discovered there were few civilian jobs that made use of his skills. Without the structure of the military, he was adrift. Civilians seemed aimless, undisciplined, lacking in planning. Perkins just didn't understand them, including his own family, whom he'd visited once upon returning from Afghanistan and hadn't seen since.

For a time, he had worked for anyone who could pay him, whether it was aboveboard or not.

He'd been thankful when Sanders hired him. His official title was administrative assistant, but his real job was bodyguard, a pretty cushy job as far as Perkins was concerned. Most often, he was simply an errand boy, and that was perfectly all right with him.

Now, Perkins tried to figure out what his boss was asking him to do. Hack the sheriff's office or the state police? Surely they wouldn't be holding anything back.

"I want you to take my son back to Connecticut, whether he wants to go or not," Sanders clarified. "And he probably won't want to. I will vouch for you if anything happens."

What am I supposed to do? Knock the kid out and put him in handcuffs? "I'll do my best, sir," he said.

"Check that coffee shop at the intersection," Sanders said. "Liam used to hang out there with... with Devon." Sanders looked away, silent for a moment. Perkins knew he was thinking that the kid who'd died could just have easily been Liam. The only time Perkins ever saw his boss emotional was when it concerned his son.

Sanders continued, "I don't think Liam has any friends he can go to, except maybe some other surfers. So check the coffee shop and then check the beaches on the way back."

"Yes, sir." Perkins turned sharply to leave, as if a general had just given him an order.

"Oh, and Jasper?"

Perkins hesitated in the doorway.

"Find him fast. If Doctor Henderson is right about the earthquakes, we need to get away from here as soon as possible."

Perkins nodded and left the room. But he didn't leave the house immediately. Instead, he made a quick search of Liam's room, and then jogged up the stairs and checked the secret hideaway. He was looking for clues, but everything looked normal. Liam's beach gear was still on the floor. Wherever Liam was, Perkins suspected it wasn't one of his usual haunts. But that was where he had to start.

He took the Humvee, which Sanders let him use as his personal transportation, and drove to the small cluster of shops that serviced the beach crowd, about ten miles down the road. In the winter, most of the places were closed except for the coffee shop, which seemed to do booming business all year long. Perkins got his newspapers there whenever he could get away.

Liam wasn't there, and no one had seen him.

"Tell Liam I'm sorry about Devon," the barista said. She was a teenage girl with tattoos running up both arms.

Perkins nodded. He quickly drove to the first beach, which was busier than usual. It was a warm day for September, and people were spending their last weekend at play. He quickly searched the crowd and moved on.

The second beach was a repeat of the first. Lots of people, no Liam.

The third beach was the most likely. Liam spent most of his time on the north side of the jetty, but he normally paddled there from the island instead of the mainland. Still, there was a beach that was accessible from the road, and Perkins thought it was his last and best hope.

He was halfway there when the first aftershock struck. The Humvee lost traction. He spun the steering wheel as the vehicle swerved toward the shoulder, then shot across the road into the embankment.

The Humvee stopped moving, but the ground under it kept shaking. Gravel and small rocks tumbled loudly onto the hood. Bigger rocks were teetering threateningly at the top of the embankment.

Perkins started the vehicle and pulled away just as a huge boulder landed where the Humvee had been and rolled across the road. The shaking subsided. Perkins pulled over, closed his eyes, and breathed deeply. He'd survived combat because he'd always been able to get ahold of himself, to gather his wits when everyone else fell apart, to think tactically when others merely reacted.

The Humvee was dented but still in good shape. The machine was insanely expensive and burned gas as if it had a private pipeline to Saudi Arabia. Then again, it had been designed for just such emergencies. It hadn't taken much for Perkins to convince his boss to buy one.

The beach was only a short distance away. On the other hand, the parking lot was well short of the beach, and he'd have to run down a long pathway. Still, if he could find Liam quickly, he could be in and out in time to get away.

But what were the odds? Perkins had lived while others died because he played the odds. He turned and headed west. He'd avoid the city and try to get to safety on one of the lesser-used roads that encircled it.

He pulled out his phone and pushed the button that was so well used that the lettering had worn off.

"Have you found him?" Sanders demanded.

"Did you feel the second earthquake?" Perkins demanded back, his voice firm and calm. It was the voice he'd used to command men, and Sanders had never heard it before.

"Of course I felt it. You need to find Liam, Jasper."

Perkins didn't answer. In the distance, he heard the tsunami sirens. Perkins had attended the risk assessment meetings when the resort was being planned. He'd heard about the odds of an earthquake and the even more devastating tsunami that was likely to follow.

"Perkins," Sanders broke in. "I've been overpaying you for years for exactly this type of circumstance. You owe me."

"Leave, Mister Sanders." Perkins ended the call, put the Humvee into gear, and headed west. The phone immediately rang, and Perkins didn't have to answer to know he was fired. Thing was, if he had any idea where Liam was, he'd go after the kid, tsunami or no tsunami. Not leaving a soldier behind was inculcated in him, but to search the greater Seattle area for a single runaway kid was a fool's errand.

There were few people on the road at first. Many of the vehicles were on the side of the road as if the occupants were trying to figure out what to do. Perkins suspected that by the time they figured it out, it would be too late. He hoped his boss had taken his advice and left the house. Liam was on his own, and John Sanders dying wouldn't help the kid.

But the one thing Perkins knew about the old man was that he was stubborn; mule-headed enough to bet against the market and wait for it to turn and make him rich. Stubborn enough not to take no for an answer when it came to building a resort on a public island. Sanders didn't care about anything but his son, and it would probably be the death of him.

Perkins figured he was halfway around the city before he hit heavy traffic. He was forced to slow and then stop. An SUV was crossways across the road, its side smashed in, the wheel well crushed. There was a pickup with a dented bumper a few feet away. Behind it was a bright yellow VW Beetle. A large, fat man argued with a diminutive woman while another man stood watching.

Perkins got out of the Humvee and marched toward the gathering. He looked in the pickup to see if the keys were there, but they were gone. He walked up to the fat man. "Give me your keys."

"What?"

"Give me the keys to the pickup *now!*"

The man almost reflexively extended his hand, the keys dangling from it. Perkins checked to make sure there weren't any kids in the SUV, then got into the pickup and drove it forward. The others stood frozen for a moment, then got out of the way just in time. The truck's bumper struck the dent in the SUV, and it almost tipped over, then started sliding to one side. Perkins didn't stop until it tumbled over the embankment, rolling over and over, gathering speed and disappearing over a cliff.

"Are you crazy?" the woman screamed.

Perkins got out of the truck, ready to give the keys back. The fat man had a tire iron in his hands, and the other man, who looked like a bank clerk who had skipped PE when he was still in school, brandished part of a jack.

Perkins pulled his Glock from the holster at the back of his belt. "Do you really want to bring a tire iron to a gun fight?"

Both men dropped their makeshift weapons and put up their hands. The bank clerk said, "Listen, mister, we won't get in your way."

"Good," Perkins said. He threw the pickup keys at their feet. "Now get in your cars and drive west. Take the woman with you. The second you can pull aside, let me get past you or I'll ram your ass off the road."

"Yes, sir," the bank clerk said, getting into his VW Beetle. The fat man nodded and bent over to grab the keys, almost falling over. He waddled to the pickup, got in, and pulled away.

Within half a mile, Perkins passed them. He knew they'd be busily taking down his license number, but if the tsunami caught him, that would be the least of his, or their, worries.

He concentrated on his driving, taking the fastest angle on every turn, speeding up on the straightaways, so he was amazed when he looked in the rearview mirror and saw the Beetle and the silver pickup almost keeping up. Apparently he had scared some sense into them.

Then he saw what they had probably been seeing all along. There was a giant wall of water bearing down on them. Backlit by the setting sun, it looked like a flow of lava, burning red in the sky. Perkins didn't slow at the next turn and nearly slid off the road. When he reached the next straightaway, he looked behind him again. The silver pickup came racing around the turn, and then the Beetle, and then the yellow car was gone. The pickup lasted a few seconds longer then it, too, was submerged.

Perkins kept his eyes on the road, not watching the impending doom. When the Humvee lifted off the road, floating for a few moments and then slowly tumbling, he could only think about how he'd been slowed by the other traffic.

"Damned civilians," he muttered. He saw a shadow approaching, and then the Humvee smashed into the side of a cliff.

CHAPTER THIRTY

Conrad Smith sat on the rock that capped the hill like a king surveying his realm. This hill was the highest of the coastal foothills, with the ocean barely visible in the distance. It was part of their tribal lands despite being surrounded by commercial resorts and condos. They called it the 'campgrounds'. Most of the top of the hill was flat enough to create camping spots for tents and RVs. A rough road had been carved out of the old paths, and the meadow below the campground was full of battered pickups and SUVs.

Almost all of Conrad's family was here, and it seemed as if half of the tribe had come along too.

Nothing like offering free beer and barbecue to get people to show up.

He'd tried warning his immediate family of the impending disaster, but they had scoffed and told him he was an old fool. Even when Derrick told his own story about the black snakes, they had just shaken their heads and said, "You and your stories, Grandfather. Now you've got Derrick believing them."

So he'd stopped warning them, instead telling them that he was celebrating his ninetieth birthday, which was still a month away, and *that* they had believed. By late afternoon, half the tribe had arrived.

Crow Mountain was a holy place to his people. The rock Conrad sat on was flat and grooved and was called Sacrifice Rock, though there was no evidence it had ever been used for that purpose.

Conrad looked out over his partying family and friends and thought the rock was there for exactly this purpose – so that a person could sit on it and appreciate the land and the sea and the People. Just below the flattened hilltop, a deep gully ringed the hillside. It was too perfect to be natural, and in the 1950s archeologists had been given permission to dig it up. They'd found layers of charcoal and unidentifiable bits of bone and decided that the circle had served a ceremonial purpose, though of what kind they couldn't seem to agree.

Conrad thought the answer was a lot simpler. When he was a little kid, he'd witnessed his grandparents tossing the garbage from a tribal cookout into the gully and burying it.

The gully was full of brush now. It seemed like every passing leaf or needle was trapped within it. The road stopped just below the circle, and wooden planks had been laid over the divide to make a bridge.

People still arrived, bringing food and more beer, which was fortunate, because what Conrad had brought was running low. He'd spent his entire savings, but if he was right, it was worth it.

He'd put Derrick in charge of the barbecue. The boy was bossing his siblings and cousins around like a tribal elder, and Conrad smiled. It was like seeing himself as a young man, before he'd started reading the legends, before he'd become the tribal historian.

A few more years of wildness and Derrick will settle down. He's too thoughtful not to.

After failing to convince the first few family members of the danger, Conrad told Derrick to keep the story of the black snakes to himself. If word got out to the authorities, it might not go well for the boy. There would be questions.

The campground was divided by two giant fire pits, above which huge pigs roasted. Adults who chose to drink congregated on one side, and on the other side, the younger and the more sober gathered. Both sides were noisy. Shouts of glee from the children were competing with the raucous laughter of the inebriated.

Seagulls soared overhead, swooping whenever an unwary camper left his or her food unattended. There was a fresh breeze blowing inland and the scent of seawater in the air. It was peaceful and joyous. Derrick looked up at Conrad with a grateful smile, and the old man's heart filled with contentment. It was hard to believe anything could break this peace.

Oh, well. What do I need money for? I'm ninety years old!

The rock beneath him seemed to shake a little. He frowned and glanced down. The soil around the base of the rock was dark, as if it had been disturbed. None of the partiers appeared to notice anything.

His perch felt as though it was floating. There was a sudden silence as the partygoers fell quiet, and then a loud *boom*. Conrad tumbled to the ground. On his hands and knees, he looked at the hairline cracks appearing everywhere around him, a few growing wider, to an inch or more.

The ancestors had chosen their refuge wisely, though, for the hill held firm.

His people looked in every direction, as if not sure where to run.

"Stay where you are!" he shouted.

As the tremors grew shorter, stuttering the ground instead of rolling it, there were shouts of relief as they realized that they'd gone through the worst.

Or so they thought.

The breeze died down. Something made Conrad look seaward.

The ocean water receded, the tidal flats extending far out beyond the broken rocks of the seashore. Conrad stood and stepped backward to the highest point of the rock, as if the extra couple of feet would make a difference.

This, too, was in the old legends. That the great waters would draw away. But they would return, greater than ever.

No, not legends, it is history, for it is all proving true.

Some of his people started down the hill toward their cars.

"Come back!" he shouted. The nearest heard him, and shouted to those further down the hill. They hesitated but, as one, seemed to realize that Conrad and Derrick had steered them right, that they were much safer than if they had stayed in the city. One by one, the families turned and trudged back up the hill.

Conrad looked out onto the expanding beach. It was as if the world itself took a deep breath.

The sounds became muted to Conrad, and his world narrowed to a single point: the ocean wave that rose up and up, and then started coming back to earth, flowing with a noise so loud that even this far away, the sound drowned out everything else.

Something about his posture must have alerted the others, who couldn't see the ocean from farther down the slope. They ran toward him, looking over their shoulders and exclaiming as they saw the wall of water surging toward them.

Then all was silent except for the roar of the wave, which filled the universe so that no other sound existed except the ending of all things.

Some of the men ran again toward their cars, then stopped as they realized they were already on the highest point of land within reach. The People instinctively moved toward Sacrifice Rock, surrounding Conrad, but no one tried to climb up next to him. He stood alone in the middle of his people and watched the great wall of water.

It seemed so peaceful, so orderly, the way the wave crashed down onto the lowlands, flowing across the reservation where many of his people still lived, across the bigger white man's town next to it, across the casino and the highway, the neon lights flickering and exploding and falling dark. Trees and homes and bridges were scraped from the surface of the land, only to reemerge riding the top of the wave.

The grinding and crashing of stone and steel, of a broken civilization rode the crest of the waters. It smashed everything within its path with thunderous impact.

There was nothing Conrad could do, no words he could say. He stood straight, facing his fate as the wave crashed into the bottom of the hill and surged upward, whitewater foaming, churning, turning over rocks and trees, adding to the broken remains of what had already been destroyed. It was as much solid matter now as water, but it was the water that moved it all, that kept the maelstrom coming. And then, little by little, the detritus was left upon the hillside until only the dark water kept coming, lapping ever upward, finding grooves and wrinkles in the terrain, trying desperately to reach the People, as if that had been its goal from the beginning.

The water came within a few feet of the edge of the circular gully and stopped. Then, unbelievably, it receded. As if in anger, another wave fell upon the first, pushing the apex of the water a few inches higher, but it once again fell short.

The water flowed around the hill as if trying to find another path, but could find no way.

Slowly, as if clawing the ground to keep its height, the wave fell backward, receding down the hill, flowing down around the giant boulders and remains of structures it had brought with it as if bequeathing a curse upon the land.

The ocean itself rose up and washed everything away, and the world was begun anew.

The outside world returned, sounds within the comprehension of man, the distant wave now no louder than a freight train, and human voices cut through the roar, shouts and cheers and cries of relief.

I stand where Crow once stood. As unbelievable as it seemed. *It really happened, just as the tales said.*

Someone slapped Conrad on the back, and he turned to see Derrick's excited face, but then his face fell as he saw something in Conrad's expression.

They don't understand yet. The people standing on this hilltop were all that remained of the People. Anyone too old or too young, too sick or too grumpy to attend the celebration were gone. Everyone who had survived had probably lost loved ones.

It is said that the darkness once came out of the ocean, and it killed everything and everyone but the People. Crow heard the distant approach, the rumbling beneath the waters.

It wasn't over, Conrad realized. And if the first part of the ancient legend was true, what of the second part? What of the blackness?

The hillside looked like a garbage pit. Shattered masonry, lumber, bricks, and twisted metal littered the ground. Everything was covered by a black substance, which, as Conrad focused upon it, began to move.

Black snakes filled every empty spot, squirming, trying to find traction and direction. And then, seemingly as one, the creatures turned upward, flowing like a smaller wave, but one that was not going to be stopped by mere height.

The People looked up at Conrad in wonder as he stood upon the rock, as the family members who'd been warned this would happen told the others and the story passed through the crowd with the swiftness of another wave.

He jumped off the rock, a movement he never would have attempted an hour before for fear his old bones would snap. He pushed through the crowd, who seemed intent on stopping him, wanting to pat him on the back and shake his hand. His giant nephew, Billy Smith, even grabbed him in a bear hug.

Conrad pushed him away, his bony hands sinking into Billy's blubber, and ran toward the barbecue pits. He grabbed the biggest burning branch he could lift and stumbled to the gully. Without hesitation, he thrust the burning embers into the dried leaves and twigs that filled it.

Frustratingly, the leaves smoldered and smoked, but didn't burst into flame.

The first of the snakes writhed to the side of the divide and hesitated as if confused. Then, one by one, they went down the side, disappearing under the debris. The leaves and twigs on top started to shudder from the wriggling of the snakes.

"Stand aside, Grandfather!" Derrick shouted behind him.

Conrad turned to see his grandson running toward him, the gas can he'd used to ignite the barbecue pits in hand. He splashed gasoline into the gully, running sideways, nearly tumbling in but managing to get a quarter of the way around the hill before the last drops were expended.

He ran back to the still-smoldering branch Conrad was holding, grabbed it, and threw it onto the gasoline-soaked leaves. They burst into flame, and the debris appeared to almost jump out of the gully as the snakes tried to escape. A few of them managed to poke their yellow-striped heads out of the gully before the flames overtook them.

There were shouts behind them. The snakes had surrounded the hill on all sides, and the first of them bridged the gap, to be met by sticks and stones and whatever else the People could find. Shots rang out as Cary Mathews pulled the pistol he always carried and started blasting.

Several women stood by the plank bridge that crossed the gully, shovels in hand, and were decapitating the snakes who wriggled across. Beside them, some of the burlier men pulled up planks and tossed them into the gully.

"There's two more gas cans in my pickup," Derrick said. Without waiting for a response, the young man turned and ran toward the bridge, yelling at the men not to throw the last plank over the side.

Cursing his slow, tottering legs, Conrad ran after him. His grandson's old, battered Ford pickup was the nearest to the crossing as Derrick had been the first to arrive to help dig the pits. Conrad managed to get to the bridge just as Derrick started across.

Conrad grabbed his arm, and Derrick turned, surprised. "No, Derrick. I'll do it."

"Grandfather..." Derrick began.

"Do as I say, Grandson. If you respect me, do as I say."

"But..."

Conrad pushed past him, nearly toppling off the narrow plank. Long ago, he'd taken to wearing heavy boots and thick Levi's he never washed, but let the grime accumulate on. When the pants started to stink, he stuck them in a freezer for a while, and they came out free of bacteria.

The first snake struck toward his steel-reinforced toes, and the second at his heels. The third snake got snagged in his jeans, just below the knee, and hung there, wriggling, trying to gain purchase. Conrad stomped on the others nearby and kicked them away, and reached the pickup. He jumped up onto the bed and saw the two red plastic gas containers strapped to the toolbox that ran along the side of the pickup.

He unstrapped them and turned around.

It was as if every snake on the hillside, thousands of them, converged on the pickup.

It's my imagination. They can't know what I'm planning.

But as he jumped to the ground and the first dozen snakes flashed toward him, he wondered. It was almost as if they had a hive mind.

Once again, the thick Levi's warded off their glancing strikes.

Then one snake managed to angle higher, and Conrad felt a sting in his belly, right where it fell over his belt. A numbing sensation immediately started spreading both upward and downward.

The bridge was only yards away, but it was as if his legs refused to move. He concentrated, putting one boot before the other. His lower body was covered in black as the snakes sunk their fangs into his pants and boots, but he struggled forward, reaching the plank and taking his first step.

His legs were numb, and he directed them by sight since he couldn't feel where they were. It was as if his old, stiff boots and jeans kept him upright while his skin and bones melted within them.

My suit of armor. He surprised himself with a grunt of laughter.

He glanced up once to see Derrick staring at him in horror, and then his eyes went to his encased legs, willing them to move.

His vision narrowed, shutting down, until he could see only a pinpoint of the plank, but that pinpoint was so clear he could see the individual whorls in the wood.

His errant boots started moving to one side.

Wrong direction! But they didn't listen. He felt himself toppling.

Strong arms grabbed him and lifted him, the heavy weight of the gas cans was taken from his hands, and before he could understand what had happened, he was on the other side of the bridge, lying in the dirt. An old woman batted at his legs with a shovel, but he didn't feel it. He saw chunks of snake falling away from his pants and boots.

His head was on a blanket resting on someone's lap, and he opened his eyes to see his granddaughter, Miriam, looking down at him, her eyes glistening with tears.

Don't touch me, he tried to say, but a whoosh interrupted him, and a circle of red fire surrounded him, and he knew that his people were safe.

Crow and his family were saved, and they came back down to the seashore, and the People began anew...

Conrad closed his eyes, happy. *I am Crow. My people are saved.*

The snakes threw themselves into the fire as if they were immune to it. A strange odor filled the air, and it seemed to Derrick that the air shimmered.

After a while, the fires died down, but still the snakes came. Derrick told the People to grab everything they could to feed the flames.

Where the coals cooled, some of the snakes made it across, scorched but still alive, but they were killed on the spot. One of the women reached down, grabbed a dead snake, and tossed it into the still-hot coals. Moments later, she straightened up and froze, then toppled backward.

"Don't touch them!" Derrick shouted, and he kept shouting it until Billy came over and said, "We heard you, man."

The blackness continued to flow toward them, and Derrick sat down on Sacrifice Rock and put his face in his hands. "What do I do, Grandfather?"

He took a shuddering breath and went to where Conrad lay. One look into his sister's eyes and he knew. Grandfather was gone.

Derrick was on his own.

Everything that could be burned had been tossed into the circle, and still the snakes came. Derrick ordered everyone to pair up, to stand back to back, it was time to make a last stand. He paced around his people, circling them, smiling with a confidence he didn't feel.

A fluttering sound rose above him, and he glanced up.

It was as if the sky was full of white, pulsating feathers that flowed downward toward him, then veered aside and skimmed along the ground. There was white among the black now, and it rose into the air. Then the black disappeared, consumed by the white.

Grandfather's words came to Derrick:

"A white cloud descended from the skies and covered them, and the blackness vanished."

CHAPTER THIRTY-ONE

Ramirez examined the lock with a sinking heart. It looked brand new. There were scratches all around the door, which was solid metal, and it was obvious from the painted-over graffiti and the chips of granite around the edges that people had been breaking into the lighthouse for years and whoever was in charge had put on the strongest, most reliable lock and hinges they could get.

Liam lay comatose at the foot of the door, while Jerry set down his backpack and rummaged around in it. Ramirez thought he was looking for a tool, but his hand emerged with a bottle of water, which he handed to the girl. "Drink up, Jennifer."

Jerry watched her, looking tired, then took the bottle and drained it. Moments later, he was nearly hopping out of his skin, and he didn't look the slightest bit fatigued. "Shoot the lock off," he said, turning to her. His eyes were shining brightly.

"What's in that stuff?" she asked. "Meth?"

"Something you've never heard of and completely legal, Deputy. So, can you shoot the lock off?"

Ramirez shook her head. In training, they'd shown videos about what happened when you tried to shoot a padlock. "Won't work," she said. "It just messes up the mechanism and jams it permanently."

"Let me try," Jerry said.

Ramirez laughed. It was such a ludicrous request that she couldn't help it. "I'm not handing my firearm over to a civilian."

"I'm the best shot you've ever seen," he said. He was so confident that she believed him, and yet...

"He really is," Jennifer exclaimed with enthusiasm. "He can hit the eye of a newt at a hundred yards."

"Yeah, sure," Ramirez said. "You still can't use my firearm. It's against regulations."

"Deputy," Jerry said, "we're about to be washed out to sea and drowned, so if you don't mind my language, fuck your regulations."

He stared at her unblinkingly. Ramirez had never seen anyone with eyes shining with such intelligence. His charisma factor was off the charts. She trusted him, which made her *distrust* him. In her experience, charisma wasn't the same thing as competence. And yet…

He was the most alive, present person she'd ever met. Either he really was what he said, or he was completely crazy.

This is the craziest thing I've ever done. But it's the end of the world, so…

She took her handgun out of the holster and handed it to him.

He examined it, but as if he'd never seen a gun before. Ramirez wanted to snatch it out of his hand.

"You guys had best get around the corner," Jerry said. "Ricochets are hard to calculate."

He moved back and forth in front of the door, staring at the lock from all angles, and at that moment, Ramirez believed he was actually calculating the angle of the ricochets.

She grabbed Liam's arms and Jennifer took his feet, and they went around the side of the lighthouse, just out of sight. From there, they could see a huge wave on the horizon.

It was breathtaking, beautiful, and terrifying. The sun had dropped behind the wall of water, and yet some of the light still shone through, refracting through it, shining with the last of that day, of any day.

How many people die with that wonder in their minds? It was a thought she had never had before.

There was a single shot, and she hurried around the corner. Jerry was bending over the padlock, examining it. The curve of metal was dented a good half inch, but it was still intact.

"That's a hell of a shot," Ramirez said, raising her voice over the incoming thunder of the tsunami. "Or you were lucky."

"I wasn't lucky," Jerry said. "Next one ought to do it."

"Go ahead," she said. "I'll take my chances."

He stood a good five feet away from the door and extended his arm. He was steady, his eyes unmoving. Ramirez didn't even see him squeeze the trigger, but then the lock dangled, broken.

The roar of the wave drowned out her shout of surprise. Jerry hurried around the corner, lifting Liam as if he was a fifty-pound sack of rice and hoisting him over his shoulders.

Jerry threw open the door and ran inside with Jennifer on his tail. Ramirez hesitated and took one look back. The wall of water hung before her eyes like the side of a building. She slammed the door shut. It latched, and then moments later the entire lighthouse shook, the vibrations so strong she was lifted off her feet and thrown toward the steps. She put her hands out to stop her fall, and pain shot through her left wrist.

The others were already up the steps and out of sight. The water seeped through what had appeared from the outside to be a seamlessly solid door. She ran. There was a loud metallic groan, but the door held for now.

The stairway circled the walls clockwise, with a waist-high metal railing. There was nothing but space beyond it. No lighthouse keeper had ever lived here. It was simply a shell housing a tool. Dim natural light filtered from above.

The caretakers hadn't bothered to paint over the graffiti inside, and every inch was covered with bright paint. It was like a psychedelic nightmare, the kind where Ramirez ran and ran and never got anywhere while the monsters closed in from all sides.

Loud crashes reverberated through the cylinder of the lighthouse, deafening and frightening. She wanted to stop at the first landing, to curl up with her hands over her ears. But the younger people were ahead of her on the steps.

I am an officer of the law. It's my duty to protect them.

At any other time, she might have laughed at the pompousness of the thought, but now it seemed proper and right. Ramirez had always thought she was in good shape, but the kids were way ahead of her despite their burden, nearly to the top.

She looked down and realized she was about halfway. As she peered into the darkening well of the lighthouse, the door suddenly burst open and water gushed in. She stared at it for a few moments, unable to move.

"Hurry!" she heard shouted from above.

The water was already to the first landing. Ramirez took the stairs two at a time. She almost stumbled at the next landing and put out her left hand to steady herself against the wall. Pain shot up her arm from her wrist and she cried out, her eyes filling with unwanted tears. Her legs felt as if the water had ready reached her and was dragging her down. The opening to the top chamber was only a few feet away.

A hand reached through the opening, took hold of her arm, and pulled her upward in one motion, lifting her the last few steps. The water caught at her ankles; then she was on solid footing. There was a loud crash as Jerry slammed the trapdoor shut and bolted it.

The metal lid bulged, then burst open, and water gushed in.

There was nowhere to run.

Cracked windows, now darkening in the twilight, ringed the top of the lighthouse. There was an empty metal pedestal at the center of the room, on top of which sat a wishbone-shaped metal device that must once have held the lamp.

The lighthouse shifted, as if the entire building had moved over a couple of feet, and all three of them fell to the floor, with Jennifer landing on top of Liam, who groaned and opened his eyes.

She figured the water coming through the hatch should have drowned them by now, but instead, it sloshed around a few inches above the floor.

The high-water mark. She closed her eyes in relief, not feeling the slightest urgency to get up.

"Watch out!" Jennifer shouted. Ramirez opened her eyes to see a long, black snake swimming on the surface of the water, coming straight toward her. More of the snakes came through the opening.

Ramirez froze. There was nowhere to go, to escape. Out of the corner of her eye she saw a hand shoot down and grab the snake around the middle. The snake reared back, wrapping around the arm and sinking its fangs into the hand.

"No, Jerry!" she screamed. The young man stood there, looking at the snake curiously. Then he reached over with his other hand and pried the snake's mouth out of his hand, the fangs still glistening with venom. With a quick twist, he snapped the snake's neck.

Jennifer also had a snake in hand, and she swung it against one of the windows, which shattered. The snake dropped out of sight.

Ramirez waited for them to collapse, but they continued to wrangle and kill the snakes without incident. *How is that possible?* Merely touching the snakes should have killed them, much less getting a full dose of pure venom.

Ramirez sensed someone behind her, and she turned with a shout. Liam was on his feet, and she recognized the glow in his eyes, the same fierce intelligence the other two young people showed when they drank their magic water.

He leaned over the pedestal, and examined it, as if trying the gauge the best angle. He grabbed the wishbone fixture with both hands and pulled. There was a screeching sound, and the metal bar came loose.

Impossible. Liam took two long steps to the hatch, slammed it shut, cutting one of the snakes in half, and then shoved the wishbone against the metal rungs on top, locking the trapdoor in place.

As Sarah sat on the floor, unable to move, the three young people tracked down the rest of the snakes one by one and destroyed them with their bare hands.

The wind blew through the broken window. Ramirez rose shakily to her feet and looked out. The ocean receded again, but she knew it would be back. They had survived the first wave, and all of a sudden, she felt confident they would handle the second wave and the third and whatever else nature wanted to throw at them.

Jerry opened his backpack and pulled out another bottle of water.

"Last one for now," he said, taking a long swig. He handed the bottle to Jennifer, who smiled and also took a drink. Then she handed the bottle to Liam.

When he was done drinking, he offered it to Ramirez.

"Maybe later," she said, and was surprised to realize she meant it.

CHAPTER THIRTY-TWO

P erkins! Damn you!"

There was no one on the other end of the call. Sanders put the phone in his pocket. The tsunami sirens screamed in the distance. He closed his eyes for five seconds, dismissing his anger. There was no point to it. Perkins was gone, saving his own skin.

The man was right, of course. Sanders should get out of the house right now. The bodyguard was still going to get fired, though Sanders understood why he ran. Sanders hadn't been overpaying the man because of his smarts, but because of his loyalty. *So much for that.*

But Sanders wasn't leaving without his son.

When the lodge was built, the architects had assured him the building could withstand a 9.0 earthquake and subsequent sixty-foot tsunami. He'd paid twice as much for that reassurance.

"Even that may not be enough," Henderson had told him. "An M9 earthquake will usually produce a tsunami well over thirty feet. The Indonesian tsunami in 2004 had a run up of forty-five feet, and the Japan tsunami was well over fifty feet in many places, with a maximum of one hundred and thirty feet."

Sanders didn't know the magnitude of the earthquake that had just struck, but the walls had barely budged. The building had swayed as if built on rollers, which in a sense it was. Not so much as a painting had fallen off a wall. The top floor of the lodge was a good fifty feet up and should be well above any tsunami wave.

Architects and safety experts tended to overemphasize danger, to overbuild and over-engineer. Sanders thought he was probably safer where he was than if he made a run for it.

If Liam heard the sirens and came running home, Sanders intended to be here waiting for him.

He strolled up the stairs to Liam's 'secret' room. Sanders had never told his son that the safe place Liam had found was literally a safe room. When the doors were closed, the occupants should be able to survive anything short of a nuclear blast. Liam had thought the room was simply a storage area for extra food and water.

Sanders stood at the doorway. Then he turned and went downstairs. He passed through the living room and stopped short. The sun's last rays were falling on an empty desolation. There was no water to be seen, only the sands and rocks draped in seaweed and strewn with creatures flopping in the open air.

Then, on the horizon, like a giant mirage, a wall of red arose and moved toward him. From a distance it seemed solid, gliding across the bare ocean floor.

Sanders realized at that instant that the architects probably hadn't overdesigned and over-engineered after all. That wave would crush everything in its path, like a giant's hand swatting the surface of a pond. He turned and walked back up the stairs, pausing on the final step to take a last look over his domain.

"Liam, are you there?" he shouted. "Have you come home?"

The roar of the approaching wave drowned out his words. He entered the safe room and swung the doors shut. The second they were latched, he heard the generators engage. Between the chamber and the generators, which produced both light and oxygen, was another two inches of steel. Sanders had been assured that four people could live for up to a week inside the room.

He lay down on Liam's little bed, and his son's odor rose from the sheets and blankets. Ever since the boy was born, Sanders had loved that smell. It reminded him of his late wife as well. The two were forever connected in his senses and memory.

Liam had often threatened to run away. It had always been a sign that he was really in trouble and that he needed help. For the first time, Sanders hoped his son had made good on his promise, because if Liam was out there, anywhere near that massive wave, he was dead.

The room shook. The bed scooted across the floor, but then steadied. A huge bang resounded in the room, and Sanders felt as if he was inside a bell. His ears popped, and he felt the pressure in the room change. Then there was a series of bangs, none of them as loud as the first, but each one seeming like it might be the last thing Sanders ever heard.

The room rocked back and forth, knocking him from the bed, and Sanders realized the room was no longer attached to the superstructure of the lodge but was floating free. The oxygen inside it kept the steel chamber afloat. Sanders almost laughed at the image of the square box bobbing in the ocean like a miniature ark.

The generators went silent. The lights went out. Sanders stumbled back to the bed, feeling his way in the dark, and sat down.

How long could he last with the remaining oxygen in the room? Dripping sounds came from the walls. Sanders stood and felt his way toward the noise, and came to one of the walls. He put his ear to the metal and heard a steady trickle of water. The emergency supplies were in a cabinet in the corner. He felt his way along the wall. His hands were moist when he pulled them away.

He stumbled upon the cabinet, fumbled with the latch, and reached in, feeling around until he touched the cylinder of a flashlight. He turned it on, certain of what he was about to see.

The outer walls had been breached, and the space between the walls filled with water. His stomach lurched, and for a moment he felt weightless, as if he was falling. He was certain the chamber was no longer floating. He was breathing harder and harder, and he tried to control it, but he couldn't seem to catch his breath.

Sanders didn't remember moving, but he fell across the bed and stayed there, his eyes closed, breathing in the scent of his son. His entire past didn't flash before his eyes, just a single moment.

Liam was five years old, and Sanders came across his son and his wife in the tiny backyard of their first house. He had just been promoted to vice president of the small company he worked for, and had gotten his first raise and his first bonus, too. He had the money to do Christmas right for once.

But when he saw his wife knitting in the lawn chair and Liam playing with his trucks in the dirt, he realized the promotion and the raise and the bonus were nothing compared to this simple happiness.

Where did I lose it? That had been the last uncomplicated moment of happiness he had ever felt.

But he'd been granted that moment, and now, in his last seconds, he was grateful.

There was a huge grinding sound, like a tin can being crushed. The walls bulged inward, and then both metal and water rushed toward him.

Mary blanked out in those first few moments underwater. She instinctively kicked for the surface, then realized she didn't know where the surface was. There were flashes of light, but no real awareness of up or down. She tumbled, rolling inside the wave.

Huge, black objects whizzed by her, and Mary felt the disturbance of their passing, the thrusting of the water against her skin. Somehow, each of the shadows miraculously missed her. She tumbled again. Her head broke the surface, and she took a quick breath. Water came with the air, and she coughed out both and was no better off than before.

A peace came over her, and she realized all she had to do was breathe in the water. There would be a few moments of panic and pain, and then it would be over. There was nothing keeping her here. Her house was no doubt wreckage, but it didn't matter. She kept expecting to run into her late husband every time she walked into a room. She could smell and hear him as if he was still alive.

The science building was now her real home, and it was gone too.

She stared down into the deep, and it was as if she could see the entire contents of the ocean swirling below her. Strange creatures smashed against intact buildings and cars, and then she saw objects with two arms and legs, lifeless people, tossed like dolls in the maelstrom.

A massive, square shadow rose toward her, and she realized that this one wouldn't miss her. She floated, waiting. There was something familiar and comforting about the object, and to her amazement, she realized it was her old desk. The giant slab of wood had been her home away from home her entire working life.

It rushed up under her, and it was as if, at the last moment, it recognized her and slowed, cradling her on its wide surface as it carried her upward. They broke the surface.

Mary grabbed the familiar curlicues on the side of the desk. Her feet automatically slotted into the deep inkwells on the other side where she had kept her assortment of pens.

Can never have too many pens in the middle of Armageddon.

A good foot of the top of the desk floated above the surface of the roiling waters, and Mary felt strangely protected, almost embraced by the old antique. The waves washed over her, but she was burrowed onto the surface of the desk like a limpet.

She'd gotten firmly ensconced just in time, for the corner of the desk struck something bigger and harder, and her vessel went spinning so fast that Mary became disoriented and dizzy. Then they were surfing again. The second time the desk struck something Mary had more faith in her old companion, and though the shock was strong she remained protected upon its surface.

I christen thee the good ship George White, naming her vessel after the professor from whom she had inherited the huge dinosaur.

She dared to lift her head and saw a hill to her left, breaking the surface of the wave, with a cluster of people huddled on top.

It was the hill on which Ernest had built their home. But her house was nowhere to be seen.

The forward momentum of the water slowed, and then it felt as if it was going backward. The wave was receding, she realized with panic. She could see the dry, unbroken land just behind the crest of the tsunami and watched it fade into the distance.

She stayed on the *George White*, and once again it rewarded her faith, for the desk slid down the surface of the wave and was deposited on muddy, broken flat land.

Mary lay unmoving for several minutes, unable to believe she was alive. She tried to let go of the side of the desk, but it was as if her hands were glued to the surface. She had to concentrate to unfurl her fingers, one by one, reaching out when her right hand became free to pry open the fingers of her other.

Now the pain came, and she remembered she was a little old lady, not a valiant sailor of a magical ship. She tried to get to her hands and knees, but her head stayed down on the smooth wooden surface, as if unwilling to detach. Finally, she lifted her entire body and staggered to her feet, almost slipping on the slick wooden surface.

The hill where her home had once stood was a short distance away. The shouts of the survivors on top of the slope reached her. Two of the men ran toward her, and she watched them approach as if she was in a play or a movie, as if she had no will of her own but was being carried along by the story.

Even through the earthquake damage she recognized her own neighborhood. The tsunami had carried her home.

The first of the men reached her. She recognized her neighbor's teenage son, Joshua Cantrell.

"Hello, young man," she croaked.

"Are you all right, Missus Stewart?"

Another young man, who she didn't recognize, ran up. "Hurry, there may be another wave coming," he said.

Mary looked down at the *George White* reluctantly. It had saved her, and she felt vaguely guilty at abandoning it.

Don't be silly, came the stern voice of the Sphinx. *It's just a desk.*

She took a step toward the two young men and stumbled. Before she knew it, they had taken her arms and legs and carried her up the slope. As light as she was, they staggered under the burden. Suddenly, a bigger man showed up and lifted her like a ragdoll and sprinted toward the top of the hill.

In the distance came the roar of the second wave, but Mary knew she was going to make it. She hadn't ridden a tsunami just to be taken away now.

As they reached the top of the hill, the first of the waters reached the flat land below, and as Mary was lowered to the ground, she turned to watch the *George White* sail away.

Kristine gripped the iron headboard and ground down on Ken despite his protests. The rough, illicit sex excited her and shamed her at the same time.

They'd checked into their regular room, and Kristine had all but torn Ken's clothes off. They left the windows open to the ocean, since no one could see in. But she didn't care about the view, she only cared about proving she was still desirable to someone.

When the earthquake came, she didn't even notice at first. Ken shouted something at her, but she'd been ignoring him for so long that he had to buck her off and grab her shoulders before she would listen.

"Didn't you feel that?" he shouted at her.

"What?"

"I think it was an earthquake."

The room looked askew, as if it had tilted somehow. She dismissed it. It was an old building and probably would have fallen into the sea if the earthquake had been anything much.

"Whatever," she said. "I'm not done yet, Ken. Lie down."

"What's got into you?" he said, but he did as he was told.

Kristine was on the verge of finally cumming when the sirens went off. Ken froze like a corpse, and all the sexual steam went out of the room.

"Now what?" she said, glaring down at him.

"Those are tsunami sirens," Ken said. He tried to lift her off him, but she clamped her legs down and grabbed the iron headboard.

"It's all bullshit," she said. "They sound the alarms at any old thing."

"Maybe," Ken said, "but do you really want to take that chance?"

"Yes," Kristine said, sliding a couple of inches up and then slamming down hard. "I'm cumming if it's the last thing I do."

She closed her eyes to concentrate. There was a strange silence, and it took her several moments to figure out what was wrong. The hotel was built on an old jetty inside a once-abandoned cannery building. Usually, there was the constant slapping of water against the pylons below. Now there was silence.

Kristine glanced out the window. Where there should have been water, there was nothing. She rose off Ken, who grunted and scooted off the bed as if he'd been released from jail and started dressing, looking panicked.

She walked to the window. The setting sun was nearly blinding, but when she held her hand over her eyes, she saw that the ocean floor had been exposed as far as she could see into the glare.

Rocks and logs and huge patches of green seaweed covered the ground. Not only that. While her own room had barely budged, it appeared that the rest of the building around them had completely crumbled. They were the only part still intact. The pylons leaned, looking as if they were going to fold at any moment.

On the horizon, a wall appeared, stretching off in both directions, backlit by the red sun, and it moved toward them like a curtain being drawn.

She looked at her clothes on the floor, then at Ken, who stood beside her with his mouth agape.

"We won't get away in time," she said. Kristine knew Charlie thought she didn't listen to him, and Lord she tried, but he had gone on and on about earthquakes and tsunamis and some of it must have sunk in.

"The tsunami will be here in minutes," she said. "The drawback of the ocean is the last stage."

Ken didn't say anything, but he also didn't run for the door.

She pulled down his pants and grabbed his amazingly still-erect member – she had seen him take the pill on the drive over – and led him to the bed. "Lie down," she commanded. "There's still time."

He groaned. "You'll be the death of me."

"Would you rather be fucked to death or killed by a tsunami?" she asked.

Kristine was finally getting her release when the ceiling came down as a single slab and swept everything away.

CHAPTER THIRTY-THREE

When Joshua reached the little old lady at the bottom of the hill, he realized it was his neighbor, Mrs Stewart. She stood there with a blissed-out look on her face and greeted him as if it was a normal day.

It's the shock. "Are you all right, Missus Stewart?" He grabbed her arm more roughly than he'd intended. She didn't budge. Joshua stood there for a moment, undecided. *Leave her?*

Dizziness overcame him, and he staggered from exhaustion. The young man who had helped him earlier suddenly appeared, and as Mrs Stewart toppled over, he caught her under her arms while Joshua grabbed her legs.

They started uphill. After a while, Joshua wasn't sure if he was helping her or she was helping him. He didn't look back but could hear the distant roar of the second wave. He fell to his knees. A shadow loomed over him, a big shadow, and for a moment he wondered if Gary had somehow managed to find the energy to help them.

But it was a man Joshua had never seen before, a big man, not mostly fat like Gary, but mostly muscle. The guy plucked Mrs Stewart off the road with a grunt and turned and trotted back up the hill.

Joshua followed the big man as best he could. His feet dragged, as if he couldn't lift them at all. It was like one of those dreams where the harder he tried to walk, the more weighed down he felt.

Meanwhile, as big as the stranger was, he staggered under the weight of Mrs Stewart. She was murmuring something about the "good ship George White", and Joshua couldn't help but look back to see if there was a boat. Mrs Stewart had to have come from somewhere.

All he saw was an old desk being washed away.

Cold water splashed up his legs, and he heard the whoosh of the wave. Even though it was only up to his ankles, it almost washed him off his feet. He struggled to keep upright. The water kept rising. It was pushing him up the hill, but he knew it could drag him down just as easily.

He got down on his hands and knees and tried to become one with the slope. *Make like a limpet.* Cold water splashed up into his face, and it had the effect of awakening him to the danger. He staggered to his feet, fought the current with his last reserves of strength, and suddenly stepped onto dry land.

It was as if someone had removed manacles from his legs. He reached Gary, who was still prostrate on his back on the ground, red faced and breathing heavily.

Joshua lay next to his new friend. He'd made it.

The ground beneath him seemed to tremble, and he could feel the flow of water beneath the road, like you can feel the water in a hose, and he knew that it wasn't over.

Tiredness fought with fear, but Joshua rose to his knees and looked out at the people sprawled on the road. "We need to get higher!" he shouted. A few people looked at him, saw his age, and dismissed him out of hand. In truth, there were only a few more yards to the top of the hill.

"Gary," he said. "I think there's something wrong."

Gary grunted as if to say, 'no shit'.

"Can you feel that?"

"Yeah, that's the main lines," Gary said, sitting up. "Water finds the easiest path."

"We've got to get out of here."

"And go where?"

The ground shook. Joshua tried to track the vibrations, and that's when he noticed the manhole covers, one every hundred yards or so, running up the middle of the street. When he realized that the water was flowing upward, following the curve of the road, he grabbed Gary's arm.

"Get up," he said in a low voice.

"Why?" Gary asked. "Another wave?"

"Something worse."

At that moment, the manhole cover farthest down the hill exploded upward, shooting twenty feet into the air, coming down with a metallic clatter on the pavement, then rolling downward toward the receding waves.

The water shooting out of the manhole was a dirty brown at first, but then it turned black and seemed to congeal into something solid, and Joshua saw what he'd feared.

It was the black snakes he'd seen wrapped around Kim in the underground, a steady flow of them, like an oil gusher. The snakes splatted to the ground and appeared stunned for a moment, then started moving in all directions.

The second manhole cover exploded upward, higher than the first, as if the pressure was increasing. The flow of snakes was unending.

The next cover was only a few feet away from where they were sitting. "Come on, big man, we gotta move."

Gary finally pushed to his feet but stood there uncertainly. Joshua looked around. The snakes below them had moved off the road, except for a few that were still or moving sluggishly. Above them, snakes were everywhere.

"Downhill," Joshua said, taking a step in that direction.

"Are you sure?" Gary said. He was looking wide-eyed into the distance, and Joshua glanced that way. Another wave was coming, and it looked just as big as the first two.

"We've got a little time," Joshua said. "Believe me, you don't want anything to do with these snakes. If we go upward, the other manhole covers will blow, and there'll be more snakes. At least below us, the snakes have started to clear out."

They moved downhill, which was surprisingly difficult, as if the downward momentum threatened their balance. The manhole cover they'd been sitting next to shot upward behind them, and a steady stream of snakes gushed into the air. Some moved down the street, but most moved toward the houses on either side.

Joshua and Gary managed to dodge the few snakes coming their way; the snakes, for their part, ignored them, as if they had their own objectives.

"Let go of me, you brute!"

Mrs Stewart was whacking away at the big man who'd saved her life, who was clutching at her. She broke away long enough to point down at Joshua and Gary. "See those two? They've got the right idea."

"Ma'am, if you don't come right now, I'm leaving you," the big man said.

"My name is Mary Stewart," she said. "I'm with the Biology Department at the University of Washington, and I'm telling you that you need to stay in the open. Avoid enclosed places."

"Look, there's another wave coming, and my house is right up the hill. We can shut these snakes out."

Mary softened slightly. "Go ahead, young man. I can't stop you, but neither can you make me come with you."

"Jesus, lady! Have it your way!" the man turned and lumbered toward a huge house with thick stone walls. It even had a turret.

Joshua watched the man go. *Damn, I wish I was with him.* And yet Mrs Stewart had spoken with undeniable authority.

The next manhole cover rocketed upward, and seconds later, three more manholes burst, and the street was covered in black.

The rumble grew louder, and Joshua turned in that direction. A wall of water rose on the horizon like a cleaver poised to fall, and he quailed.

He looked behind him. The snakes filled the road.

Through the open door of a house, he could see water gushing out of sinks and toilets, and with them came the snakes, shooting up over the counters and across the tiled floors, finding purchase and wriggling forward through unlocked doors, up and down stairs, anywhere that was accessible.

The people inside stood and stared, not quite believing what they were seeing, and by the time they turned to run, the snakes had surrounded them sinking their fangs into their soft flesh.

When they fell to the floor, the snakes swarmed over them and moved on.

Joshua looked down the road. The wave was white capped, crashing down.

A yard of bare pavement opened above them, and they took a step backward, and then another. The wave roared up the hill toward them, and then two yards uphill, and the water lapped at their feet.

Finally, there was nothing but swirling water downhill and blackness above them, and they stood frozen.

"Pick your poison," Joshua heard Gary say.

Joshua had always feared water, had nightmares of drowning. He refused to see movies about water-related disasters, and when his parents had talked about moving to the Midwest, he'd been all for it.

He stepped backward, expecting to feel something squishy, to feel numbness move up his legs, but his heel hit pavement. With each backward step, he held his breath. The water moved up to his shins, then above his waist, then splashed against his chest. There was a small tree on the side of the road, and as the water began to recede, he grabbed it. Beside him, Gary was hanging onto a fire hydrant, and Mary was hanging on with both hands to the top of a picket fence, her legs floating downward. Though they struggled against the furious pull of the water, grunting and groaning, they all managed to hang on until it receded.

They lay gasping on the road, alert for any movement on the hill above, but the snakes were also gone.

Black ribbons littered the driveways and lawns around the houses. A white bird floated down from above, snatching one of the snakes in its sharp beak. It wasn't a seagull; its body was small compared to its broad wings. Joshua felt like yelling at it to stay away, but it was too late. He watched it land on the turret of his neighbor's house and start tearing into the snake.

He expected the bird to topple over at any moment, but it kept eating. "What's that?" he muttered, hardly aware he had spoken aloud.

"I believe that is a frigate bird," Mary said. "Interesting birds. You don't usually see them this far inland." She caught what she was saying and laughed. "I guess we're on the seashore now, aren't we? Anyway, they are interesting birds. They can stay aloft for as long as two months."

"What do they eat?"

Mary was watching the frigate bird. "Apparently, black sea snakes. Must have a genetic resistance to the toxin..." she mused.

Gary spoke up for the first time. He looked relaxed, the redness gone from his face. "What kind of professor are you?"

"Who, me?" Mary looked amazed. "I'm no professor, dear. I'm a secretary."

This information took some time to reach Joshua's tired brain.

When it hit him, he put his face in his hands, and then he couldn't help it. He started laughing. And once he started, he couldn't stop.

CHAPTER THIRTY-FOUR

Charlie kept his eyes on the surface of the water, but it was impossible to tell if anything more was happening. It looked the same, but he hadn't imagined that shock wave. He had the eerie sense they were rising, that they were being carried inland. He looked along the sides of the Strait of Juan de Fuca, but they looked the same, too: flat beaches on one side, a barren cliff with a single large tree on the crest on the other side.

"What was that?" Monson asked.

"Underwater earthquake," Charlie said. He turned to Tom, who was nearby listening. "We need to get out to deeper ocean."

"We're almost out of gas as it is," Tom said. "We'll have to use the reserve gas cans."

"If I remember right, we need to be out in at least six hundred feet of water."

"A hundred fathoms," Tom agreed. "That's what the emergency manuals say." He was already turning the wheel. The open ocean was in sight.

"We're almost to landfall," Monson objected. "Can't we just land and make a run for it?"

Carol spoke behind them from the cabin door. She looked shaky, but alert. "Not enough time."

"You all right?"

"Never better," she said. Despite her pallor, she sounded like she meant it.

"An earthquake this close to shore will create a tsunami pretty quickly."

Charlie looked back toward land, but his eyes caught Marty leaning over the stern. He looked as if he was moving from side to side, not just hanging over the gunwale and puking.

"What's your brother doing?" he said to Monson.

"Marty? When he gets ten feet from shore, he starts throwing up." But Monson had followed Charlie's gaze and frowned. He walked over to his brother. "What the hell *are* you doing, Marty?"

"I'm burning those bastards all to hell."

At that, Tom poked his head out from the steering cabin. "Shit. Where are the gasoline cans?"

Charlie somehow knew what Tom was going to say before he said it, because he was running for the stern. He reached Marty just as the little man triumphantly threw the last red gas can into the water. Two other empty containers floated behind them.

Before Charlie could take it all in, Marty had a flare in hand. They'd been stored in the same place along the gunwale as the gas cans. He swiped it against the side of the boat. The flash blinded Charlie for a moment. Then the *whoosh* of heat rose and he threw himself backward onto the deck. He looked up to see Marty's cap burning, but the man just stood there, seemingly unsure of what was happening. The man had to be a little unhinged after all he'd been through.

Monson grabbed his brother and pulled him down. At the same moment, Tom gunned the engines and they were all pushed to the stern, toward the fire. Flames licked along the deck for a few moments, then sizzled as spray put them out.

Then they were moving away from the fire, out to sea.

Carol marched over to Marty, whose hat had fallen off. As he was completely bald, there was no hair to burn but his forehead was red, and Charlie knew it was going to blister and hurt like hell.

But not hurt enough, as far as he was concerned. "You damn fool," he said. "Those are sea snakes. They can escape the flames simply by diving."

"Oh?" Marty said, getting unsteadily to his feet. "Then why are they doing that?" He pointed to the sea of snakes. The snakes squirmed over each other, setting one another on fire.

The flames seemed to be spreading, beyond what the

gasoline alone could account for. Charlie frowned as he watched them. *Something in the creatures' makeup is flammable.* Perhaps the very poison they use on their prey. Why would it have ever been a problem to them?

But why weren't they diving?

"They're all tangled up," Monson said, slapping Marty on the back. "Damn brother, you done good!"

"He nearly killed us," Carol said.

"Well, we're good now," Monson said. "Let's get further out, make sure the tsunami doesn't take us in."

The boat slowed to a steady chug and Tom appeared at the top of the stairs. "That was the last of our gasoline, guys. We needed that to get to shore."

"I don't think we should be in a hurry about that," Charlie said. "I hate to say it, but Monson is right. Let's get further out."

The boat shook violently, as if it had struck a rock. Tom disappeared into the cabin. There was a high whine as the motors exerted what power they had, but the boat had stopped moving. Charlie ran up the metal steps, poked his head in.

"Have the snakes fouled up the propellers again?"

"I don't think so," Tom said. "It doesn't feel like that. It's like we've run into something."

"Burn you lousy snakes!" Marty's voice rose from the deck. From the doorway they could see him dancing, pointing tauntingly at the still burning river of snakes. "Burn, baby, burn!"

Marty turned toward the cabin and grinned. A shadow rose over him, swaying back and forth, and Marty seemed to sense the dimming of the twilight and turned.

A giant snake hovered out of the water, until only its tail was beneath the surface. It hung for a moment, then its massive head and body slammed onto the gunwale, throwing Marty off his feet. He slid down the deck as the snake slithered away. With a scream, Marty tumbled over the side.

Charlie heard a loud splash. Despite his every instinct to get away, he ran to the side and looked over. Marty was still alive in the water, eyes bugging out, his mouth open in shock, gasping for air.

Suddenly, he levitated into the air to his knees, as if he was walking on water. He jerked, moving side to side unnaturally. With a whooshing sound, he glided through the water.

Then slowly, almost gently, he disappeared beneath the waves. Bubbles emerged. Everything turned red.

In the pool of crimson bobbed a severed leg.

Charlie retched over the side of the boat. The ocean was still, almost peaceful. Charlie stared at the widening pool, unable to believe it was over.

It wasn't.

Marty popped to the surface, flailing his arms, screaming. He splashed toward the boat, his arms churning uselessly. With every motion, he seemed to become more lethargic.

The poison.

Monson, who hadn't moved since the snake appeared, finally roused himself and rushed toward his brother. Charlie pushed him away. Still wearing gloves, he reached down to pull Marty into the boat.

"Do something!" Monson shouted at Carol.

She lifted the pistol but hesitated. "I might hit him!"

Monson grabbed the gun out of her hand.

Water splashed over them. The creature rose out of the water. With a shout, Charlie fell backward. Monson fired three shots. The first two missed everything. The third bullet hit Marty between the eyes.

"Marty!" Monson shouted. The pistol clattered to the deck from his hands. Carol picked it up and turned.

The snake's jaws unhinged, opening twice as wide. It lunged downward. The top half of Marty's body disappeared. Blood geysered, bits of flesh splattering the deck as the rest of Marty disappeared into the water.

The snake came down into the boat, its head nearly filling the transom. Then it reared back up, Marty still in its jaws as he was devoured. Charlie watched, mesmerized, as the massive snake's neck bulged with the passage of the body.

It then began to slither in. Its body was at least three feet in diameter, its head as big as a man. It reared as it came closer, and its gills were more obvious than its smaller brethren. They spread out like the fringe of a cobra, the light of the setting sun shining through the yellow skin.

Carol stood frozen. The snake opened its mouth and Charlie dove through the air, knocking Carol to the deck. He heard the spray of liquid go over them, threw his arms over his head, hoping none of the droplets would fall on him.

As they rolled, Carol held onto him for a moment, then pushed him away. Before he could stop her, she rose, lifted the pistol and fired the last three bullets into the body of the creature, just below the head.

The snake didn't hiss. It roared. The sound of a wounded monster. It reared upward, and it stared down at them with rage-fueled eyes.

But behind the rage was calculation, intelligence, and that scared Charlie more. He looked at the weapon in Carol's hand. She hadn't lowered the pistol, as if to intimate there were more bullets. The creature dived backward in a startlingly serpentine and graceful motion and splashed into the water, sending a wave of over them.

Charlie got to his feet, careful not to touch the deck or the gunwale. Miraculously, none of the spray had hit him.

Carol finally lowered the pistol but didn't move further. Charlie put his arm around her, venom be damned. She looked up at him with clear eyes.

"She'll be back."

CHAPTER THIRTY-FIVE

D id you kill it?" Tom asked from the top of the steps.

"I doubt it," Charlie said. "Nine millimeter bullets probably stung, but I don't think it would mortally wound a creature that big."

"Forty feet long, at least," Carol said. "Bigger than the largest anaconda."

"No shit," Tom said. "That thing is prehistoric."

Charlie said, "I think..." he gulped at the memory of Marty being bitten in half, glancing at the still red waters before looking away. "I think Marty antagonized her by burning her offspring."

"Goddam it, Marty!" Monson shouted at the ocean. He sounded angry at his brother – who he'd just shot between the eyes.

Probably a blessing.

"Couldn't leave it fucking alone!" Monson raged. Then it was as if the realization of what had happened fully came over him and his legs gave out. He thudded to the deck, breathing heavily.

Tom clambered down the steps, giving a worried sideways look at Monson. In a low voice, he said, "What do you mean 'her'?"

"I don't think she's the mother of all these snakes, that's impossible, but I have a feeling she is their progenitor, their queen, that they come from her and her forebears. She's guiding them."

"Do snakes do that?" Monson asked, pushing to his feet, his voice as shaky as the man himself.

"Hive mind?" Carol said. "Not that I've heard of. Just like I've never heard of sea snakes that are both venomous and poisonous to the touch. Nor has anyone ever seen a forty-foot snake, at least not in the modern era. But something is guiding that river of snakes toward shore."

"How can you not know what they are?" Monson said, taking a step toward Carol.

She turned to him and snapped, "Eighty percent of the ocean is unexplored. My guess, they probably evolved in an isolated spot, maybe the southwest Atlantic. They put Napoleon there on the island of St Helena for a reason. It's thousands of miles from anywhere. Someplace like that."

"But why now?" Monson asked. "You act like it's a fucking scientific curiosity. Why here? Tell me!"

Monson sank to the deck again, his back to the gunwale, eyes fixed on the gore on the deck, the remains of his brother. Carol went to his side and whispered something. He nodded, his face slack, but rose when she put her hand under his elbow. She led him to the cabin.

Charlie followed her, waiting until she'd sat Monson down. "Just rest," she said.

She turned to Charlie and he nodded toward the door.

"We have no way to fight something like that thing," he said. "Unless you've got more bullets."

She didn't answer at first, then she took his hand and led him down the steps. Where the gas cans had been stored there were loose straps, and under them, almost unnoticeable, a small box. She opened the box, and pulled out a flare.

"Just one," she said, holding it up.

"Well, Tom probably thought two was too many. I like the guy, but he's cheap. Have we even checked to see whether there's a life raft big enough for all of us?"

"If it comes to that, we might as well just jump in the ocean," she said. She examined the deck. "Where's the survival suit?"

"What remains of it? I think it's in the corner of the cabin."

"It might provide some protection until I can get close enough to *her* to use the flare."

"Not this time," he said. "I'm doing it."

"The suit doesn't fit you, remember?'

He shook his head. "It doesn't fit *anyone*. We cut into it to get you out. I'm pretty sure there's enough slack for me to put it on now."

She opened her mouth as if to argue more, then caught the look on his face and nodded. "You have to get close enough."

Tom yelled from the cabin, his hands still on the steering. "Hey, guys! You'd better get a look at this!"

They went to his side and looked at where he pointed. The river of sea snakes behind them was breaking up.

Monson got up from the cot. "You think Marty really hurt them?" he asked, an element of pride seeping into his voice.

"I don't think that's what's happening," Carol said. "Look ahead of us." The snakes undulated past the boat and out to sea, but instead of scattering, they reformed, linking with the existing stream. Waves slapped rhythmically against the side of the boat, as if they moved in concert.

With us on the inside.

"How do they know to do that?" Monson said.

"I doubt they do," Carol answered. "But the queen snake does. Did you look into her eyes? There was intelligence there."

"But how are they communicating?" Charlie asked.

"Hive mind," Carol said. "That has to be it."

"Which means *she's* alive," Monson said, his voice rising.

As if responding to a summons, there was a splash inside the newly formed circle of snakes. A hump rose, and a few yards back another hump, and then another. It undulated across the surface of the waves, and then the snake's head breached and turned to look at them.

Charlie inhaled sharply at the malevolence in her eyes. Beside him, Carol said, "Oh, shit."

With a splash of its tail, the monster submerged beneath the waves..

"We have to get out of here," Monson said. "We have to get to shore."

"It isn't safe," Carol said. "We'd be dashed against the rocks."

"Jesus," Monson spat. "I'd rather take my chances with the tsunami. Wouldn't you?"

A splash came from the other side of the boat as the giant snake reappeared, her head dipping in and out of the water. Charlie wasn't sure how he could read the queen snake's intentions, but there was vengeance there, an unreasoning hate.

"What's she doing?" Monson asked, hysteria bubbling just below the surface.

"She's circling us," Charlie said. "Checking us out."

"She's looking for our weak spot," Carol agreed.

They watched as the creature circled them twice more, each time getting a little closer. On the third circuit, she kept going, heading toward the deep ocean. They watched it until she was out of sight.

"Do you think she's coming back?" Monson asked.

Charlie looked down at the flare in his hand, then at Carol. She squinted and nodded slightly. He knew her now, he knew she wordlessly said: *It will work.*

He turned, not saying anything and marched to the middle of the deck. And waited.

There was a splash in the distance. The queen snake breached, fully extended above the waves, then dove head first into the water. She turned straight toward them, at twice the speed she had been moving before. Surf flew in all directions, her tail thrashed and her head dipped in and out of the water. Her body was one long muscle, all straining to move as fast as she could, gathering momentum.

"Hold on!" Charlie cried, though he himself was in the middle of the deck. At the last second, he dove onto the wooden slats. The boat stopped suddenly and violently as if it had hit a wall. He slid across the deck, splinters piercing his arms and legs. The hull shuddered beneath him.

Charlie got to his knees. He'd expected her to rear up as before, instead she had rammed the boat amidships. He saw the tail rise above the gunwale and come down and slap the side of the boat.

Monson, crouched close to the bow, turned and shouted. "She's biting into the side of the boat!"

"Good!" Tom shouted from inside the cabin. "Let her! The *Cirdan* is good and solid."

Charlie got to his feet, waiting.

The queen seemed to understand the futility of her attack on the hull and, with a last slap of her tail, surged away. Again she circled the boat, this time gathering momentum with every glide of her body.

With a final rush, she turned and slammed into the boat again, so fast that Charlie didn't have time to brace. He staggered, and despite himself, put out both hands to catch the port side. The flare jumped out of his hand, rolled along the top of the gunwale. He jumped for it, and caught it just before it dropped into the water.

He barely had time to stand before the queen snake rose above him. He could see the individual scales, the yellow stripe seemed to be pulsing, her gills fully extended. She opened her mouth and her fangs glistened with venom. He was close enough to hear the fluid moving up her body, approaching her gullet.

"Charlie!" he heard Carol call, and knew she was telling him to strike.

Not yet. Not until she's full of it.

The liquid dripped down, splattering on the deck next to him, and it sizzled, burning into the wood. And then, at the edge of his hearing, he heard the venom rising, gathering.

He slammed the tip of the flare against the side of the boat. Too hard, it bent in half but didn't ignite. With the last of his courage, with deliberate speed that seemed agonizingly slow, he swiped it against the rough wood.

It ignited, almost blinding him. The queen's mouth was fully open, a huge, darkened maw of death and destruction. It looked as if the spray was halfway to him, though how he could have seen such a thing he didn't know. He brought the flare up to meet the flow of liquid. A blast of intense heat threw him off his feet and he slid backward along the deck, splinters stabbing into his back, his head striking the far side of the boat. Above him, the giant snake wove back and forth as if merely puzzled by the flames, as if it was something she had never encountered.

Through the halo of fire, those furious eyes locked to Charlie's. Then the creature roared again and flames spat out over the boat. The queen reared upward, as if swimming in the air, her long body rising higher and higher. Her head was on fire, but she was still coming forward.

At the same moment the flames that swirled about her head brightened.

Charlie closed his eyes. The explosion was deafening. He put his arms over his head, felt something wet slap against the survival suit. Black skin slid down his arm. He looked up to see the giant snake seeming to float in the air, a gaping wound in her head. Slowly, without movement, she slid into the waves.

Charlie rushed to the side of the boat, caught a glimpse of the queen snake's flayed head sinking downward into the murk and disappearing.

Flames licked over the surface of the water and then blinked out.

"Is the bitch dead?" Monson demanded, standing over him.

"She has to be," Charlie said. "Nothing can survive a wound like that."

Tom yelled from inside the cabin. "I don't think it's going to matter."

"What is it?" Charlie asked.

"Unless I'm mistaken, we're going backward."

Tom tried to keep the boat out of range of the snakes but they pushed the *Cirdan* toward land. The captain revved the engine into the red zone. Extending across the entire width of the strait was the river of black snakes. When Tom eased up, it was immediately apparent that they floated backward again. The bow of the boat rocked upward and then turned inland.

Charlie turned to Carol, but she wasn't there. It occurred to him that he hadn't seen her since the fight. "Where's Carol?" he asked Monson.

"She was right beside you," he said, unable to stop his gaze flicking to the chunks of flesh littering he deck, to the remains of his brother.

Charlie ran to the side of the boat, though he knew it was too late if she'd fallen in or...

"She's back here," Monson yelled from the stern. Near the transom, there was a canvas square he hadn't even noticed before. The life raft.

Carol was out cold behind it. Charlie knelt at her side, intending to take her in his arms.

"Careful," Monson said. "She got some of that stuff on her."

Charlie hesitated, then pulled back his hands. She looked otherwise unharmed. He had to hope that by now she'd gained enough tolerance to the poison that she would be all right. He stood. The boat shuddered beneath his feet as if they were riding rapids.

The tree on the point shook, then disappeared. Charlie blinked, trying to make sense of it. Then he saw the rockslide, the tree at its center, plunging into the ocean.

Another earthquake. And unless he was mistaken, this one had been centered just a short distance away. The first one had probably been the Cascadia fault, Charlie realized. This was the more local Juan de Fuca fault. One earthquake had triggered the other, both near the mouth of the strait, and now the passageway was acting like a funnel, directing all the water from the quakes eastward, toward the cities of Everett and Seattle.

The tremor from this earthquake struck the *Cirdan*, and the transom rose, and it was as if they were riding a wave. Tom had been staring off into the distance and was caught off guard.

Charlie saw him stumble backward, hands outstretched, trying to grab something. Charlie's arm shot out, but it was too late. Tom fell backward, toward the open doorway. His feet went out from under him and he went down, his head striking the stair railing.

Charlie reached him in time to keep him from sliding off the side of the platform. Now Tom was out cold, too. Charlie held his hand over the man's mouth and felt breath. He felt under the captain's head, and though a large welt already formed, there was no blood.

"Is he going to be all right?" Monson asked.

"I don't know."

"Who's going to guide the boat?"

"I will," Charlie said. "Help me get the captain into the cabin."

Getting Tom inside took longer than Charlie expected. Both men looked nervously to the sides to see if they were about to hit land, but they stayed almost directly in the middle of the flow.

They placed Tom on the cot.

Charlie hurried back down to the deck to Carol's side. This was the second time she'd been exposed to the toxin within a matter of hours.

She appeared to have turned over, and that had to be a good sign. He went to put his hand on her shoulder when she murmured something, as if she was dreaming.

"Carol?"

There was no response. Charlie sighed; Carol was safe enough there. He turned and went to the helm. *It seems simple enough. Left, right… how hard can it be?*

"Why you?" Monson asked. There was a challenging tone in his voice. "You ever done this before?"

A vivid image came to Charlie. When he was about ten years old, his family had visited Multnomah Falls in Oregon. His father had fashioned a paper boat out of one of the tourist pamphlets they'd been given and had thrown it into the water. Charlie remembered it because the ranger had caught them, and his father had been lectured sternly. He also remembered how the current had caught up the boat as if it was a leaf and how it had disappeared into the mist of the falls, never to be seen again.

He laughed. "I don't think it's going to matter who guides the boat. You want to give it a try?"

Monson backed down instantly. "No, no... you do it."

Charlie turned the helm one way, then the other. It had no appreciable effect. *I might as well just take a chair and watch, for all the good it's doing.*

"I'll do it," said a voice. Carol stood behind them, looking drawn but determined. Her voice was soft but firm. Her eyes were shining brightly, and her jaw was clenched. She was ramrod straight, as if being lifted up by something.

He went to her and hugged her, toxin be damned, and for a moment she returned his hug; then she gently pushed him away. "Keep your gloves on and away from your skin," she said.

She took the helm and did the same thing Charlie had done, moving it back and forth like a child pretending to drive a car.

"Have you done this before?" he asked.

"Please be quiet, Charlie. I love you, but I need to concentrate."

Charlie frowned. She'd never spoken to him this way before, but there was no denying the forcefulness of her tone and posture. Monson looked at Charlie with his eyebrows raised.

"It's all yours," Charlie said.

CHAPTER THIRTY-SIX

Carol awoke to loud voices. She'd struggled to open her eyes for what seemed an eternity. It was a horrible feeling, as if she was being dragged to Hell and couldn't fight it. Just being awake was a huge relief, though the residue of the nightmare clung stubbornly.

Where am I? Even as she asked herself that, she knew. She could feel the deck under her back. She was on the *Cirdan*, and snakes surrounded them.

Was I bitten? No, I would be dead by now.

She'd watched Charlie face the queen snake, saw him hesitate. She'd run toward him, thinking he was frozen. Instead, just as she reached his side, he ignited the flare. The flames had tossed her backward, but that isn't what had knocked her out. Some of the spray had splattered on her face.

She felt vaguely ashamed that she hadn't trusted Charlie to do the job.

The arguing voices, though seemingly distant, brought her back to the now. She opened her eyes, rolled over onto her hands and knees. Grabbing the gunwale, she pulled herself to her feet and staggered toward the cabin.

One of the raised voices was Charlie's, and the fear she'd felt began to fade as she thought of his smiling face. Then she heard him say, "I don't think it matters who guides the boat."

A different voice rose, this time from within Carol. It was her, and yet it wasn't. It was her at her most certain, her most imperious, the way she sometimes felt in front of her class when she was in full command of her subject and knew she had the rapt attention of her students.

Her late husband had always teased her about this part of

her. He'd tap her arm and say, "An arrogant mood just struck you." With the snake poison surging through her body, she almost laughed at the thought.

Charlie had never seen this side of her personality, but here it was, stronger than ever. She knew what she was doing, and no one else did.

Her doubts disappeared. It *did* matter who guided the boat. How she knew this, she couldn't tell. She climbed the steps and stood at the doorway.

"I'll do it," she said.

Carol had calibrated her commanding tone and posture exactly, just enough to get her way without embarrassing Charlie. He was a good man, and ordinarily as smart as she was, if not smarter. But right now, every painfully slow thought was reflected on his face. He moved as if he was covered in lead weights. She had to control her own movements so that she wouldn't look so frenetic that the two men wouldn't trust her.

She dismissed Monson as a player, but gave him a quick smile to keep him mollified.

Carol had known the instant she woke there was a side effect to the snake toxin. Her mind was clearer and faster than ever before, even those few times she'd taken uppers or snorted coke in college. This was like that, only so much more. It was stronger and clearer and deeper. It felt as if parts of her brain that had never been used before were now in play.

She was a biologist, but her least favorite part of her job had always been mathematics. Now, equations she thought were long forgotten flowed through her mind as she instantly calculated the distance and speed of everything around her.

The computing part of her estimated their odds, and the answer sent the more humanitarian part of her into a panic. Sweat trickled down her back, and her heart was racing, even as her brain seemed above it all.

We don't have a chance of surviving this wave.

She tested the helm and felt a tiny response. They were little more than insects on a leaf on the surface of a whirlpool.

The currents they rode moved so fast and powerfully that the engine might as well have been oars. But even oars, directed at the right moment in just the right way, could eventually change the direction of an ocean liner.

It was the butterfly effect, but in real time, as if the butterfly was conscious of the effects of its own flight.

Carol had merely glanced at the navigational chart spread on the side table earlier that day, but now she remembered it as if it was in front of her. Halfway through the strait was a narrow channel that they were quickly approaching, then it was clear shot into Everett, which she didn't want. She wanted to ride this wave on open water until there wasn't any water.

Facts flashed through her mind. Everett had the largest public marina on the West Coast. She didn't question how she knew these things, the information was simply there. The tsunami would make the harbor a deathtrap.

She turned the wheel all the way to starboard. The *Cirdan* moved slowly, ever so slowly, to the side. It shuddered as the full length of the boat was exposed to the ever-increasing speed of the current.

"What are you doing?" Monson shouted.

She ignored him, counting the seconds, then turned the wheel back to port. Her mind flashed to the chart, and there was a blank spot there. She remembered Charlie had passed through her line of vision at that time, something that never would have mattered or been remembered, but which now left her wondering about the depth of the channel.

"Charles," she said. He wanted to be called Charles, she knew at that moment. She didn't question how she knew that. From now on, she would call him Charles. "I need to know the depth of the Puget Sound south of Everett. Check the chart."

He moved with a maddening ponderousness to the table and looked down. Seconds passed. "These small numbers?" he asked, finally.

"Yes," she said, trying to keep the impatience out of her voice.

"It's too dark to see them."

She reached over and turned on the floodlights. Again, with a slowness that made Carol want to leave the helm and hurry over and examine the chart herself, he leaned down.

"Hurry," she said calmly.

Then he read off a series of numbers.

She followed the first few, and then it was as if her brain slowed down in mid-thought.

It's wearing off.

It all started to fall apart. The imperious voice was still there, but it sounded tinny, as if coming from a distance and not to be trusted.

"I don't know what I'm doing," she said out loud.

Monson had been watching her, doubt radiating off him, and until now, she had been able to ignore him. Now, she turned to him. She backed away from the helm, motioning him to take over.

Monson gulped and looked away.

"Keep going, Carol," she heard behind her. "You've gotten us this far." She felt Charlie's big hands on her shoulders, and he turned her toward him and took her in his arms.

"I... I don't know how," she said.

"Try," he told her. "I doubt we could do better."

"Whatever that was," she said, "it's gone."

"Do you remember what you were thinking?"

"I... I couldn't remember the depth of the channel south of Everett. But I don't know why that was important."

Tom's binoculars were on the counter. Carol picked them up and lifted them to her eyes. The tsunami was obviously wreaking havoc on land. Lights blinked out as she watched. *Jennifer. Oh, god, Jennifer.*

Carol focused on the here and now; she had to survive this to get back to her daughter.

There was a huge shadow ahead that seemed to move back and forth across their path. She tried to make sense of its shape. While they'd been riding the current, darkness had rapidly fallen.

But when she concentrated, it was as if her eyesight suddenly sharpened.

It was a freighter. It had put out its anchors and was trying to keep from being dragged into the flow of the tsunami. It wasn't succeeding, except in blocking the channel for everyone else.

"Move everything you can to the starboard side of the boat," Carol said. She couldn't remember why she had decided that, but it was the last clear idea she'd had when in the throes of the toxin.

"Everything?" Charlie asked.

"Everything that isn't nailed down," she said. For the first time, she let her fear show. "Including yourselves."

They hurried to grab everything they could. Carol closed her eyes and tried to get a sense of the movement, to see if it was doing the slightest bit of good.

There. The boat moved ever so slightly to port. It wasn't much, but it would compound over the next mile and a half.

When she opened her eyes, she no longer needed the binoculars to see the freighter. It looked as though the *Cirdan* was going to strike it dead in the middle.

Then as quickly as the new clarity had come, it was gone. Worse, Carol suddenly felt as if she was going to fall back into the nightmarish dreamscape. She struggled to keep her eyes open, to stay on her feet.

She looked at the helm. *What I am I doing here? How useless this all is.*

They were going to hit the freighter, and there was nothing she could do about it. She turned away from the wheel and staggered to the cot, barely managing the step over Tom before sprawling onto the blankets.

She must have blacked out for a moment, because when she opened her eyes, Charlie was sitting next to her, smoothing her hair.

"I'm sorry," she said. "I tried."

He leaned down and took her in his arms, nuzzling her neck. She heard his quiet words as if from far away. "I know you did. And we almost made it."

"Shit!" Monson's voice echoed through the cabin. He was at the helm, moving the wheel back and forth. "How do you steer this thing?"

Carol rose, helped by Charlie. She stumbled to the helm, and Monson gladly gave it up. *What was I thinking before everything became hazy?*

The freighter swung across the channel, back and forth.

There was a fifty-fifty chance that it would be blocking the left side or the right side when they reached it.

Carol turned the wheel all the way to port and kept it there. The last few hundred yards seemed to take forever, though it must have been only moments. For most of that distance, she thought she'd guessed wrong.

"You're going to hit it!" Monson cried. He tried to shove her aside, to turn the wheel, but Charlie pushed him away. Carol stayed committed. She closed her eyes as the sides of the freighter dwarfed them. Tall and rusted red, the hull blocked the entire horizon. And then, at the last moment, the huge wall moved ponderously aside. The *Cirdan* glanced against the stern. Carol held tight to the wheel, and Charlie held tight to her, while Monson careened across the cabin. There was a loud metallic screaming, and then silence.

They were past.

Carol had no more energy. Her thoughts were sluggish, as if she was sleepwalking. Now that they were past the worst, she thought she should be steering the boat to safety, but she couldn't summon the energy. She went over to the cot and sat heavily.

Charlie took over. *Charlie or Charles? I can't quite...*

His steering had little effect. The docks of Tacoma were in sight. There was wreckage everywhere, and it looked as though they were going to join the pileup.

Then the wave lessened, dropping them lower and lower until they were in the harbor.

The *Cirdan* slowed, and the engine finally caught, burning the last bit of gasoline. Charlie guided the boat to the nearest pier. There was a single vacant spot, and he slid the *Cirdan* into it as if it was made for just that purpose.

Monson ran to the side of the boat and leapt over the gunwale, landing on the slick pier and stumbling. Then he was running full speed for land.

Charlie and Carol watched him.

"The second wave won't reach this far," Carol said. "I remember that much."

"What happened?" They turned to the voice to find Tom Bailey sitting on the edge of his cot, his head in hands.

Charlie barked a laugh. "You just missed the ride of your life."

CHAPTER THIRTY-SEVEN

As Charlie helped Tom up, he watched Monson's retreating figure disappear from view. The little man didn't even look back, made no effort to take care of what was left of his brother. Charlie turned to Carol. "We should have left the bastard on that crow's nest."

"You don't mean that," she said, but she couldn't help but smile. Monson had been a pain in the ass, but he was a person, and they'd saved him, and she was proud of it.

"No?" Charlie said, grinning back at her.

"How long have I been out?" Tom asked, rubbing the back of his head as if that would clear away his stupor.

"An hour," Carol said. Her mind was still ticking like a metronome, as if she could measure the seconds, but the clarity was fading rapidly. "Maybe less."

"Where are we?"

"Tacoma," Charlie answered.

"Tacoma... in an hour? That's impossible."

"We rode the whirlwind, Tom," Charlie said. "Carol surfed the tsunami like a pro. You wouldn't have believed it."

"You're right," Tom said, standing. He swayed for moment but managed to stay upright. He looked out over the docks and shook his head. "If I wasn't seeing it with my own eyes, I wouldn't believe it."

Carol brushed past him, barely making it to the cot before her legs went out from under her. A sprinkling of stars danced before her eyes, and she groaned.

"Are you all right?" Charlie knelt beside her, gazing into her eyes with touching concern.

She reached out and stroked his chin gently. "Shazam. I think my superpowers are gone."

She lay back on the cot, her head spinning. It had been pretty amazing, but she realized she didn't miss the machine-like precision her brain had operated with. It was as if it had drawn energy from every other part of her, physically, emotionally, and spiritually.

"Hell of a drug," she murmured.

She was shaking. No, it wasn't her. The *Cirdan* was shaking. She sat up, her sudden certainty a last gift of the toxin.

Tom rushed to the gunwale and stared over the side. He froze. "Oh, shit."

Carol tried to rise and almost fell back onto the cot, but Charlie grabbed her by the elbow. "We have to get out of here," she said.

Tom backed toward them. "Where are all these fuckers all coming from?" he said. "Are they following us?"

"They came the same way we did," Carol said. "They followed the same course of the tsunami."

There was a flash of yellow and black where Tom had been standing seconds before. The snake fell back with a splash, but thuds rattled the boat as other snakes tried to leap upward. It was only a matter of time before one or more of them made it over the side.

All three of them looked around the shattered cabin, realizing it provided no safety. They rushed to the dockside. In the water between the boat and the dock, the snakes writhed. It was as if the ocean was a boiling black soup, churning over and over.

Tom jumped onto the dock and turned to help Carol down, and then Charlie leaped down beside them. They couldn't see the shoreline through the labyrinth of masts and boats. As they hesitated, a large snake slithered onto the dock.

Carol ran, her head clearing sufficiently to understand that they needed to get out of there. She felt foggy but realized it was the fog she had always lived with, had always thought normal.

Monson was certain it wasn't over. Let the others stand around and congratulate each other; he wouldn't feel safe until he put a hundred miles between him and the Washington coast.

I'm never leaving home again. Suddenly, the tornado alley of his own state didn't seem so bad.

He ran straight down the dock and almost slid to a stop as he realized the wooden planks suddenly ended in a T. He looked down both sides, confused. On one side he saw the lumpy, lolling bodies of sea lions. They'd been barking in the background since the *Cirdan* landed, but he hadn't really paid attention, figuring they were probably out on the rocks somewhere. Instead, they completely blocked further progress – huge, lumbering creatures that didn't look like they'd move aside for anything or anyone.

Monson turned left, but didn't get far before that dock also ended abruptly. He was forced to backtrack until he found a platform that appeared to be heading in the direction of land.

It was a maze. For every few hundred feet he progressed landward, he had to retreat an almost equal amount. The adrenaline that had filled him upon reaching the docks was dissipating, and his breathing was ragged. His legs didn't want to lift, and he stumbled.

Finally, he reached a dock that looked to be clear sailing all the way to shore. He trotted down it.

Just get on land, then you can rest.

Something moved onto the dock, and Monson did slide to a stop this time. At first it was a single stripe of black, and then another, and then a third. Monson jumped onto a small boat to one side and looked for weapon. He slammed his shoulder into the door of the cabin, busting through. The cabin was shipshape and tidy, and hanging on the wall was a long gaff with a wicked-looking hook.

He grabbed it.

Back on the dock, the snakes coiled around each other, as if fighting for space. Before he could talk himself out of it, Monson ran toward them, swinging the gaff. The last snake got hooked, and no amount of shaking could get the whipping creature off.

Monson tossed both the tool and the snake into the water and kept going.

He ran up a slight embankment before he realized he was on solid ground. A set of stairs was ahead of him, leading to a parking lot on the hill above. He fell to his knees and almost toppled over onto his back. He couldn't seem to catch his breath.

He glanced behind him. The snakes had made landfall, coming out of the water and down the docks, slithering up the sandy embankments. Monson groaned but pushed to his feet and stumbled up the steps.

The parking lot ran parallel to the beach, long and narrow. On the other side was a busy freeway, and Monson almost stopped, confused by the sight.

Don't they know what's happened?

It looked like business as usual, as if these people were unaware that less than half a mile away, the largest tsunami in living memory had made landfall just minutes before. But they had to be fleeing.

He sensed rather than heard the snakes reach the parking lot.

I can't run another foot.

He stumbled along the row of cars, looking in each driver's side window as he passed. About halfway down, in an old, rusted VW bug, a pair of keys hung from the ignition, attached to a pair of fuzzy white dice. He opened the door and threw himself into the seat. It seemed to him that he felt something brush against his shoe as he turned and slammed the door.

The black asphalt of the parking lot undulated. He leaned back in the seat, closed his eyes, and concentrated on his breathing, on slowing his heart rate. It felt at first that the more he focused on the pounding beats, the faster they went, but a lassitude slowly overtook him.

The car shook, as if from an earthquake. Monson sat up, his heart pounding again, not quite believing he'd nodded off.

He reached out for the keys and turned them. The motor turned over a couple of times, then stalled. He tried again, and felt the entire car shake and heard the thunderous sound of a backfire, then nothing.

He craned his neck over the seat, looking out the back window, and saw a spray of red blood and black flesh spewed upon the asphalt behind the exhaust pipe. He groaned and leaned back in the seat again. "Great!" he said aloud. "I'll just wait you guys out."

He almost dozed off again. The VW stopped rocking and his eyes snapped open. The asphalt appeared to be clear of snakes, but he didn't trust it. *Just a little longer.* He was thirsty and hungry and dirty and tired, and he fantasized about a clean motel room, a long, hot shower, and room service. He reached over to the glove box, hoping to find something, anything, to read, even if was just a user's manual. Reading always calmed him.

There was a square piece of mat on the floorboard that didn't seem to fit the rest of the car. A carpet sample? It looked bright red and sickly green… and it moved.

He leaned down with shaking hands and lifted the carpet.

A snake crawled into the car. The rusted metal of the floorboard had developed a hole beneath the mat—just big enough for the snake's head to get through.

Monson screamed, scrabbling for the door latch, unable to find it. Finally, his hands found the slender hook, and he pulled on it.

It broke off in his hand.

He turned just in time to see the snake striking and felt its fangs tear into his shoulder. His throat constricted, his scream choked off. He couldn't breathe. He felt something wet move under his shirt, and it seemed as if every nerve in his body was dead but the ones in his stomach as the snake tore into his soft flesh.

All I wanted was an exotic fish on my wall.

Carol reached the T in the docks and stopped, confused. To one side, sea lions leaped and lunged. They tore into the snakes, taking one bite and tossing the remains into the ocean. A sea lion rose up, barked a cry, and flopped down on the pier, its fat suddenly loose and lifeless. The other sea lions paid no attention but kept feasting.

The dock on the other side led to clear water.

"Turn around!" she shouted.

They retreated the way they'd come, retracing their steps. Charlie led the way, kicking at the snakes, and Tom followed, also jumping and kicking like a young boy. The snakes were headed for shore, and so it wasn't until they found a dock that gave them a clear path that they ran into too many snakes to deal with.

They stopped, a heaving black carpet between them and safety.

Tom jumped onto a yacht tied next to them, and after a moment's hesitation, Charlie and Carol followed. Tom ran to the stern, and then nodded.

"Come on," he said, then appeared to jump into the water.

Carol almost cried out, but she reached the stern and saw that he'd jumped into a large yellow dinghy, almost as long and wide as the *Cirdan*.

"These rich bastards always have a smaller boat alongside," Tom shouted.

Snakes swam in the water, but the creatures appeared to be intent on heading for shore. Tom sat at the rear of the boat and started the outboard motor, and the dinghy shot away from the dock with surprising speed, almost toppling Charlie, who had just landed on board.

The seashore was covered with snakes. "There must be millions!" Tom shouted. "Billions! Where did they all come from?"

Carol just shook her head. She didn't feel like trying to shout above the roar of the motor. The oceans covered seventy percent of the Earth's surface. Plenty of room for a species like this sea snake to thrive, to hide until some event brought them to land.

But, yeah, there seemed to be an impossible number of snakes.

Tom steered toward a tall rock that jutted out into the bay. Snakes flowed to either side, but couldn't climb the slick incline. The outboard motor gave out just a few feet away, and Tom reached out at the last second and grabbed an overhanging outcropping with his gnarled hands, holding the dinghy against the rock.

"Can we climb it?" he grunted to Charlie, who got up and examined the rock.

In answer, Charlie stepped up onto the rubber side of the dinghy and, as it began to slip away under his feet, stepped over into a small crevice and started climbing. Carol saw that the rock's surface was broken, full of holes and crevices, and she quickly followed.

Before long, all three had surmounted the rock. They kept climbing. There were cliffs on either side, but on top of the rock there was a gentle slope that led to the summit of the bluffs. They reached the top before they saw snakes again.

A narrow earthen bridge led to a parking lot. Beyond was a freeway. Snakes swirled together in knots like giant creatures, then broke apart and spread out, and then, a few hundred feet farther on, they combined again in a heaving mass.

The freeway was a slaughterhouse of smashed snakes. The cars were slowing but wisely not stopping, their windshield wipers going full blast as they bumped over the increasing carnage.

"We could get into one of those cars," Carol suggested, pointing at the parking lot.

"Hell no," Tom said. "I want to see them coming."

He had a point. She didn't think anything could keep these creatures out of an enclosure if they wanted inside. As if to prove that point, a snake squeezed out of a hole in the cliff a few feet away, a hole so small she doubted she could've fit two fingers into it. Charlie stamped down on the snake before it could fully emerge.

"What do we do?" he said.

"I see only one place where there aren't any snakes," Tom said, pointing toward the freeway median.

There was a broad green swath amid the four lanes of the highway, and it was clear of black. None of the snakes made it across the highway.

"Do we make a run for it?" Carol asked doubtfully.

"Unless you want to wait," Tom said. "Do what you want. I'm going for it."

He started running, weaving his way through the clusters of snakes. As he passed them, the clusters broke apart, and a stream of snakes followed him.

Charlie looked at Carol, his eyebrows raised. She nodded and took his hand. They crossed the land bridge and ran.

She made it only halfway across the parking lot before her legs gave out. She found herself sprawled on the pavement, looking up at Charlie. His eyes darted to one side, and she saw the bottom of his boot flash by, then land with a thud next to her head.

"Carol, dear, we have to keep going," he said.

She tried. She really tried. Her muscles simply wouldn't respond. She reached over to the door of the nearest car and tried to pull herself up.

Monson stared out at her from within the rusted VW, his expression showing the usual anger and disappointment. But his eyes weren't moving. As she watched, a black swirl appeared around his neck, sliding up the side of his head and down his back.

She looked away. Her gaze landed on the snake that Charlie had stomped on. She reached out and grabbed it.

The shock was instantaneous, as if a needle had been jabbed between her eyes, and all thoughts narrowed to that point, became clear and hard, and she looked around and saw the path, as if everything but her was moving in slow motion.

Chemistry had been her least favorite course in college, but now all of old Professor Martin's lectures and lab experiments came back to her. She'd been exposed to the toxin in small doses at first, all the way back to helping Jerry to the ambulance. She did rough calculations in her mind's eye, saw how in every case the exposure had been just light enough to keep her upright, though now that she thought of it, she had felt pretty woozy a couple of times. She'd just attributed that to fear and stress.

She remembered Jerry's sudden willingness to interact, which had been so startling at the time. It was clear the toxin acted differently with each person. She was lucky.

She reached out with her free hand and grabbed Charlie's. "Follow me exactly," she said, pulling him after her.

It was as if she could tell where the snakes were going to be before they started moving. She had to slow down a little, because Charlie pulled on her hand, holding her back. *Come on,* she wanted to shout, but knew it would be counterproductive.

Tom reached the side of the freeway before them, and Carol winced as he darted into traffic. Her brain did a quick calculation and realized he was going to make it, barely.

Then they were there. She stopped abruptly and started counting.

"Where's all the traffic coming from?" Charlie asked aloud. "Don't they know what's happening?"

Carol had a clear vision of a traffic map, though she couldn't remember ever looking at one about this area. No, she had seen one, about ten years before, when she and David thought they were going to take a road trip back east. Ironically, this was the part of the freeway that came closest to the shore before turning due east.

There, in what looked to be an impossibly crowded block of traffic, was their chance. It was a measure of Charlie's trust that he followed her into what seemed a solid block of cars.

They crossed the lanes at a quick, measured walk, the vehicles whizzing by them, dead snakes under their feet, squashed, blood and gore everywhere. Bits of flesh flew into the air, and Carol watched each one, and when one almost reached Charlie's face, she reached out and snagged it from midair.

They were almost there. Tom was already standing on the green grass, waving them forward. Charlie let go of her before she realized what he was doing and ran those last few feet.

A truck clipped him in the leg and he flew through the air, almost landing on his head next to where Tom was standing.

Carol walked the last few paces, the truck missing her by inches. They'd made it.

The truck, however, had slammed on the brakes and was sliding sideways across the freeway as other cars slammed into its side. It slid to a stop, blocking all lanes of traffic. More cars slammed into the truck, and other cars slammed into them, horns blasting. Then all was silent.

People emerged from their vehicles.

"Get back inside your cars!" Tom shouted.

Carol knelt next to Charlie. "Can you stand?"

He nodded and tried. His leg was bent at a strange angle, and he fell with a shout.

She knew even before she turned to look. The snakes wound their way through the carnage, headed toward them. A young couple got out of a car a few yards away, then cried out as the snakes struck, then they fell out of view.

"Go on without me!" Charlie said. "Carol, please. Keep going."

She shook her head and flopped next to him. He groaned but maneuvered his head into her lap.

Beside them, Tom said, "I'm tired of running." He sat cross-legged next to them. "I'm not even going to fight the bastards."

Wouldn't do any good. Carol calculated their chances of escape had been about fifty-fifty. Now they were zero.

The snakes flowed toward them, and they wove a pattern that was beautiful to Carol now that she could see it. Magnificent creatures. No doubt they'd been swarming for millions of years, but only now had they run into modern man. She'd bet anything that if she went back and explored the legends of the native peoples, she'd find references to just such a plague.

Charlie moaned beside her. She looked down at the hand that had grasped the snake and tried to calculate how much of the venom was still on her skin. No way of knowing, too many unmeasured factors.

She pulled up Charlie's trouser leg, trying hard not to jostle his leg. He gritted his teeth but didn't say anything. She rubbed her hand along the skin above the broken bone. He started, and for a moment she was afraid it was too much.

But maybe that would be a blessing.

He looked up at her, and the look in his eyes said he understood what she had done. The snakes came closer, seemingly in no hurry. *They were never in a hurry. We just perceived it that way.*

It seemed to her that she could sense their thoughts, they wanted only to feed and breed. The queen snake had guided them to a new land where they could flourish, and she'd paid the ultimate price.

The first snake crossed over to the median, stopped, raised its head as if to sniff the air, and then slithered toward them.

A flash of white covered the snake, and it disappeared, and then the sky was full of white birds, as plentiful above the ground as the snakes were upon the ground, or more. The feeding frenzy began.

Snakes sank their fangs into their winged attackers, but the birds didn't even seem to feel it. The air churned, currents striking Carol's face in such a chaotic motion that even her sped-up brain couldn't make the slightest sense of it.

"What are they?" Tom asked.

"Frigate birds," Carol said. It must have been every frigate bird alive, all converging on this spot as if this had happened before.

Out of sight of mankind, these two species had probably evolved together. The sea snakes needed to swarm to breed on land, and the Frigate birds had fed upon them, gaining tolerance. In response, the poison of the snakes had grown in strength, but so had the frigate birds' immunity.

The snakes had been starving in their old lands. The rumbling of the earth had drawn them, and here they would make a new home.

Her phone rang, and while she was surprised she still had it, with a mother's instinct, she knew who it was.

"Are you safe, Jennifer?"

"I'm fine," her daughter's voice said, calm and clear. "My friends Jerry and Liam are with me. And Deputy Ramirez."

Carol breathed a sigh of relief. Of all the miracles that had happened today, this was the biggest. Around her, the white cloud swarmed the black waves, and she smiled at the rightness of it.

EPILOGUE

Ben Barker paddled toward shore, careful not to touch the sides of the raft. After he'd bailed from the *Knotty Girl*, he'd lain on the rubber bottom of the raft, feeling the snakes squirming beneath him, afraid to move an inch.

He'd landed on top of the snakes, smack in the middle, and froze. As night fell, he stared up into the stars, trying not to think about his brother. He wondered if his boat was nearby, but didn't dare look up.

Somehow, despite it all, he'd fallen asleep, dreaming of being in a wriggling mass of snakes, pretending to be one of them, feeding on his brother's body. He woke so shaken that he didn't fall back to sleep before dawn.

The sun wasn't that hot, but it beat down on his confined space. The snakes beneath him seemed to grow sluggish.

With a splash, he felt the raft drop a couple of inches, and realized the only movement he felt was that of the waves. Still, he didn't dare move for a long time.

Finally, he rose just enough to poke his head over the side. The snakes were nowhere in sight. Somehow, their movement had slowly pushed him along until he'd come free.

He explored the emergency kit. There was one store-bought bottle of water. It was stale and warm and wonderful. He forced himself to save half of it for later.

He picked up the pathetically flimsy and small paddle and started rowing for shore, vowing next time to get a state-of-the-art life raft.

Next time.

It was his brother's good credit that had allowed them to buy the boat. There was no chance, unless the insurance settlement was a good one, that he'd be able to replace the *Knotty Girl*.

I made the last insurance payment didn't I?

He wasn't sure where he was when he finally sighted land. There had been an unusually strong current carrying him eastward, but it was just another strange thing among many and he hadn't thought much about it.

But even as he approached the shore, he didn't recognize it, and he thought he knew every nook and cranny of the Puget Sound. Then he saw the old tower, part of a building that he once thought of as a castle, a vanity project by some nutcase who had never finished building it.

But only the tower still stood, and it leaned precipitously.

What the hell?

The land shifted in focus and suddenly he saw the overlay in his mind's eye of the old landscape laid over this new one.

The Big One hit, just like they always said it would. And I was at sea.

The fast current was explained and he realized he'd probably been just far enough out not to have been carried in on the tsunami.

Well, bad luck turns to good luck.

He paddled harder, anxious to feel the earth beneath his feet again. There were clouds of smoke rising over the landscape, and he wondered just how big the Big One had been.

But as hard as he paddled, he drifted backward. He leaned over the side of the boat, saw something massive moving in the water below him.

A whale? Just his luck if it breached where he was.

The creature rose higher and Ben grabbed the sides of the raft, poison be damned. He saw the mouth opening, as big as the raft.

Whales don't have fangs, he had time to think before the giant snake closed its jaws over him, and he slid down the maw, still conscious, still screaming.

Thanks for reading.

We hope you've enjoyed the book as much as we did putting it together.

Please consider leaving us a review if (and anywhere) you see fit. Any and all reviews are gratefully accepted. If you have any questions, or want to quote from the book, please contact us at any time.

I would ask please, if you DO review online, send a link to Geoff via editor@cohesionpress.com or via our Facebook page messaging system. If you review for a magazine or paper, let us know and we'll buy it.

Thank you.

+ + +

Geoff Brown - Director, Cohesion Press.
Mayday Hills Lunatic Asylum
Beechworth, Australia

Amanda J Spedding - Editor-in-chief, Cohesion Press
Sydney, Australia